"In *No One Tells Everything*, a quiet, shut-in of a New York copy-editor finds herself obsessed with the murder of a coed. Meadows is a confident and compelling prose stylist, whose sophomore effort [is] more charged than even her debut." —*The L Magazine*

"*No One Tells Everything* is a brave and moving novel. Presenting her struggling and overwhelmed characters in near-translucent prose, Rae Meadows makes a plea for the wounded humanity of all of us: the golden children and the loners, the murderers and the killed." —Martha Moody, author of *Best Friends*

Praise for *Calling Out*
A *Chicago Tribune* Pick for Best Books of the Year
Winner of the 2006 Utah Book Award for Fiction

"A stunning debut." —*St. Petersburg Times*

"Rae Meadows's keen, often humorous take on living, loving, and moving on is like a glass of cold water after a long run. Deeply satisfying." —*Marie Claire*

"No *Pretty Woman* rescue fantasies here: Meadows, who once worked as an outcall phone manager, presents the profession in all of its sad, banal, dangerous complexity." —*The Washington Post*

"[A] beautifully crafted novel about a woman who has lost her way . . . satisfyingly complex." —*The Capital Times*

"A strong author, a brave female voice." —*Venus* magazine

ALSO BY RAE MEADOWS

Calling Out

No One Tells Everything

MERCY TRAIN

a novel

RAE MEADOWS

St. Martin's Griffin ❧ New York

MERCY TRAIN. Copyright © 2011 by Rae Meadows. All rights reserved. Printed in the United States of America. For information, address St. Martin's Press, 175 Fifth Avenue, New York, N.Y. 10010.

www.stmartins.com

Design by Kelly S. Too

The Library of Congress has cataloged the Henry Holt edition as follows:

Meadows, Rae.
  Mothers and daughters : a novel / Rae Meadows.—1st ed.
    p. cm.
  ISBN 978-0-8050-9383-4
  1. Mothers and daughters—Fiction. 2. Motherhood—Fiction. 3. Family secrets—Fiction. 4. Domestic fiction. 5. Psychological fiction. I. Title.
PS3613.E15M67 2011
813'.6—dc22

2010028953

ISBN 978-1-250-00918-0 (trade paperback)

Originally published in hardcover format by Henry Holt and Company under the title *Mothers and Daughters*

First St. Martin's Griffin Edition: April 2012

10 9 8 7 6 5 4 3 2 1

For Alex, Indigo, and Olive

MERCY TRAIN

SAM

Sam was hungry for pound cake. Or at least for the making of it, for the recipe's humble simplicity—one pound each of flour, butter, eggs, and sugar—which had a certain elegance. The old-fashioned-ness of pound cake appealed to her, too, its satisfying solidity and lack of pretension, its buttery richness. Blame it on Wisconsin, she thought.

The trees had begun to change with the sugar maples leading the way, their golden-red leaves glowing through the rain-spattered windshield. It was October. Sam loved the ephemeral majesty and beautiful decay of fall, yet she couldn't enjoy it. Winter loomed. The promise of cracked lips from parched indoor heat, burned cheeks from pinprick winds, the grit of sand and salt everywhere. This would be their third winter in Madison, and she wondered how she would bear it, stuck inside with Ella, who was increasingly mobile, crawling circles around the living room, as darkness closed them in by four o'clock.

She sat in the backseat nursing Ella across the street from her friend Melanie's large Arts & Crafts house near

Vilas Park on the Westside. She ran her thumb across Ella's forehead, the skin poreless and heartbreakingly soft, and then traced the tiny curlicues of her ear. Ella's hot baby hand braced against Sam's chest in close-eyed concentration. How easily Sam was forgetting the last eight months, each developmental milestone quickly replaced by another. When had Ella first smiled? Rolled over? Sat up? It would soon be lost in a fuzzy hodgepodge of that first year, of "when Ella was a baby," the specifics no longer interesting or important.

Today was the first time she would leave Ella with a babysitter. She didn't want to, but she was doing it to show Jack that she was normal. He had been urging her to get back into her studio for months. She knew he was starting to find it worrisome that she never wanted to leave Ella, that she thought she was the only one capable enough to look after her.

Jack was right. Sam did think that. The fear of something going wrong with the baby was overpowering. No one would be as watchful and anticipatory as she was. What if Ella fell back and cracked her skull? Swallowed a penny and choked? Got stung by a bee and went into anaphylactic shock? At times she resented the primacy of her role as mother. She felt all-consumed by her daughter, a need to smell her neck and see her breath and feel her weight and warmth. Jack was bemused by her irrational scenario spinning, wondering what had become of the woman who used to exude composure. A twenty-pound being had inverted their life together and made it unrecognizable, his wife unrecognizable.

But it was more than just leaving Ella. There was the matter of the commission. A teapot for the head of the English Department, an old-guard scholar whom Jack needed to win over. A gift for the man's wife, requested almost a year ago. Sam knew Jack had to restrain himself from mentioning it as the months ticked on. She hadn't used her studio since she was six months pregnant, when her belly made it impossible to center clay on the wheel properly. She did miss the damp-chalky smell of her porcelain. The luminous gray-white glow of pots not quite dry. The centrifugal birth of opening a shape, a vessel, from a lump. Something from nothing. But now going back to work spun an anxiety that was new and ferocious. With porcelain she had to bring total consciousness, to be vigilant with form, because there was no roughness to hide behind. She had a lingering fear that her hands would no longer work in steady tandem, that she had lost her ability, her eye. Or, almost worse, that her pieces would be lackluster, relegated to craft fairs or a tent at the farmers' market, her creativity lost to motherhood. Cobwebs now ran from the window to her tools, and a strange crystalline mold grew up from her wedging table.

Ella pulled away and sat up gurgling and, with a large burp, dripped milk from her satisfied lips. Sam still got up a few times a night to nurse her. She couldn't bear to let her "cry it out"—to let her scream for an hour until she collapsed in exhaustion—as if a baby's need was something to be drained. Jack didn't mind Ella's wake-ups since he slept right through most of them. To the pediatrician and her friend Melanie, Sam lied and said Ella was sleeping through the night, not wanting to defend herself, expose her weakness. Sam had become the type of parent she used to disparage: the pushover, the hoverer, the handmaiden to the royal empress.

The rain had stopped, and the stately neighborhood was drenched in shiny yellow and red leaves. Ella twisted and squawked, climbing up Sam's front.

"Okay, okay, baby," Sam said. "We're moving."

Her phone rang as she got out of the car, bobbling Ella and baby gear. She banged her knee against the door and spilled the diaper bag.

She answered her husband with a clipped "Hi," trying to keep the baby from flipping out of her arms.

"Hey," Jack said. "Are you okay?"

"I'm fumbling everything. Heading into Melanie's."

"Oh, sorry. I thought you'd be on your own already. I'm proud of you, you know," he said.

"It's just a babysitter."

"Still."

"We'll see how it goes." She felt herself love him again. Since the baby, it seemed her feelings toward him required moment-to-moment readjustment.

"The rooter guy is coming today," Jack said.

"I know," she said quickly, irritably. She had, of course, forgotten.

Roots from the big maple tree in front had invaded their sewer pipes, and every six months they had to be drilled out. Sometimes Sam would lie awake and feel their old house decomposing around her, the foundation cracking, the roof leaking, the wooden clapboards rotting. What a transparent metaphor, she clucked to herself, but she was still powerless against the feeling that their home was going to seed faster than they could repair it. One of these days as she bathed Ella she was sure the claw-footed tub would fall through the soggy floorboards into the basement.

"Hey, you know how I told you about the committee search for David's job? How Samuels wants a theory person even though that would leave no one to teach Modern American?"

"Uh huh."

Sam still didn't know much about the esoteric workings of academia, but she supposed Jack didn't know what *raku* meant, or what *terra sigillatta* was, or how a glossy brown-black *temmoku* glaze would turn yellow-green in a salt firing. Their professional lives were secret lives, to some extent, the details not really part of the marriage. She wondered if this made their work dangerous or necessary or both.

Jack lowered his voice. "There's some stuff going on here."

"Dadadadada," Ella said, yanking Sam's hair with her dimpled fist.

"Got to go," Sam said to Jack. "I'll call you in a bit."

Sam squatted to pick up the diapers, now wet and dirty from the pavement, and tried to stretch her free hand under the car to get the pacifier that had rolled underneath, all without bumping the baby's head. She stood, blew the hair out of her face, and kicked the door closed behind her.

"I'm walking, honey," she murmured. "Let's get inside, shall we? I'll only be gone for a few hours. Nothing to worry about."

Sometimes Sam thought that having a baby allowed her

to act like a crazy person, talking to herself in public, even singing, and not always in a desperate move to placate her child. Her old self would surely have mocked her.

"Samantha!"

Melanie waved from the porch, her hair in a tousled shag with just the right highlights. She wore expensive jeans and an olive-hued, crushed velvet jacket, so chicly unlike the crunchy non-style of Madison. She and her husband, Doug, had moved from San Francisco—he was an anthropology professor—and she liked to complain about the provincial quality of Madison, the awkward Midwest pauses, the lack of irony and edge, even as she loved being a big fish here, a novelist (her book had been made into a movie) and a local celebrity. Jack found her aggressive and self-indulgent—and, Sam was pretty sure, attractive—but he liked Doug, who was quiet and cerebral, and the two couples had fallen into an easy sociability, their get-togethers never coming around too often to feel stifling.

Melanie and Sam had met three and a half years before in prenatal yoga, both newly arrived in Madison, both newly pregnant. And when Sam dropped out of class at week eighteen of her pregnancy, Melanie sought her out, and Sam would always be appreciative of that. It was her unadorned, to-the-point manner, her self-preservationist spirit that made Sam tell her the truth about the first baby. In fact, Melanie was the only person other than Jack who knew. Everyone else, including her mother, believed the pregnancy had ended with a late miscarriage. Sam tried to remember this when Melanie irritated her.

Sam waved and bounced Ella back onto her hip. "Hey." She smiled. "You look as fabulous as always."

"Your standards have dropped. Come on in. This weather is ridiculous."

Melanie's daughter, Rosalee, careened by and disappeared upstairs. Melanie took Ella and nuzzled her.

"Look at those cheeks. God, she's cute. I can barely stand it. You know I *really* don't want to have another one, but I still sometimes crave giving birth. I ogle pregnant women. I tape those ridiculous Baby Stories on TV and watch them one after another in a misty-eyed trance."

"I'm sure there's a support group for that," Sam said, setting the diaper bag on the polished concrete counter. She was surprised by Melanie's admission and liked her more for it.

"Don't tell anyone. I wouldn't want to lose my heart-of-stone reputation."

"Believe me, I get it," Sam said. "I didn't know my mind could capitulate so easily to my body. Or what is it, to the propagation of the species?"

"Gross," Melanie said. "And here we thought we were evolved."

Sam looked around the newly redone kitchen, a pasta water spigot over the stove, a deep rectangular stone farmhouse sink, a butcher-block island, a Subzero refrigerator. She wondered if all this was thanks to movie rights or if there was family money. It certainly wasn't funded by Doug's university salary.

Melanie, having had her fill, handed back the baby. Her large sapphire ring—"Diamonds are tacky"—caught on Ella's sweater.

"Shit," she said, freeing herself. "So sorry. This sweater is charming, by the way."

"My grandmother knit it. For me. Eons ago," Sam said. Her mother's mother had died when Sam was just an infant, and Sam cherished the small sweaters and blankets— complete with MADE BY GRANDMOTHER tags sewn in—she'd made.

"Ah. You have craftiness in your genes, " Melanie said.

Sam smiled but felt a slight rankling. Of course pottery was craft in the traditional sense, and she was proud of the utilitarian nature of her ceramics. But was a set of her nested bottles in a crackled jade glaze less a work of art than Melanie's book about a woman's relationship with her Jack Russell terrier? Melanie, she thought, is someone who believes the compliments she receives.

Sam put Ella on the floor to crawl around on the terracotta tiles.

Melanie downed the last of her coffee, and Sam saw that the mug was one she had made, one of her earlier styles with an hourglass middle, glazed in a milky *shino* with deep orange flashes, fired in a wood-fire kiln that she had helped feed for ten hours, a quick flare-up singeing her eyebrows. She remembered the giddy thrill she'd felt when they'd pried the door open the next day to see what had become of their pieces. The base of the mug was a little too narrow, she saw now, with a bead of glaze that had crawled, lodging itself clumsily at the base of the handle in a smooth nub.

Sam felt abashed for her snide thoughts about her friend, who had always been loyal. What is wrong with me? she thought. How puerile. How unattractive, her mother would have told her.

"Oh, that reminds me," Melanie said. "If all goes well

today, you could start dropping off Ella a few days a week. Sarah told me she's looking for more work. She's game."

Sam inwardly shrank. Before she could say she wasn't ready, Ella bumped her head on a drawer handle and, after a long pause, her face red, her mouth wide, unfurled a howl. Sam rushed to her and swept her up, cradling her head against her shoulder, Ella's cry still a painful tripwire to Sam's core. She felt her breasts harden with milk and begin to leak.

"Think about it and let me know, okay? It would be good for you. If it's the money, we'll figure something out." Melanie waved her manicured hand in the air. "I would love, love, love to have you cranking out pots again."

Rosalee, her dark hair cut in a flapper's bob, ran in and crashed into her mother's legs.

"Careful, please."

"Mama," Rosalee said. "Mama. Mama. Mama."

Melanie sighed. "Yes, Rosa."

"Juice, juice, juice, juice."

Melanie poured a little apple juice into a sippy cup and doubled it with water.

"Sarah?" Melanie called to the nanny, and then said quietly to Sam, "She was on the clock at nine."

"I'll be right there!"

Sarah jogged down the stairs and into the kitchen. She was what they called a "Sconnie," a UW student from Wisconsin, apple-cheeked and sturdy-framed, as opposed to the "Coasties," the more sophisticated, moneyed kids from New York and California who lived off-campus and ate sushi.

"Sorry about that. Hi," Sarah said, waving to Sam. "Oh,

and hi to you." Ella smiled as Sarah touched the pad of her little nose.

"Hi, Sarah," Sam said. "Here's her diaper bag. I'll put the bottles in the refrigerator. There's a jar of squash and a jar of sweet potatoes. And a thing of Cheerios. She's not a great napper, but she'll fall asleep in a sling if you don't mind wearing her around. Oh, and she can sit up okay, but you have to watch her because she's not that stable and can fall back and hit her head."

"No problem," Sarah said. She exuded a warm confidence that Sam had never been able to pull off. "We'll have a great time together."

Melanie crossed her arms and smiled, amused by Sam's worry. Sarah expertly fashioned the sling around her body and waited for Sam to relinquish the baby.

"And my cell phone number—"

"On the refrigerator already," Melanie said, grabbing her keys from a pewter hook. She had an office space near the wine store on Monroe Street where she went to write every day until four. She'd gone back to work when Rosalee was just four weeks old and said she'd never regretted it. She was not about to relegate the importance of her creative life, her career.

"It's better for everyone," she had said, "not the least of whom is me."

At the time Sam thought it impressive, a model for her to aspire to. After she had Ella, though, she couldn't help but think her friend selfish.

"Mama, Mama, Mama, Mama. Come with me. Come to my room," Rosalee whined, tugging at her mother's hand.

"Come on, Rosalee," Sarah said. "Why don't you show me your new Pocahontas dress?"

Rosalee thrust out her bottom lip and stamped her foot.

Sam held out Ella to Sarah and tried not to let the tears leak out.

"Believe me, Samantha, you're going to get used to this," Melanie said.

From Sarah's arms, Ella smiled at Sam with six little teeth, the two front ones spaced far apart, her eyes gray-blue and impossibly large. Sarah tucked Ella's chubby legs into the sling and hammocked her, and then took Rosalee's hand and whisked out of the room with a "Bye" over her shoulder.

"I'll walk you out," Melanie said, picking up her laptop bag.

Sam was embarrassed to be crying in front of Melanie, who was derisive of the earth-mother culture of Madison. "Spare me the hippie bullshit," she'd say.

The sun streaked through the cloud breaks, warm on Sam's head.

"We'll talk," Melanie said. "Get back in the studio, woman. Okay?"

They hugged, and Melanie clicked away in her heeled boots toward Monroe Street. Sam stood in her open car door and strained her ears through the birds and a leaf blower down the block, thinking she could hear Ella's cry. But she couldn't be sure. She sat behind the wheel.

She wished she could call her mother. She called Jack.

"So?"

"I'm out here and she's in there."

"You did it," he said.

"I don't feel liberated."

"You don't have to."

"I guess I'm headed home."

"Your studio awaits."

"I'm scared."

"I know. Just get a feel for things. Get your hands dirty. Clear out the cobwebs."

"Literally. Have you seen it in there? It's like *Tales from the Crypt*."

"I thought I'd bring home Matsuya for dinner."

"What if I suck?"

"Sam."

"Okay. I miss her already."

"You're a good mom."

"My usual. Spicy tuna roll, shrimp tempura roll."

"I'm going up for tenure."

"Already? What happened?"

"The department is shifting. Daniels was forced out. He'll retire at the end of the year. I think the timing is right."

"Wow. That's huge. Not that I didn't know you were the 'it' kid."

"It doesn't mean I'll get it."

"You'll get it. You get everything."

She'd meant this as a compliment, because he was one of those people who got the grants, the jobs, the fellowships he applied for, one of those people who was well liked because of an easygoing exterior that belied the smart and driven man underneath. But her words hung in the air a moment too long and she couldn't tell if she'd sounded a little bitter. She couldn't tell if she'd been mean.

"That's not true," he said. If he was stung, he didn't let on. "I'll tell you more about it later."

"I love you," she said.

"I love you, too. Hey, Sam?"

"Yeah."

"I hate to be a nudge. But."

"The teapot."

"I need Franklin's support. He's already on the fence. I don't want to give him a reason, you know? He asked me about it last week."

She hid her face in her free hand. She had to throw the body, the spout, and the lid, trim a base, pull a handle, assemble the parts, making sure that the piece actually worked, that it poured easily, while still looking graceful and light, with smoothed joints and upward lines and energy. Then the bisque firing, which might bring out cracks and warping, which would mean starting over. All this before figuring out the colors that would best suit the shape, the precise measuring of chemicals and minerals, and applying the glaze. And then another firing. It was an exhausting, teetering climb to imagine, and she couldn't get quite enough air.

"When?" was all she could get out.

"Two weeks."

Sam dropped her head against the steering wheel. "Oh, Jack."

"You can do it. I know you can. For me."

She chucked the phone into the passenger seat and tried to regain her breath. She glanced back at Melanie's house and started the car, willing herself to drive away from Ella. But she couldn't bring herself to go home and face her studio. She felt a curious new sensation of being cut loose. The day stretched out in front of her.

She could do whatever she wanted.

VIOLET

Violet skipped, laughing a little as she slipped on the rain-slick cobblestones. The air was heavy with fish and soot, but it was familiar and it was welcome. The sun had just cracked the sky, the morning still cool in the shadow of the Great Bridge. The sky was a spring-water blue. She stopped atop the small hill on Roosevelt Street to watch the masts of the few ships in the East River, black spindles and dirty sails, moving slowly under the bridge's span. She had never been across to Brooklyn, had never been on the bridge itself for that matter, but she didn't think she was missing much. Boston, maybe, or California, or some other place she had heard about—that would be different.

Violet had escaped from the Home before the sun came up, through a window near the laundry, leaving behind two weeks of hourly bells, bread and molasses for breakfast, bread and milk for lunch, soup for supper, and Bible verse recitation with the Presbyterian ladies who came in every evening to help purify the children's still salvageable souls. She would not miss the coughing, hiccupy cries of the babies, their faces pink and their noses gooey, or their heavy-footed wetnurses—Italian women with thick eyebrows and ample bosoms—who scowled at the children as they trudged to the nurseries. But she was sorry to have missed today's bath. She was filthy, her fingernails edged in dirt, her head itchy. Upon admittance to the Home, they'd hacked off her long black hair, leaving it short in back with a jagged line of bangs high on her forehead. The attendant, Miss Nickle, had said it made her eyes look bluer and prettier. Violet didn't see this as any kind of benefit, but she did like that she felt lighter without all that hair. She felt harder to catch.

It was a rare still moment in the neighborhood, the small space between the exhale of night and the inhale of morning. No clopping hooves of carriage horses, no puttering automobiles, and even the elevated trains were not yet roaring and screeching. The Fourth Ward was an overstuffed slice of the Lower East Side: tenements, docks, boardinghouses, saloons, dance halls, factories, shops, warehouses, a slaughterhouse, a bone boiling plant, a tannery, a coal yard, a mission, a manure dumping ground, and a police station. No grass, no trees, no open space save the cold river. It was a hive of small dark streets that angled and turned in odd directions, and to outsiders it was an iniquitous place to be avoided. But Violet was glad to be back.

In just her muslin dress and plaid apron from the Home, she was chilled by the breeze along the wharf. The rigging of the harbored ships clanged against the masts as she walked along South Street, passing grubby kids asleep, tucked in among barrels and shipping containers and crates waiting to be loaded. Garbage and ash wagons were lined up to dump their foul freight onto a barge in the river. Violet held her nose in the crook of her arm. At least it wasn't yet summer, when dysentery hit the tenements worst, when the noisome smells of filth and decay would become unbearable.

Violet walked up to Water Street and stepped over the gutter stream churning brown. The neighborhood was coming alive: shopkeepers opening up; sailors, fleeced and pilloried, blundering back to their quarters; the box factory night-shift workers stopping for cheap rum; the ragpickers scavenging the heaps of refuse left from the night's debauchery. Violet looked up to the second floor above the vegetable store, but it was too early for the women in the windows; their services weren't generally offered before noon.

Across the street, the two Dugan boys searched the pockets of a drunk slumped outside of a bucket shop called the Tiger Eye. The older one had copper hair and freckles; his little brother had dark hair and olive skin. The others teased them about their mother, calling her a bed warmer or a sailor screwer. But they were just jealous. In the Fourth Ward, having a mother around was a silent, collective longing.

"What'd you get?" Violet called, as she crossed over to the boys.

She had learned fast in the city, and she had done her fair share of pocket picking. She liked the surprise of it, the endless possible discoveries. A licorice whip, a deck of cards, a gold nugget—anything could be awaiting quick fingers.

He held out his palm, dirty in its creases, displaying a nickel and two pennies. Violet tried to grab them, but he snatched his hand away.

"I'd knock you if you weren't a girl," he said.

Violet teased him with a quick-footed shuffle-ball change, a step she had learned from her mother.

"You were put in the Home, huh?" he asked.

"Ran off this morning."

"Good thing," he said. "They might have put you on one of them trains."

She'd heard rumors about the trains at the Home, but she didn't understand why they wanted kids or where they went. She'd seen the Aid Society women in their black coats and fretted brows scurry about, holding the hands of some of the youngest charges, bitty ones she never saw again.

The younger boy rubbed his runny nose and kicked the drunk's foot.

"Let's go," his brother said to him, jingling his new coins in his fist.

"Hey, Red," Violet said. "Seen Nino?"

"Nah. I heard some of the newsboys got busted."

The barkeep pushed through the swinging doors and dumped a bucket of dishwater into the gutter. When he saw the boys he feinted a lunge.

"Go on," he barked, as they scampered away. "You too," he growled at Violet.

She stuck out her tongue at him and jumped into the fetid stream, splashing his feet. The water seeped through the soles of her boots, but it was worth it, she decided, for the zing of retaliation.

As she neared the Mission, she saw Aid Society women milling about in heavy black wool dresses, their stiff bonnets encasing hair that was pulled tightly into puritanical buns. They had baskets of sweets, which they held out for children who made a tentative approach, their desire for candy outweighing their fear of authority.

"How about you, little sir," said the oldest of the women, her nose like a small gourd, bending down to a boy with a dirt-streaked face and bare feet. "You want to live with a nice Christian family?"

He grabbed a handful from the basket and took off down the street.

Three little girls, no older than five, sat on the curb. One of the women directed a couple of scruffy boys to sit next to them.

"Train leaves tomorrow! Hot meals. Clean clothes. Need a mother and a father? Don't be scared, children. Gather round."

Two dark-skinned boys were given candies and then told to move along. The women began to sing:

"There the weary come, who through the daylight
Pace the town and crave for work in vain:
There they crouch in cold and rain and hunger,
Waiting for another day of pain.

"In slow darkness creeps the dismal river;
From its depths looks up a sinful rest.
Many a weary, baffled, hopeless wanderer
Has it drawn into its treacherous breast!"

Violet stood behind a lamppost and watched the ragged children collect on the curb, each devouring a lollipop, each looking relieved to be in someone's charge. The women herded the group down the street to a waiting carriage.

Violet was thankful she had a mother. She just needed to

find her. She took off toward the Mission. She figured her
mother would not be there—Lilibeth was never quite desperate enough for God—but she checked anyway.

Reverend Mackerel, his dark beard grazing his shirt,
paced in front of a motley collection of seekers—mostly
drunks and sailors this morning—and yelled out his ser-
mon, the same tale he told day after day.

"If heaven had cost me five dollars, I still would've spent
it on drink if there was a rum hole within spitting distance.
You say you can't be saved? Jesus took hold of me just like
He saved wretches, and don't you suppose His arm is long
enough to reach across nineteen hundred years and get a
hold of you?"

Violet scanned the audience, and then she slunk backward toward the door.

"You, girl," Reverend Mackerel said, pointing. His left
eye bulged.

"I was looking for my mama," she said. "I best keep
looking."

She quickly ducked back out before he could command
her to take a seat.

Before the Home, Violet and Lilibeth had lived for a
month in a rear second-floor room on Frankfort Street.
When they moved in, the walls had been freshly white-
washed and the window cleaned, and in those cold tail-end
days of winter, it was a welcome relief to be settled. But
when it had warmed, the thick black dust from the coal
yard and the putrid fumes from the nearby tannery—green
hides on drying racks were visible from their window—had
meant they had to shut the window and stuff rags around
the casing.

At the entrance to the tenement, Violet stood and took a breath before walking on the plank bridge over the sewer channel. In the courtyard, women pumped water into their washtubs, a naked baby cried, and muddy cats dived at vermin. She pounded on the door to the room where she and her mother had last lived.

"The longshoreman's got it now," a girl said. She was pregnant, her arms like sticks. "I ain't seen the southern lady for a long time now."

Violet held her disappointment in a tight knot in her stomach, trying to keep the fear from springing loose. She had not thought much about what came after getting out, had not considered that she might not find her mother. A girl alone was easy prey. She knew where she needed to go. If her mother had gotten money from one of her boyfriends, she would surely be at Madam Tang's.

Back out on the sidewalk, Violet's stomach gurgled in complaint. She saw a cart on the corner, manned by the one-legged Sicilian who couldn't chase after her. She ran, picking up speed, and swiped two bananas, knocking other yellow bunches to the ground, and kept on running, dodging big-skirted women and top-hatted men who never saw her or didn't care enough to respond to the old man's curses.

She zigzagged through traffic, making drivers shake their fists, zipping through the crowded streets, running, running, until her breath gave out and she had to stop. She wolfed down her haul and threw the peels into the gutter. The sun burned hot on her newly exposed neck. For a moment she closed her eyes amidst the staccato hooves, the grind of carriage wheels against gravel, the jangle of harnesses, the *putt-putt* of motor cars, the clang and hiss of the box works, the hum of conversation and transaction, the cries of seagulls, and sank into a cool muddy stillness—her soul, she guessed—as the world spun in dizzying discord around her.

A year before, as the train had clattered northeast through Kentucky and West Virginia, the second-class wooden seats worn hard, the car stale, Violet had watched the trees and the towns, the fields and the farms, her forehead red from leaning against the window. Violet and Lilibeth switched trains in Charlottesville, and from there they headed north, leaving behind the softness of low-lying southern land-scapes, and hurtled by cities, tall buildings of brick and limestone, smokestacks, and behemoth steel train stations. Violet sat up tall, excited by the enormous scale of it all, the motion and commotion, the people rushing around with someplace to be. Lilibeth slept, a blank composure in her face.

"Mama," Violet said, placing her sweaty palm on her mother's pale hand as they approached New York.

"Mmm," Lilibeth said, shifting and wrinkling her nose.

"What are we going to do when we get there?"

"I don't rightly know," Lilibeth said, her baby-blond hair rumpled from sleep and travel. "It was always about getting away, wasn't it?"

Violet shrugged. She hadn't known they were leaving until they left, but it wouldn't do any good to point this out.

"We'll be okay, Vi," Lilibeth said. "Some nice person will direct us where to go."

Her mother sat up and stretched her arms overhead like a child. She had never been a planner or a worrier. For most of her life, beauty had allowed her the indulgence of having others take care of things. Her father had owned a creamery and had done quite well, certainly in comparison to most Aberdeen residents, and Lilibeth, the youngest child and only daughter, was adored and adorned, the jewel of the family. But when her father was caught cutting the butter with tallow and yellow textile dye, he had to struggle like everyone else to scratch a living from the fickle earth. Yet Lilibeth never wavered in her sense of entitlement. She felt deserving of refinements, and when she met Bluford White he seemed to agree.

Violet's father was a lumber grader, a man with hooded eyes and prematurely white hair—how funny, people used to say, that his name was Bluford White—who was neither kind nor clever and was most of the time sullen and mute. Lilibeth said she had been fooled, as a girl of seventeen, into believing his quiet brooding was evidence of dignity. He was a little older, a man of experience, she'd told Violet— he'd lived for a time in Lexington—a man of taste, surely, who recognized that she was a different breed from the farm girls. He said her ivory skin was a sign of purity, her graceful fingers further evidence of her goodness, and to show his devotion he gave her a white silk sachet embroidered with an owl that he had purchased in a shop in Louisville and a silver-plated swan pin with a pearl chip for an eye. Lilibeth hadn't considered that these gifts might be extravagances that would cease, or that when they married Bluford would expect her to clean and cook. She had known he worked in the lumber mill, and even that he ate fried squirrel brains with his fingers, but she'd imagined they would move away to a city where he would make it big doing something or

another, and she would assume the life she was always
meant to have.

That nice person Lilibeth had chosen to approach, once
they arrived in New York City and disembarked from the
train into the station's frenzy of travelers, scammers, and
beggars, had been Fred Lundy, a man too red-faced and
puffy to be handsome, but who retained the imprint of
youthful attractiveness. He wore a shabby, dandyish striped
suit and ascot, his hair oiled sleek like an otter's pelt under
his bowler, and Lilibeth misread his flamboyance as sophistication. He smoked a cigar, scanning the crowd, as a boy
shined his shoes.

"Excuse me, sir," Lilibeth said, so softly he had to lean
forward to hear.

Violet stood a pace behind her mother with their small
suitcase. Though she sensed things at work she did not
understand and felt uneasy about the way this greasy man
looked at her mother, she was savagely tired. She just wanted
to do as her mother told her. She tried to focus on the shoe-
shine boy, who was about her age, his hands black from
polish, his black shoes gray from dust.

"Why, hello," Fred Lundy said, looking Lilibeth up and
down, appraising her country dress, her southern accent,
her refined beauty. "What can I do for you?"

"My daughter and I have just arrived here in town, and
you look like the sort of gentleman who could help us get
our bearings." She set down her bag.

He laughed a little, glancing quickly at Violet and then
back to Lilibeth. He tossed a coin to the boy and stood.

"You have good instincts, my dear," Fred Lundy said, picking up Lilibeth's bag. He didn't offer to carry the suitcase.

They ended up on the Bowery where, by the time the carriage delivered them, night had fallen and the street had turned into a circus of lights, music, and crowds, with the bone-shaking screech and rumble of the elevated train overhead. Violet clutched the suitcase and her mother's hand as the man ushered them into the parlor of a dilapidated rooming house that smelled of mold and oranges. He paid for the night as Violet and her mother sat on the edge of a wooden bench, both of them stunned silent at where they found themselves—the insouciant depravity of the neighborhood, the blatant untidiness of the lobby. Once inside the crummy room, the ceiling mildewed and water-cracked, the bed covers unwashed, Fred Lundy gave Violet five cents and shooed her out to buy candy.

"Take your time," he said. "Half an hour at least."

He pushed her out before she could catch her mother's eye. The door locked behind her.

Violet, just two days out of Kentucky, did not feel frightened because it was all too topsy-turvy to sort through. She walked tentatively into the stream of flowing revelers, moving along, sure she would be stared at, her dress handmade and patched, her hair unbrushed for days. But no one looked at her. She wandered the block, her eyes wide and blurry, the coins damp in her hand. She nearly stumbled over the feet of two boys leaning up against the columns of a theater smoking cigarette butts. When she started to look closely at the darker edges of the street, she saw more kids—scrappy, scratched, dirty kids—laughing, teasing, fighting, stealing. Boys mostly, but a rough-looking girl or two as well.

She found a brightly lit candy store, the first she had ever seen, a decadent array of colors and sugar. The confections she recognized—lollipops, saltwater taffy, horehound drops, jelly beans, and molasses chews—took up barely a shelf of the jar-lined shop. Violet let out a laugh at the selection and thought, New York City!

A woman whose dress was too short, her cheeks heavily rouged, swayed by as a trio of men entered the store. The group talked quietly in the corner.

Violet stared at the woman, transfixed by her brazenly loose walk, her uncovered shoulders.

"Never you mind about that," the shopkeeper said.

Violet reluctantly turned away from the transaction.

"I want some peppermints," she said.

He pulled down a large jar of red-and-white swirled candies and held up a tin scoop attached to his apron.

"How much?"

"Five cents." She held her palm open with the coins.

The woman walked out of the store with one of the men, her arm linked through his.

The shopkeeper took Violet's money and handed her the candy.

"Go on now," he said.

The waxed paper sack in hand, a peppermint melting sugary and comforting on her tongue, she went back out into the teeming nightlife, dodging a group of sailors, hats cockeyed and cheeks blazing, as they heaved out of a saloon.

When Violet returned to the rooming house, her ears buzzing, too tired to sleep, she found her mother with red-rimmed

eyes and snarled hair. Fred Lundy had left, and their room
had been paid through the week.

The merchant wagons lined up daily in front of RW & Sons,
packed with crates of bruised turnips, quinine tonic, walnuts,
flour, smoked oysters, chicory coffee, oleomargarine, and
powdered soap. Violet was not up for another run-by—she
had nowhere to stow whatever she might be able to grab—
but she did see a cigar box on one of the driver's buckboards.
It was shiny black, and on its lid was an image of a girl holding a rose blossom. Her friend Nino had admired one just
like it in a shop window: a place to put his things that wasn't
his pockets. She pretended to play alongside the wagon, whistling and hopping on one leg, before she snatched the box and
set off to find him.

She reached Slaughter Alley and peered into the darkness.
"Nino!" she called. "Hey, Nino!"

"Shut up!" a man yelled back.

Nino's Italian parents rode a mule-led wagon through
the surrounding neighborhoods sharpening knives. Their
apartment was so crowded that when the weather was fair,
Nino slept in a rusted straw-padded boiler at the base of
one of the bridge supports.

Nino leaped over a puddle into the light of the street.
"You look like a boy in a dress," he said, frowning at her
chopped-off hair.

"You don't exactly look like the King of England," she
said.

He pretended to straighten a tie against the neck of his

ratty flannel shirt. His knuckles were swollen and scarred from street fights, and around his eye was a fading yellow bruise.

Violet was warmed by the sight of him but tried not to give herself away.

"Where you been?" he asked.

"She put me in the Home," she said, "but I escaped."

Nino shifted his coal eyes sidelong to her. He shook his head, not swayed by her bravado.

"You should have stayed in as long as you could."

She held the box out to him.

"What do you got there?" He took it and looked it over, opening and closing the hinged lid.

He didn't say anything, but she knew he was pleased.

He walked away, and Violet ran to catch up, stepping over the putrescent frothy blood running in a crooked stream from the slaughterhouse. The drainage line to the river was always getting clogged.

She was struck by how Nino looked older, his shoulders broad, his arms long and muscled. Gangs didn't bother with the boys until they were old enough to be valuable, but Nino had already been approached by the Batavia Boys on account of his size. He didn't want to be a gang runner, but he didn't have any illusions that he wouldn't be one. Newsboys graduated to be criminals. Violet knew what her options were. She could be a sewing girl, a paper-flower seller, or a prostitute. She didn't like to think about the future; none of the kids did. They feared growing up because, when they became adults, they would no longer be invisible. They would live in flophouses or sagging tenements and drink and gamble away what little they had. They would fight. They would be picked

over by kids as they slept off their hangovers on the sidewalk. Or they would be dead.

"What'd I miss?" Violet asked.

"Same old garbage," Nino said. "Some lady jumped off
the bridge. Filled her stockings with sand. But she lived,
I guess."

Nino couldn't read, but Ollie, the newsboy captain, read
them the headlines before they headed out with their papers.

"Your grandma'am still sick?" she asked.

"Coughs and rattles the whole place. She'll be dead by
fall, my papa says. Not soon enough, he says."

"My mother's gone again."

"So?"

"I can't go up there alone."

Nino shook his head. "Ollie's giving me Cherry Street.
Evening edition."

"You'll be back in time," she said.

Nino crossed his arms and clamped his hands into his
armpits.

"I got to do something on the way," he said.

They walked. Nino kicked a stone along the sidewalk
until Violet intercepted it and sent it skidding out into the
street.

"There he is," he said. "Wait here."

Violet leaned against the wall of the post office on watch
as Nino tussled in the adjoining alley with a boy who owed
him money. She wanted to jump in and help, but she knew
better. A policeman rounded Oak Street and she hopped up,
whistling three times through her fingers.

Nino stormed back out into the street, wiping blood
from his nose with his palm.

"Little bastard," he said, over his shoulder.

Violet turned away from her friend's battered face, secure in knowing that the other boy surely looked worse.

She carried the cigar box as they walked.

"You get it from him?" she asked.

"Nah. It don't matter, though. He won't try it again."

He held one nostril shut with his fingers and shot bloody snot out onto the sidewalk at the feet of an old woman cradling her market basket.

"*Che schifo!*" she yelled at him. .

"*Lo scorfano!*" Nino hurled back, startling her with his Italian.

The woman scooted away, looking back once to make sure Nino wasn't following her. Violet laughed. She had stopped caring about disgusted looks and diminishing comments long ago.

"What'd you call her?" she asked, handing him the box.

"Ugly. It's a real ugly fish."

As they reached Chinatown, Violet thought this was what a foreign country must be like, the faces unfamiliar, the words indecipherable. She and Nino found the building and looked up at its crooked façade, a worn Star of David over the rusty front door left over from the old days. She had been here before in search of her mother, but it didn't make her feel any more comfortable. Inside it was hot and close and, despite the hour, too dark to move about. They waited until their eyes adjusted before trying to find the stairs. The building's residents were indentured to various brokers and smugglers, packed ten to an apartment, their narrow windows lined from the inside with newspaper in a cursory attempt to curtail Board of Health raids. From under the doors seeped smells of frying food and urine, of smoke and men. The building's communal cat dragged a fish skeleton from floor to floor, his black fur bare in spots from hot grease.

Violet reached down to rub the cat's head, but it hissed at her and skulked away down the rank hallway. She and Nino climbed another flight of stairs.

"It stinks in here," he said.

"So do you," she said.

He shoved her shoulder roughly and she knocked into a wall, something sticky against her sleeve.

Madam Tang's was on the fourth floor. For the initiated, a separate entrance with a chutelike staircase led straight from the street to another door. Violet knew better than to attempt access that way. She and Nino had to wait until Li emerged to set out milk for the cat. They sat and watched the door.

A skinny Chinese boy slipped through the door and squatted with a saucer.

"Li," Nino whispered.

Li squinted into the grim light and scrunched his nose, waving them away. They knew him from the docks. When the boy wasn't at Madam Tang's, he hawked the scraped-out tar from opium pipes to foreign sailors.

"Let me in," Violet said.

"No way," Li said. "Scram."

"Leave the door unlatched or I'll beat your face in," Nino said.

Li twitched in resignation and disappeared, leaving the door open a crack.

Nino stood and clapped the cigar box at Violet like it was a mouth.

"I got to get my papers," he said.

"Okay," she said. "Go on."

"We're celebrating tonight. Jimmy's back."

"Where'd he go?"

"Jail. He got nicked trying to rob a police."

She knocked her head with her knuckle.

"We're meeting up behind the tavern," he said.

Nino tucked his cigar box under his arm and saluted her with his free hand before bounding down the stairs, jumping two-footed onto each landing with an echoing boom, all the way down.

When she could no longer hear him, Violet knelt on the grimy floor and pulled the door open with her finger. She had never been inside. The last time she had come looking for her mother, an old man had chased her away, swinging a walking stick at her and screaming in Chinese. The ceiling was high, and bands of sunlight stole through fabric nailed across the windows. Patrons lay on their sides on straw mats or on flat mismatched cushions, their heads on their arms like napping children.

Madam Tang was a middle-aged Chinese woman with parchment skin and corncob teeth, a layer of flesh between her chin and her neck. She reclined on a frayed divan. Peeking out from beneath the hem of her long silk smock, her small feet were fat and bare, her toes contracted and gnarled.

The smokers were all men except for Lilibeth, who curved her body gracefully around her tapped opium pipe. Her eyes were at half mast, but they seemed to smile in spite of her slack, slightly parted lips.

"Mama," Violet said.

Madam Tang whipped her head to the door, a snarl

slashed across her face, but she knew better than to disturb her customers by raising a fuss.

Lilibeth lifted her eyes slowly to her daughter. "Vi," she said, in a low, throaty voice. "Vi, Vi, Vi, Vi, Vi. What am I going to do with you?"

She patted the mat. Violet lay down under the crook of her mother's arm and breathed in the smell of stale, sweet smoke from her sleeve, the faint hint of lilac from her perfume. Violet took hold of Lilibeth's delicate fingers, and then closed her eyes.

IRIS

Iris decided that her birthday would be a good day to die. That gave her three more weeks. She would have liked to see the end of the millennium, out of some desire for the tidiness of reaching a milestone year, she supposed, but this was not an option in even the most hopeful of scenarios. She had always thought cancer would be a banal way to go, but in fact it felt personal, almost intimate, an insidious march beneath the surface of her skin. Seventy-two years didn't seem like an unfair sentence. She had lived plenty. She had tried to express this to her children in an attempt to curb their need to find a solution, some other specialist, treatment, or drug to prolong the inevitable, but her passivity—her equanimity, really—frustrated them more than it comforted.

Morning was the least painful part of the day. Iris sat up in bed and placed her feet on the floor, waiting for the stars to recede from her vision and her blood pressure to stabilize. Even as her body had gone to hell from age and sickness, her feet still looked girlish, her toes painted petunia pink. She had been barefoot every summer of her Minnesota childhood, her soles tough and dirty, the tops of her feet tanned deep. The older she got the more recent those years seemed, while the decades she spent as a suburban housewife grew flat and faded. That wasn't completely true, she thought, rubbing her feet lightly against the white Berber rug. There were her children, and sometimes memories of when Theo and Samantha were little would strike her with vivid wallops. Motherhood was its own universe with its own nonlinear time line, its own indefinable pain and reward.

The overhead fan spun lazily above her head, the air cool through the open window. Iris wondered if she would ever need to turn on the air-conditioning again. This was a game she played with herself: would this be the last manicure, shampoo purchase, mu shu pork, thunderstorm, visit to the post office, Saturday crossword puzzle? This musing imparted ceremony to the mundane, which she appreciated. There weren't many things she longed to do again, though she would have liked to revisit her childhood home near the south fork of the Root River. She was sorry she had not made that trip north in the thirty years since her mother had died. Her father had been so fiercely, silently, proud of the farm, even as he sold off the land toward the end, with no one to pass it on to, Iris having long ago stepped away from rural life.

The early morning was overcast, the clouds above the ocean slate-gray and pink, spongy, the light in the room soft and flat. Her father. He'd been a gentle and quiet man, with thinning blond hair and a weedy frame that belied his strength and tirelessness. He'd spoken with the Scandinavian-Minnesotan cadence and accent, the *yahs* and *ehs* and flat vowels. Iris remembered her father's voice raised only once,

a sorrowful yell, when he'd learned that his brother Peter
had been killed, the lower half of his body sucked into the
combine teeth before his boy could cut the engine. Her father
was from the old world, her mother had often said, in explanation for his taciturn nature and his almost spiritual devotion to land and work.

Her mother had been tough and capable, a woman who'd
done man's work readily and never complained. She didn't
talk about herself and seemed to have no needs of her own.
"How is it you are my daughter?" she said sometimes to
Iris, who'd been lazy at chores, a girl given to daydreams
and wandering. Her mother was not prim and did not like
to dress up, wearing a dress only to church, and she had a
surprisingly quick and boyish laugh. Much to Iris's dismay,
she was the only mother around who wore pants. She loved
to knit, her hands never still, churning out blankets, scarves,
and mittens, sometimes late into the night. On rare afternoons, she and Iris would go to the river and fish, squishing
their toes into the cold, slippery clay along the bank, and
pass a bottle of milk between them. Iris wondered if her
mother had been lonely after her father died, or if she had
been, as an old woman, happy finally to be alone. Why did I
never bother to ask? Iris thought.

She picked up the splayed book on her bedside table and
slipped in a bookmark. She knew it would be her last book,
and she was savoring it all the more, reading slowly, feeling
the words tumble through her sleepy mind, getting lost in the
interminable sentences. The bespectacled boy at the library—
visiting his grandparents on fall break, he'd told her—had
recommended it as she'd perused the new arrivals cart next
to him.

"Any good ideas?" she'd asked.

"It's tough to choose, isn't it? So many books to read. I'm on a postmodern kick myself, but that might not be your style."

Iris smiled. "I'm not sure I have a style."

"How about Virginia Woolf? Do you like her?" he asked.

"I couldn't say," Iris said. "I don't think I've ever read anything of hers."

She felt, ridiculously, the heat of a blush in her cheeks. He was a handsome boy, tall, his brown eyes slightly magnified by his small round glasses, and he was unknowingly earnest. He reminded her of Henry, or what Henry must have been like long ago. Their affair had lasted for less than a year, but she still thought of him every day.

"Follow me," the boy said.

He jogged over to the literature section, scanned the shelves, and finally pulled out a book.

"I read this one last semester in my Western Civilization class. It's, like, amazing." With both hands, he'd held out *To the Lighthouse* to her. "It's going to rock your world."

"That's quite an endorsement," she had said. "I'll take it."

Iris used to frown at literature—who had the time or attention for it?—preferring the zip and ease of thrillers or the colorful, mind-numbing predictability of magazines. And yet here she was, having discovered at the last minute that she had been wrong. Something else to regret, she thought. Add it to the list.

Her mind was cottony from painkillers, but she felt okay to stand, to begin the day. She pulled on the apple-green robe she had draped over the back of the rocking chair the night before. She didn't like to see herself in her nightgown in the bathroom mirror. It wasn't the slack fabric where her breasts used to be or even the smooth red edges of the scars that peeked from the neckline that bothered her as much as her concavity, her diminishing physical form. As if she needed reminding of her wasting body. Since her divorce, Iris had cherished her independence, her solitude, her lack of need— she had chosen to move to Florida after all—but she knew her run was coming to an end.

She could no longer tolerate coffee, but she made a pot anyway for the smell that filled the kitchen, for the illusion of energy and possibility. As an English muffin toasted, she watched the palm fronds whip in the brewing storm and listened to the measured rhythm of Stephen, who lived in the condo next door, jumping rope. Stephen was tan and shiny and worked at the front desk of the Holiday Inn. On those rare occasions when they passed in the parking lot, he called her Irene, which she had never bothered to correct. When she had first moved to Sanibel, she'd found his revolving love interests a source of amusement. She'd watched the beefy men he brought home scurry away into taxis in the morning. But as the years passed, and the men kept coming, and Stephen got older, it made her sad to think of him after the men had left, gelling his hair, plucking his eyebrows, buttoning up his gray hotel uniform suit. She wondered how long it would take him to notice that she was no longer living on the other side of him.

As she buttered her muffin, the phone rang. It was her son, of course. He called every morning, dutifully, from the office. She imagined his daily to-do list: attend partner meeting, orchestrate bank merger, call dying mother. This was not fair, she knew, but he had grown increasingly patronizing as her illness progressed, spurred on by his fear of her death and his inability to do anything about it. But it was tiresome nonetheless. Iris sighed and picked up the phone after the fifth ring.

"Hello?"

"Mom? Are you okay? How come it took so long for you to answer?"

"Just having some breakfast, sweetheart. No need to send an ambulance."

She could sense her son bristle at her making light of his concern. Iris pictured him at age three, marching around the kitchen, livid at the indignity of not being able to go outside in the snow.

"How are you feeling?" he asked, as if taking a deposition.

"Oh, pretty good today," she said. "Your sister arrives tomorrow."

"Listen, I wanted to talk to you. There's this guy up at Mayo—"

"So you've told me. Theo, please."

"I could have you on a flight this afternoon."

"I know you could."

"Mom."

"Enough," she said, with as much motherly force as she could muster.

"Okay," he said. "We'll come down soon. A few weeks tops."

"I'm not going anywhere. Love to Cindy," she said, hoping she didn't sound disingenuous. What he saw in her, Iris would never know. Her daughter-in-law was humorless and persnickety, though pretty, she supposed, and well maintained.

So much effort went into appearances—Iris had never seen
Cindy without makeup, even early in the morning—it seemed
an exhausting existence. But maybe it was just because Iris
recognized a familiar keep-up-the-façade streak in herself,
and that made her critical.

She took a bite of English muffin, but chewing was an
effort, and the toasted surface was sharp against the roof of
her mouth. The rain began in fat drops. She breathed in the
smell of the wet wood of her deck. She tried to think about
what food might appeal to her—the other day she'd tried a
McDonald's cheeseburger, only to give up halfway through.
Maybe one of her mother's puddings or trifles, she thought.
She'd been famous for them at bake sales and after-church
socials. They had been too sugary and rich for Iris, but now
a bite would be nice. What had she done with her mother's
recipes? When she'd cleaned out the farmhouse after her
mother died, Iris didn't save much. She kept her mother's
worn wooden sewing box, the rounded corners and dove-
tail edges so lovingly crafted by her father. Inside, under the
sundry spools of thread and rusted scissors and fraying pin-
cushions, she'd been surprised to find a little old Bible, as if
her mother had hidden it there. But somewhere in the ensu-
ing thirty years, Iris had lost track of the box. And, appar-
ently, the recipes. She could envision that neat rubber-banded
packet she'd found, oddly, in her mother's top dresser drawer.
Iris wouldn't have thrown them out, even if she'd never used
them, never even taken the rubber band off, for that matter—
what was she going to do, make a Jenny Lind cake?—but she
knew she didn't have them here in Florida. She could account
for everything here, part of the beauty of containment.
Maybe Glenn had taken them; he'd always had a big sweet

tooth. Glenn. It was amazing that she had been married to him for forty years. Forty years! For the most part they had been a compatible pair. They'd had disagreements but had never really fought. He had been providing and nice and a decent weekend father. She had never asked herself if she was happy, so she had never had to answer. But familiarity is not the same as love, she knew now, and when he'd finally left her—she'd known about Marie for years—and the anger and fear had settled down, Iris had felt unburdened.

It was time for the day's first fistful of pills. Iris poured a glass of milk and pulled the amber plastic prescription bottles down from the windowsill, each with a clack against the lemon-yellow tile counter. Sanibel, this condo, this tile even, had been such a pointed turning away from the look of her former life. It was quite strange how all at once, after the divorce, she no longer cared about the trappings she used to: the Windsor chairs, the refinished chests, the oak dressers, the eighteenth-century mirrors, the colonial brick house, the North Shore country club. Her children misread her move— "A condo in Florida? You don't even like the sun. What are you going to do, play shuffleboard?"—as sadness, running away, depression. Leaving Chicago for Sanibel was a type of flight, she conceded, but she had felt better here than she had for so long. She had found solace in the small, impersonal series of white-walled rooms she had filled with "Florida" furniture (pastels, bamboo, white lacquer) and artwork (seascapes and shell prints). She had felt content in the hotel-like austerity, away from the intrusive weight of memories and history, and freed from sentimentality. No one else's schedule, no one else's mess, no one else's needs. People change, she had told Samantha and Theo. I have changed.

The rain had been brief, and now the darker clouds moved out to sea, a sliver of lightning in the distance. Iris knew she should walk on the beach or take her cold-weather clothes to the Salvation Army or write a letter to the granddaughter she would never meet. But all she wanted to do was get back to her book, back to the Ramsays in their tattered summer house by the sea, with the beautiful, self-absorbed, comforting, maddening Mrs. Ramsay trying to orchestrate the experiences of everyone around her. The incessant emotional recalibrations. Was that a woman's curse? Iris thought. And whatever did Mrs. Ramsay see in needy, tempestuous Mr. Ramsay? Not to mention eight children.

One had been enough for Iris: her son, Theo. Ten years later—she'd been forty, for God's sake—she'd discovered she was pregnant again. She'd sat in the front seat of the car outside the doctor's office, as the snowflakes swirled and melted on her windshield, and wept. She cried more than she had at the news of her father's death the year before. She felt betrayed by her body. Reentrenched in motherhood just as Theo needed her less and less. But abortion was illicit then, seamy, even dangerous. People she knew didn't even use the word—"I heard Mary Jo Surrey had something taken care of by a doctor on the South Side"—and she wouldn't have known how to go about it anyway. So Iris feigned excitement for Glenn, whose eyes turned dewy with the news, and as the weeks passed she waited for a miscarriage that never happened. Samantha was a calm baby who slept well, as if sensing she needed to be good to please her mother, to make herself easier to love.

As a toddler, Samantha grew increasingly shy, clinging to Iris, hiding her face. She would only go on the slide or the swings if the playground was empty, and only with Iris by her side. Even with Glenn, if Iris left the room, Samantha would collapse in a heap of tears. Iris wasn't that concerned. She'd been a shy child after all, and part of her liked being so desperately needed.

"It's not normal," Glenn said.

"She'll grow out of it," she said. "It's a phase."

"Theo wasn't like this."

"Boys are different."

"Take her to the doctor. Just to make sure."

The pediatrician, old and stern Dr. Kimble, told Iris she coddled Samantha and that was the problem. "Give her less attention. Let her cry. She'll get over it."

So Iris signed her up for a music class held in a Sunday school room of the Presbyterian church. Carpet squares were spaced out on the linoleum floor. A picture of a kindly Jesus holding his hand out to the Samaritan was on one wall, a constellation of God's eye crosses on the other. Mothers kissed their kids, told them to behave, and left. Samantha tightened her grip on her mother's hand, pressing her body into her leg. Iris knew it was not going to go well. She knew Samantha would not settle down after she left. She knew it, yet surely the doctor knew better?

"No Mommy go out," Samantha said.

"I'll be right outside the door, honey. It's going to be fun!"

"No Mommy go out. Sama and Mommy go home."

"Are you going to bang on the drum? Look at that. That's a tambourine. Why don't you go get it." Iris pried her fingers loose and pushed Samantha forward. "Be a big kid like Theo, right?"

The teacher, with a helmet of tight white curls, came

over and tried to usher Samantha to the circle as Iris walked quickly away. The sobs began before she got the door closed. Iris counted the seconds on her watch for two minutes before she marched back inside to the pitying eye of the teacher and swept up Samantha, who buried her burning, wet face in Iris's neck. Dr. Kimble—even Glenn, for that matter—could go to hell. What did men know of mothering? She'd decided to ignore everyone and let Samantha come out of her shell on her own terms.

Iris rolled slowly over onto her side to relieve her sore hip. Hogwash, she thought. The truth was a lot less flattering. She had always feared that somewhere in Samantha's cells, or in her limbic brain, perhaps, she knew she had been unwanted, that Iris had wished her away. And Iris wouldn't force a separation because of her own guilt. Within a year, Samantha had become an independent little creature who never seemed to need her much at all. Or maybe that was a myth Iris had spun to make herself feel she'd been a better mother than she actually had been. Did it matter now?

Iris awoke on the couch, her book fanned across her chest, a black, meaty fly buzzing in a circle around the room. Her joints ached. Her head felt too large for her body, blood pounding behind her eyes, and she felt she could not lift it. She lay for a moment trying to fill her lungs, knowing she was late for her pills by the way her skin hurt.

She had awakened thinking of her mother at her father's funeral, one of the last times Iris had seen her. It had been so windy at the graveside. That was the most visceral memory Iris had of that day in 1965. She had to keep one hand around her hair, to keep it from whipping across her face, and the other on her skirt. She couldn't hear the old Lutheran minister's slow, hushed words above the rush of air, the rattle of poplar leaves. For such a stoic man, her father sure knew how to make an exit.

Iris stood next to Glenn—solid as a tree trunk in his dark suit as leaves whirled around him on that early fall afternoon. Her mother stood alone, dry-eyed and stolid, her hands clasped in front of her dress, an ill-fitting black jumper she'd bought in town the day before. Glenn tried to urge Iris forward.

"It's her husband's funeral. She's your mother," he said, right into her ear so the wind wouldn't carry his words away.

"It's not her way," Iris said, dried salty streaks crisscrossing her face. She knew how uncomfortable all the attention and well wishes and country hugs were for her mother. She knew she wanted to be alone.

Iris grieved for her father, but it had been so long since she'd been home or even talked to him—he didn't talk on the phone, his wife acting as the go-between—he'd been a distant figure for most of her adult life, and it felt like she had been mourning him since she left Minnesota. Later, at the farmhouse, she traded tight smiles with old neighbors as they circled the dining room table laden with hotdishes and lutefisk brought by the Sons of Norway. Mrs. Ingebretson, the ancient church secretary, had made a kringle. Iris had bought two apple pies on the drive up from Chicago, which sat untouched on the sideboard. She overheard Glenn talking to the mailman, who'd asked, "What will she do now?"—as if being alone made one's life stop, which annoyed Iris even as she knew it was a genuine concern—and went looking for her mother. She waded through the rooms of the house she'd grown up in, glided through them really, knowing the layout in the memory of her muscles, and then she ventured outside behind the house. The wind had died down some, the day mild and clear with the smell of woodsmoke, old hay, and pig shit in the air. She found her mother in rubber boots, a large canvas coat over her mud-splattered dress, raking out one of the pig stalls.

"Mother?" Iris stepped on her toes in her pumps, trying to avoid the soft rain-soaked patches in the yard. "Did you get something to eat?"

"I don't know why I bother with this," she said. "He's just going to kick it all up again as soon as I let him back in." She stopped, leaned the rake against the wall, and brushed off her hands. The two pigs snorted, and then one of them, pinker and hairier than the other, threw its weight into the pen divider. "Elsie, you behave." She looked squarely at Iris. "I wish you'd brought your boy. It's been such a long time since I've seen him."

"He's with Glenn's mother," Iris said. "I thought it best."

Her mother nodded and wiped her wrist across her forehead. "I have something for him. A scarf. Make sure I give it to you before you leave."

"Okay. Do you want to come inside?"

"Lord, no," she said.

Iris rubbed her arms, aware that in her chic black sheath she looked profoundly out of place, yet that was part of it, wasn't it? To be the city girl, returned. She looked out at the grassy field of newly sown winter wheat behind the barn, owned by the Jensens now, and she was sorry that she didn't feel a loss for the land itself. It was shameful, she thought.

"I think the guests would like to make their condolences," Iris said.

Her mother shrugged. "They'll live." She unlatched the metal gate. "Here, hold this. I'm going to let Elmer back in."

The mottled pig had made a low grumble and heaved itself onto its tiny feet. Iris had held the gate, unsteady in her high heels, trying to spare her dress the filth.

"You look like you're cold, Iris," her mother had said. "Why don't you go on in. I've got this. Get yourself some tea. I'll be fine."

Iris folded her book and set it down on the floor, her arm shaky with fatigue. Her mother was always fine, even when she wasn't, and Iris had never bothered to distinguish between the two. It had been easier to believe in her mother's stoicism than to risk a glimpse of her vulnerability. I'm thirty years too late, she thought, rolling onto her side.

Through the window she could see patches of sky through the shifting clouds, the air warmer now, the rain forgotten. She slid her feet off the couch and onto the floor. Get up, Iris, get up, she told herself. Don't wallow. Don't waste the day. I'm a dying woman, she answered. I'm allowed to do as I please.

SAM

She would start by making the pound cake. With Ella breast-feeding, Sam could easily eat the whole cake by herself. She could not eat enough these days. By the time Jack got back from campus, all that would be left would be a nondescript, homey baking smell, enough to make him wonder at the source but not enough to ask about it.

She pulled out the flour and sugar and then checked the refrigerator. She had a little less than a pound of butter and nine eggs. How was she to weigh eggs? Or flour and sugar, for that matter? She closed her eyes hefting the butter in one hand and the eggs in the other. Close enough.

She rummaged through a cupboard for the bread pan she inherited from her mother's kitchen, along with the Mixmaster and the velvet-lined chest of silver that had begun, the last time she had looked, to tarnish. Sam had dumped the rest of her mother's belongings into boxes and delivered them to the Salvation Army in Fort Myers, along with the furniture, the seascape paintings, and the driftwood frame mirrors. She had saved only a yellow glider chair and a white dresser that

were both now in Ella's room, along with a few other odds
and ends she carried in her bag on the flight home. When
Sam's parents had divorced, her mother had gotten rid of all
the antiques she had spent her married years collecting, the
refinished chests and colonial rocking chairs and iron beds.
She had left Chicago, moved to Florida—to Sanibel Island—
and bought a condo, where she had lived until her death last
year, four months before Ella was born.

The pan wasn't anywhere. How could that be? Sam
thought. She'd last used it to make pumpkin bread for some
English Department thing. She bristled. Jack must not have
brought it home. Domestic details were not part of his
frame of vision. She was pretty sure that in the five years they
had been married he'd never once bought toilet paper, garbage bags, or laundry detergent. Or soap. Or toothpaste. You
chose to put your baby's needs and the home first, she said
sometimes, to calm herself. But she knew it wasn't really a
choice. Sam still felt at the mercy of her biology, and sometimes she quietly raged against not having a say about the
intensity of feeling she had for Ella. It was like she had given
birth to one of her own vital organs, requiring a subversion
of her self that was instinctual, non-negotiable, complete.
"You're postpartum, Samantha," Melanie had said. "Obvi-
ously." Maybe she was right. Or maybe everything was just
different now.

Sam grabbed her keys and pulled the front door shut
behind her, nearly tripping on a box on the landing. She
wondered where it had come from, given the hour. But then
again, she hadn't received a FedEx package since moving to
Madison. By the blocky left-handed scrawl of the address
slip, she knew it was from her brother, Theo. Something for

Ella, maybe, though that would be uncharacteristically thoughtful. He left such duties to his wife. Sam slid the box closer to the door with her foot—what in the world could be so heavy?—and went to the car.

They lived on the Eastside near the north shore of Lake Monona in a funky-shabby neighborhood of old Victorians and Craftsman bungalows, a few blocks from a food co-op and a vegan coffee shop, a soup kitchen, and a single-room-occupancy residence. The area had gentrified, its dilapidated skid-row roots smoothed over, but it still retained a leftover seediness that Sam appreciated. She was glad to live away from the university and the too-pretty and suburban Westside.

She didn't miss a lot about New York, but she missed the color and the grit. At her old shared studio space in downtown Brooklyn, she'd loved to look down from the seventh-floor balcony—the cold air a relief from the kilns' oppressive heat—and watch ebullient crowds coming in and out of Junior's and the lights and honking and Spanish and Arabic and luggage stores and cell phone hawkers on Atlantic Avenue. At times she even missed the sad and sinister mall she had to pass on her walk to the subway, the *R* burned out of the Toys R Us sign, the beauty supply store with its cracked window, the parking garage that seemed dangerous at any hour of the day. She missed the dark and light created by millions of people bumping up against one another.

Her cell phone rang: Theo. She ignored it.

Her brother was a lawyer at a big Washington, D.C., firm, the mergers and acquisitions arm, and his wife, Cindy, with her shellacked blond pageboy, was an interior decorator whose traditional style bordered on the rococo, with an overabundance of toile and stripes. She had a thriving business along the Potomac and the Chesapeake Bay. Sam found their Georgetown townhouse pristine and gaudy at the same time, and a spread in *Town & Country*—sent to her by Cindy—did little to disabuse her of that impression. Theo was ten years older than Sam, and they had never been close. He treated her with older-brother condescension, which in turn made her petulant and defensive, as if they were forever twenty-six and sixteen. In the last year, they had spoken more than they ever had because of the multiplicity of details to decide upon, from the large (coffin or cremation) to the mundane (the font of the memorial service handout) to the ridiculous ("Mom's hairdresser claims she was promised a jade ring") necessitated by a parent's death.

Their mother, Iris, had had breast cancer. The double mastectomy and removal of lymph nodes and radiation had not been quick or thorough enough to contain all of the stealth cancer cells that had taken root in her body and come roaring to fruition six months later. In the end, to Sam's dismay, her mother decided against the ravages and slim odds of chemotherapy. Iris played neither victim nor martyr, but she had always been stoic. It was her Scandinavian genes—her father had come from Norway—she liked to say. When Sam tried to get her to move to Madison, Iris chuckled and said she'd rather die where it was seventy-five and sunny, thank you very much. So Sam went to her instead. She left Jack and moved to Florida for what turned out to be only a three-week stay. Iris had died on her seventy-second birthday. Theo and Cindy had finally shown up a day too late.

She turned onto East Washington, the commercial strip that ran down the isthmus between Lake Monona and Lake

Mendota, from the Capitol to the interstate, peppered with check-cashing outlets, fast-food places, liquor stores, and a 24-hour X-rated shop, which, she had read, had been robbed five times this year. Out of habit she glanced in her rearview to check on Ella, and the empty car seat panicked her heart before her brain could catch up. She drove past the Lotus House, a massage parlor tucked in near Highway 30, a strip club, and the low-slung Admiral Motel, rooms $31.95. HBO and in-room phones! Astroturf lined the area around the motel office, and a brown broken-down Monte Carlo camped in front of the first room, where it had been for months. Another room door gaped hopelessly open. She'd been surprised the first time she had driven this stretch. She had expected Madison to keep its vices midwesternly hidden away.

As she drove, she tried to isolate why she was so quick to get angry at Jack. For being able to go about his day unhampered by worry about the baby. For not knowing the right type of wipes to get. For wanting her to snap out of it. For everything and nothing. He was a convenient outlet. She breathed deeply through her nose, and then caught a glimpse of a spot of drool and a smear of sweet potatoes on her shirt. Now that Ella was eating food and nursing less, Sam's once-robust breasts were sadly flattening. Somehow this was Jack's fault, too.

When she'd been pregnant, Sam had loved the feeling of giving her body over to something else, and, for the first time since adolescence she had not been concerned about what she looked like, had not wondered if she should eat the extra donut, had not cared that her thighs strained against the seams of her sweatpants. It had been a revelation—so much time she had wasted—to be happy about how her body was working, nourishing life, fecund with purpose. And how quickly this had faded after Ella was born and she began to care that the extra skin on her stomach bunched, that crooked, silvery fingers of stretch marks striated her hips. In baby swim class she eyed the bodies of the other mothers as they sang "Wheels on the Bus" and spun their babies through the water, calculating how her flaws stacked up against theirs, while she knew she should have been enjoying Ella's squeals and kicking little legs. The return of her vanity was a disappointment to her.

Inside the drugstore her post-baby brain—shrunken four percent, she had read—sputtered and groped to recall the reason she was here. She walked the aisles. Baggies? Batteries? While standing next to the Wonder Bread she remembered.

At the checkout line, Sam set the loaf pan on the counter behind a skinny girl with bad posture, not much older than twenty, dwarfed by her hooded sweatshirt and a pink nylon miniskirt hanging off her hips. The girl's hair was scrunched shiny and covered half her face, as if she were trying to obscure her prominent nose. She wore heavy makeup, a thick layer of cheap powder that didn't quite match her skin, blue eyeliner, and metallic berry lipstick.

"These are expired," the middle-aged clerk said too loudly, sighing and handing two coupons back to the girl. "And you can only use one per item." She handed back another.

"Sorry. I didn't notice," the girl said to the floor, shoving the coupons into her pocket.

Sam looked down at what the girl was buying: shampoo, soap, Skittles, Lean Cuisine, and then a bag full of small packets that had already been rung up. Condoms, individually packaged, thirty or so. And then she saw the girl's shoes, Lucite platform heels. She is a prostitute, Sam thought, feeling instantly sorry for her, sorry for having seen the condoms, sorry for the scorn of the clerk. She wanted the girl to look at her so she could smile to say, I'm not judging you. We do what we can to get by. Things will get better.

The girl dragged her bag off the counter and slunk off, shoulders hunched, as the clerk shook her head. Sam would not look at the clerk, not collude; she would punish her for being rude.

Outside, the sky was opening up enough to promise the rain was past. The breeze was cold and smelled of damp leaves.

But as Sam started the car she looked up and saw the girl again, sitting in a dented, rust-edged white sedan one row over, plucking her eyebrows in the sun-visor mirror. Did she work during the day? Or watch TV until the appointed hour? Where did a prostitute live in Madison? What did her life look like?

Sam waited. The girl backed out. And Sam followed her.

She kept a little distance between her car and the white sedan as they turned west on East Washington. She knew she was acting foolish—or downright weird—by following a stranger, but she didn't care. She didn't want to go home.

The girl signaled left, and Sam did the same. They turned into the Sunrise Inn. It was not as rock-bottom as the Admiral, but it was decrepit and shady, with a whiff of illicitness about it. Through hazy windows was a dank indoor pool, a sure repository of germs and STDs. The motel was only a short strip mall away from the massage parlor. Sam pulled in next door in front of a dingy day-care center called Kid-zone, its painted sign chipped and faded, the window glass cloudy yellow.

When the girl got out she looked even more furtive than Sam had remembered, her possum-nosed profile wan, her narrow shoulders rounded as she struggled with a large soda and her drugstore bags. She worked the key into the door-knob, jamming it in and shimmying the handle before the door bucked open. She turned then and looked straight at Sam, who froze, hoping she was obscured by the windshield. The girl went in and the dark room swallowed her up, the door banging closed behind her.

A large black-haired woman in sweatpants and a tube top, despite the cool temperature, sauntered out of another room smoking a cigarette and leaned her back against the balcony. She sniffed her armpit without reacting. Her shoulders were acne scarred, her elbows ashy. A boy in a Batman mask peeked his head out the door. Sam had the flash of thought that he was the age her son would have been, and she felt the prickly heat of guilt. She had never allowed herself to mourn him. She didn't deserve to.

The woman yelled at the boy and pointed with her cigarette to get back inside.

Sam shook her head. What am I doing? she thought. She played her brother's message.

"Sammy. It's Theo. You should have gotten a box I over-nighted you. I've been trying to sort through the last of Mom's stuff and I thought you might want to look through some of it. Faded photos, this and that—keepsakes, I guess you'd call them. All in some old wooden box. I don't know. Not to sound cold or anything, but I don't want any of it.

It'll just sit in the basement. You were always more senti-
mental. And you have Ella now. Call me."

The pointed reference to Ella felt accusatory. He and
Cindy had tried for years to conceive, then Clomid, five
attempts at IUI, and six rounds of IVF at $15,000 a try.
Sam, unfairly she knew, thought Cindy, a closet purger and
compulsive exerciser, had been too thin to get pregnant.
When Cindy turned forty-two, they had finally stopped try-
ing. The one time Sam had raised the issue of adoption,
Theo had quickly shut her down.

"We want to have our child, not someone else's," he'd
said. "End of story."

Sam had a friend Mina in New York who'd been a gesta-
tional surrogate for her gay brother and his partner. The
magnanimity of such an offering, and the beatification it had
bestowed upon Mina, appealed to Sam, but she didn't think
she loved Theo or Cindy enough to even broach the topic
with them. Not that they would want her to carry their child
anyway, to always feel that they owed her. It was all too intimate, and intimacy had never been a family strong suit.

When Sam had gone to Florida she had steeled herself to
find her mother emaciated and sickly, and she'd feared she
would have to avert her eyes. But Iris had picked her up at
the airport looking remarkably unremarkable. Her brunette
hair was newly cut in a smart bob, and she wore a white
linen tunic and khakis, her large sunglasses perched on her
head. In a hug her smallness was disconcerting, her pros-
thetic breast inserts firm and high, but her face was sun-
touched and Sam was, on the whole, relieved. Perhaps there

would be more time. Her own pregnant belly had emerged, a taut low mound, and Iris patted it with a little smile.

But the illusion of Iris's wellness dissipated quickly. By the time they arrived at the condo, Iris had used up all the energy she had put into her first impression, and she was exhausted. She needed her daughter's help just to get up the few front steps. And it was later, when Sam helped her with a bath, that the frailty of Iris's body came into devastating relief. When had she last seen her mother naked? She remembered as a girl seeing Iris—who must have been in her late forties then—after a shower unself-consciously hanging up the towel that had been wrapped around her body, exposing her womanly rounded hips and full breasts and the pouch at her stomach.

Now there were no more curves, no more softness around her bones. Her skin was slack, dry, and thin. Two ragged diagonal scars angrily crossed her chest where her breasts once were.

"I made it easy for them," Iris said, "since I wasn't getting reconstruction. Quick and dirty." She shrugged. "It wasn't that big of a loss, really. Though the scars really itch. That I could do without."

Iris gamely kept her tone light and Sam tried to comply, running a washcloth over the remains of the body that had given birth to her. Sam's pregnancy made the bath an awkward dance, each movement recalibrated to fit her changed shape.

"I like your haircut," Sam said, and they both laughed.

"Someday you will understand how hard it is for me to have you here," Iris said, as if Sam didn't already have a pretty good idea.

"I'm glad I could be with you, Mom," Sam had said. "I wish you would stop seeing it as some kind of sacrifice."

"I'm sorry for what I will have to ask of you," she had said.

In front of Sam's car a group of children, three little girls with short black hair and pierced ears, toddled out of the door of the day-care center ushered by a tiny old woman in a black stovepipe hat.

They were Hmong, most likely, a Southeast Asian ethnicity Sam hadn't heard of before moving to Madison. She'd first seen Hmong people at the farmers' market, petite in body with wide lovely faces, their ordered produce cheaper than that of the other stalls. During the Vietnam War, the CIA had recruited them to help fight the "Secret War" in Laos, and when the United States withdrew from the region and the communists took over the Lao kingdom, the Hmong were singled out for retribution. Hundreds of thousands fled, and many of those refugees ended up in Wisconsin.

How could I ever have the nerve to complain about anything, Sam thought. The first Wisconsin winter for the Hmong must have felt like banishment to a frozen hell.

One of the little girls was crying, snot running down into her gaping mouth, but the old woman ignored her. She marched her charges—not dressed warmly enough for the chill, Sam thought—through the parking lot out toward the commercial strip. Sam watched in her rearview as the miniature group trundled in a row along the busy street. After a while the bobbing black hat was the only thing visible. Sam had never seen public housing in Madison, but she knew it was close by, tucked behind the fast-food restaurants and the tire stores. Was that where they were headed? Should she have offered them a ride?

A hard knock on her window froze her breath. It was a policeman, his radio a loud litany of static, chirping, and a garbled voice of a female dispatcher, as Sam rolled down the window.

"Is your kid in there?" he said, pointing to the center.

"No. She's with . . . I was just. Sitting here. Thinking."

"You're loitering. At a child facility."

"What? Oh, no. Really. I'll move." She straightened up and reached for her ignition.

"Hold on a minute. You're not going until I say you're going. License and registration, please."

As the officer walked away with Sam's documents, she saw the reflection of her car in the Kidzone window and had the awful realization that he was checking to see if she was some kind of pedophile on the registered sex offender list. She was molten in embarrassment, sweat dripping down her sides, at a loss even about what to do with her hands, finally hooking her fingers on the bottom rung of the steering wheel. The cop returned and handed back her license and registration card.

"I'm sorry I caused any concern. I'm a mother," she said, as if that exempted her from suspicion.

"Move it along, ma'am," he barked, quickly taking his leave.

She started the car, her hand quivering, and backed out in front of the cruiser. She wanted to wave and smile, to

erase any doubt the officer had, but she refrained, not trust-
ing herself these days to know how to appear normal. In
the last year she had lost the conception she used to have of
herself, as if her internal filter had been knocked askew. But
when she shifted into drive and looked up, there was the
girl she had followed, standing in the doorframe of the
motel room eating from a large bag of Skittles, her hair in a
ponytail now, accentuating the sharp trajectory of her nose.
Her lips were wet with purple lip gloss, her feet bare, one
foot perched on the inside of her knee like a flamingo. She was
someone's daughter. A few wrong choices and here she
was. Surely Sam could talk to her, reach out to her in some
way, couldn't she? Who are you trying to convince? Sam
said to herself. You can't even talk to your husband. She
could see the police officer in her periphery, and she slowly
moved forward.

She knew she was losing her grasp on the day, and she
had to get to work. The thought that her output was now
absurdly tied to Jack's career made her eyes ache. She
drove back to her familiar neighborhood, trees afire, sun
high, Tibetan peace flags and bicycles on porches, lawn signs
sprouting from overgrown yards—THERE IS NO SUCH THING
AS CLEAN COAL, NADER IS MY HOMEBOY, WHERE ARE WE
GOING AND WHY AM I IN THIS HANDBASKET?—scarecrows
and elaborately carved pumpkins on stoops, and the purple
moose head mounted on her neighbor's front door.

When she got out of the car, she felt the odd freedom of
nothing to carry but a nonstick loaf pan—no groceries, no
diaper bag, no baby. She reveled in the buoyancy of being
an unencumbered body. But as she approached her small
white house, she could see the box waiting for her on the

front steps. Dread replaced lightness. Perhaps it would be better not to know any more about her mother. Didn't she already know enough?

She hoisted the box up to her hip, carried it inside, and plunked it down on the kitchen table.

VIOLET

Violet led her mother by the hand from Madam Tang's, through Chinatown, and back into more familiar territory, where they settled into an easy stroll down the sunny side of Park Row, part of the late-day stream of hucksters and shoppers spilling over from Chatham Square. As they made their way around the street's curve, ahead of them rose the towering Park Row Building that, when completed, would be the tallest in the world.

"His name is Mr. Lewis, and he is a prosperous gentleman," Lilibeth said. Her mother was dreamy, her hand on her throat as she talked about her latest boyfriend. Violet warmed to her when she was like this, felt less vexed by Lilibeth's mercurial moods.

"He's a loan officer at the bank," she said, as if she had already forgotten that she was married.

The once-neat waves of Lilibeth's pale hair were mussed, her hairpins crookedly replaced behind her ear. Her dress was white linen and lace, muddy at its hem, and when the wind blew, the slender outlines of her arms were visible through its blousy sleeves.

"He doesn't know about you yet," her mother said. "I didn't want to scare him off. You understand how it is, Vi."

Violet understood. There had been a string of men—pawnbrokers, philanthropists, cardsharps, politicians—since they'd arrived in New York City. Lilibeth played up her lilting accent and delicate demeanor, which Violet found confusing at first, and then annoying, and then ignorable. If city people—men especially—wanted to believe she came from a white-columned plantation house, so be it. As her mother spun tales, Violet never let on that Aberdeen—all of Barren County really—was the pits. There was nothing genteel about it: prairies, caves, and sinkholes, rife with muskrats, wild turkeys, and copperheads. Nino said it didn't matter anyway because everyone in the city was from someplace else, and really he'd rather be from Kentucky than Calabria, so she should feel lucky.

Violet didn't like to think about how her mother would have an easier time without her, and she was still willing to believe Lilibeth knew that there was a chance for something more this time. Her mother could have left her in Aberdeen, Violet reminded herself, and she had not.

As they approached City Hall, the pigeons scattered, abandoning the crumbs of an old roll, which crunched under Violet's feet. A group of boys, their pants rolled up to the knees, played toss-penny in the adjoining park. She recognized a thief who worked up on Doyers Street, and Buck, a newsboy with two protruding front teeth. He squinted his rodent eyes at her, always peeved that Nino paid her any mind.

The thief looked up from the game and whistled—
Lilibeth usually elicited reactions—and pulled his shirt out
in two points. Violet scowled at him, but her mother didn't
notice as she floated along, smiling a little at the twitter of
starlings in the bushes.

The gas lamps were being lit, and the electric lights of the
bridge—a blue-white light every hundred feet that made a
chain from Manhattan to Brooklyn—blazed against the veil
of dusk, their reflections like dots of fire in the windows of
the sooty tenements that skirted the bridge's massive supports.

They reached Water Street, the twilight bringing on an
air of glittery possibility and sin. In an alley, a ring of wool-
capped men, dockworkers, yelled and jeered at a cockfight.
Violet lingered to glimpse the birds, which danced around
each other, landing bloody jabs with their chipped beaks
and sharpened claws.

"Come on, now," her mother said. "Stop your dawdling.
You, child, need a bath."

Lilibeth, with the help of Mr. Lewis, had rented a new
room in a building near the wharf, a dormered attic with a
window and a sink. The ceiling was low but the room was
surprisingly airy, and when Violet sat at just the right angle,
she could see a tiny triangle of the river flashing in the city
lights. She wanted this to be home.

"I have a job," Lilibeth said, her hand flitting to her hair.
She turned from the pot of water on the stove and smiled at
Violet, a girlish, pleased smile.

"Really?"

"Some ironing. For the grocer's wife, you know, Mrs.

Baker. With the funny squished face. Maybe you'll help me with it?"

Violet nodded, wanting to keep her mother buoyed.

"I won't go there anymore. To the Madam's." Lilibeth turned away, her eyes glossy.

The air from the open window was cool and only a little fishy. Violet tapped the pane with her finger, forcing herself not to grab for the hope that threw out a new line whenever her mother was her mother again.

"You aren't sorry you came with me, are you, baby girl?" Lilibeth's face threatened to fold, her eyes water-clear, exposed.

"No, Mama," Violet said. And she wasn't.

Her mother filled bowl after bowl with cold water from the sink and emptied them into a tin tub on the floor. She wrapped towels around the pot and added the boiling water.

"I didn't know they would cut off your pretty hair," she said, helping Violet pull the dress over her head. "I'm sorry about that."

The warm water turned Violet's skin pink, and her dirt turned the bathwater gray. She closed her eyes as her mother cupped water over her head. She had missed her mother, an instinctual, wordless ache, no matter how she had tried to convince herself otherwise, no matter how much she did not want to need someone whose eyes seemed permanently cast on some distant shore that no one else could see.

"You look more like your father with your new hair."

"No, I don't."

"He was handsome," Lilibeth said. "In his way."

When they had married, and it became apparent that Lilibeth could not maintain the cookstove or take care of the chickens or even bake biscuits—"Why should I know those things?" she had said to Violet—Bluford made it known that he felt cheated. Any fondness between them had dried up and blown away like crackled remnants of dead leaves.

"Do you think he misses us?" Violet asked.

"I don't think he does," her mother said, slowly lathering Violet's hair. "But we don't miss him neither, do we?" She giggled. "That stupid way he used to walk, all hunched like, you remember? Like he was afraid frogs were going to start falling from the sky."

"How about how he ate a biscuit? Tearing the whole top off with his mouth and chewing so the whole world could see what was going on in there," Violet said.

"What about his mother? That ugly woman. Her face all pebbled. Belching at the table."

"I hated how he called me *girl*," Violet said.

The bathwater was quickly cooling to tepid. Lilibeth rinsed Violet's hair and helped her dry herself with a thin towel they had brought from Kentucky. She was calmed by her mother's touch, soothed by her closeness.

"You were never his," Lilibeth said, lying on the bed. "I mean, one look at those ice-blue eyes. You were always mine. You made me a mother. You're the only one who can ever say that." She closed her eyes.

Violet pulled one of her old dresses on over her head. "I'm hungry," she said.

"Check the cupboard. I can make you something in a bit."

"Are you going out later?" Violet asked.

"Mr. Smith is taking me to the cabaret. I think it will be quite marvelous."

Reginald Smith was a poet with sleepy eyes who wore a frayed pauper's coat but checked the time with a gold watch. His wealthy uptown family gave him a handsome allowance, which kept him in shabby comfort in a sprawling, rattletrap apartment, where, Violet guessed, her mother often slept. When he wasn't locked away, wringing out a poem that would surely cause a sensation if only he could get it to the right people—"He writes beautiful things, Vi; they wouldn't know what to make of him back home"—he would dote on Lilibeth and call her darling, and promenade her around town. Violet had met him once. She'd accompanied them to watch elephants being unloaded from a ship, bound for the circus. He jumped around with twitchy enthusiasm, waving his hands like a magician. When the elephants didn't appear, he bought Violet a giant pink lollipop and exclaimed she was a picture of innocence and beauty. Lilibeth had switched into her languid southern voice in his presence, much to his delight.

Violet didn't much care for him, but she didn't think he was dangerous. She thought he was foolish, a flimsy paper doll. But Lilibeth grew wan and began to stay away for longer than a night here and there. She was both listless and agitated, sleepy but never sleeping, complaining of headaches and sore hips, disdainful of light. It was Nino who figured it out as they watched Lilibeth duck into the staircase to Madam Tang's while other fuzzy-eyed customers came out.

"It's a dope den," he said. "They smoke the pipes up there."

It shouldn't have been entirely surprising—Lilibeth had been looking to give herself away ever since they had arrived in the city—but Violet felt like a trapdoor had swung open, pitching her into cold darkness. The world had become newly incomprehensible, opaque and shifty. Lilibeth had taken her out of Aberdeen, but now that they were here, Violet had begun to see that she was too much for her mother, begun to understand that her mother might be better off alone.

Lilibeth rolled over toward the wall. "You'll be okay tonight?" she asked.

Violet nodded, even though she knew her mother couldn't see her, and rummaged through the odd bowls, jars, and pots. The only thing she could find was an onion with one end gone soft and wet, but then in a coffee tin she found a package of pecans and a roll of dollar bills. Maybe Mr. Lewis was all right after all. She sat for a while, watching the last of the light leave the room, crunching on the sweet meat of the pecans, sipping tea, strong and hot. She felt clean and warm and good. She set her cup in the sink, pulled a dollar from the roll, and replaced the can on the top shelf.

The lanterns were lit, the lights on the bridge switched on, the saloons ablaze. It was night in the Fourth Ward, and Violet sat in the alley behind the Water Street Tavern, a dance hall and saloon, with the boys: Nino, Jimmy—just out of jail—and Charlie, fat-faced and short, who spent his days scooping out rendered fat from giant vats boiling bones and offal. They made Charlie sit down a ways because he smelled like rancid meat.

"Mikey left on the train," Nino said, chucking oyster shells.

Violet took a look at him to see if he was serious. "How do you know?" she asked. "He'll show up."

She reached down to scratch at a scab on her knee; she'd fallen climbing out of the window of the Home.

"His pops told him he had to go on it. Came at him with a belt. Mikey tried to hide out at the depot, but they must have got him."

"Why'd he want Mikey to get on it so bad?" Violet asked.

"They pay cash money for kids," Charlie called down.

"I thought it was preachers who run it," Violet said.

Nino shrugged.

"Well, shit, where do I sign up?" Jimmy said, laughing. "I never said no to free money."

"You're too old," Nino said.

"I don't look a day over fifteen," Jimmy said, grabbing the jug out of Nino's hand.

"Where's it go anyhow?" Violet asked.

"West somewheres. Where the farms are," Nino said.

Violet pictured the Christmas display she had seen, with kindly animals and baby Jesus in a cozy manger.

"They make you a slave is what I heard," Charlie said. "Now pass me that bottle down here."

Violet took a swig of the searing rum before handing him the jug. She could not leave her mother, not that her mother would ever let her go anyway.

The musicians were warming up inside. Violet went

around to the front window and positioned herself in front of one of the few uncracked panes, the light inside the bar a smoky golden orange.

"Twenty cents a dance," the host called out.

Twelve girls, their hair decorated with ribbons and flowers, their skirts barely below the knee, milled about on the side of the dance floor until the music struck up, and then they formed two lines, swaying in time. Men in the bar stood and blocked Violet's view. Now and then she caught a glimpse of the dancers, marching, spinning, and right-about-facing in a quadrille.

Violet marched in place to the music, even as the fiddler broke two strings. Nino came around the building. He stopped a few feet away from her.

"Don't," he said.

Violet stopped moving, confused by his tone and his anger shimmering just below the surface.

"You're no cherry," he said, spitting.

"What's it to you?" she said, trying to sound angry to cover up the quaver in her voice. Inside, the musicians began a Scottish reel.

But then Jimmy and Charlie came careening out of the alley, two sailor boys in pursuit.

"Run!"

Nino and Violet took off with them, dodging and weaving until they got to the river and collapsed, choking down air and laughing.

Li, Madam Tang's errand boy, leaned against a lamppost near them, outside a sailor house.

"Well, if it isn't Chinkaroo," Jimmy said, as Li approached.

"Don't you come up there no more," Li hissed at Violet.

"I thought you missed me," Violet said.

Nino laughed.

Li wedged himself between two barrels next to them. A big-ended rat trundled by, and Violet tried to hit it with a stone.

"What's that smell?" Li asked, covering his nostrils with the tips of his two fingers.

Nino nodded his head toward Charlie.

"I don't even smell anything," Charlie said. "Hey, Kentucky, do you think I smell?"

"You reek," Violet said.

Warm with rum, she leaned back against a burlap sack and looked up at the ship masts, which shot up and disappeared into the sky. The moon hovered in a sickle. Here she was and she was happy not to be in the Home, happy not to be in Aberdeen. She wished that nothing would change. But if she thought anymore about it she would have to admit that things had already changed. Nino had told her to stop dancing, and she'd felt a shame that was new and ominous. She was a child, a girl, who soon would no longer be one.

Li jumped up to try to sell his pipe dregs, but the young sailor he'd approached scurried away.

"Have you tried it?" Violet asked Li when he returned.

"It's for fools," Li said. "That's what Madam Tang say."

"Shut up," Nino said.

"What?" Li asked, exasperated.

"I done it," Jimmy said. "It's like tobacco but makes you drunk."

"You're full of shit," Charlie said.

Jimmy shrugged and spit.

Li unfolded a piece of newspaper. Inside were black sticky ashes.

"Who wants to smoke?" he asked, pulling a small reed pipe from his pockets and waving it in his fingers like a cigar.

"Atta boy," Jimmy said, his voice deep. He had slipped past childhood, no longer one of them, no matter how hard he pretended it wasn't so. Nino had told Violet that Ollie was going to pull Jimmy's papers; he had aged out of being a newsboy. A scar bisected the back of his hand.

"I got a dollar," Violet said. "What should we do with it?"

"Where'd you get a buck, kid?" Jimmy asked.

"I stole it from my mother."

"That ain't stealing," Nino said. "What'd she ever do for you that wasn't really for herself?"

A group of white-suited sailors walked by, singing a drunken round of "Row, Row, Row Your Boat."

"You boys want magic oriental potion?" Li said to them. He jumped up to make a deal.

"Don't get yourself shanghaied, fellas!" Charlie yelled.

"Woo-hoo!" Jimmy whooped. "Let's really get drunk."

Outside of the Tiger Eye, they saw the police clubbing a man, an Italian Nino recognized from the slaughterhouse. The blows were wet thuds, the man already out. In the shadows, men watched, their eyes hungry and hot. Bloody sludge ran in the grooves between the cobblestones.

"Come on," Violet said to the others.

As they moved in from the water, the carrion scent of the bone boiler grew stronger.

"Hey, Charlie, it's starting to smell like you around here," Jimmy said, kicking over a pile of rotten vegetables outside a shuttered market.

The Dugan brothers sat on the stoop of their tenement, throwing rocks at passersby.

"Mother busy in there, Red?" Nino said.

"Fuck off," he said. "At least she ain't as poor as Job's turkey."

They went to Willy's, where they would get served as long as they sat out back in the alley. Violet had been drunk many nights since arriving in New York, and once even before she'd left Aberdeen. She'd sat in the outhouse with a jelly jar of her father's homemade potato brew and choked down the firewater until her face flushed and her limbs felt loosey-goosey, and going back in that house, with its rough plank floor and tilted walls and parched woodsmoke air, which held on to the ghost of the dead baby boy her mother had given birth to, didn't seem as bad as before.

The alley was a rubble of passed-out men and garbage. It was late and cold, and Violet shivered.

"I'm sleeping out tonight. If you're wandering around," Nino said to her.

"She got us a room. I wouldn't want her to worry," Violet said, too eagerly, embarrassed by the naked hope in her voice.

Nino chuckled a little. "Okay," he said.

"Hi-ho cheerio, lads and lady," Jimmy said, clanking their tin cups so hard the rum sluiced over the sides.

Lilibeth did not return to the room that night. Violet lay in the bed that smelled of smoke and flowers and listened to the fighting in the room below, fists on flesh, broken glass, drunken sobs, until the crack of the early morning sun. She wondered what it would be like to know pure quiet, to sleep without the fits and starts of her heart catching, to hear her own breath.

When she finally sat up, her head throbbed and her tongue felt like sandpaper. The room was marble cold. There were a few chunks of coal in the bin, which she tossed into the stove, struggling to get a flame to catch. Thankfully there was old coffee in the bottom of the kettle. She rooted around for a shawl in Lilibeth's floral carpetbag, a gift from Bluford before they were married, to take on their honeymoon, a night in a hotel in Lexington that never happened. Sometimes Violet thought Lilibeth left Aberdeen just so she finally had a reason to use her bag.

In the corner of the room there was a teetering stack of laundry Mrs. Baker had brought over: shirts, trousers, petticoats, and dresses. Violet ran her finger along the brocade trim around the collar of one of the dresses, a velvet ribbon tie at the neck. She held it up to her front and wondered how it would feel to wear it, to feel the skirt swishing about her legs, to feel like someone new. But her fingers fumbled on the complicated buttons and laces, and she got tired from holding up the unbearably heavy dress, her hands shaky with hunger. She draped the dress back on top of the pile. She poured coffee into a chipped little cup—it tasted bitter and burned—and set the iron on the stove.

She had never actually ironed, but she figured it couldn't be that hard. She spit on the iron and it sizzled. She spread a man's white shirt on the bed, and placed the iron on it, but when she moved it up the front panel it left a scorched yellow trail. The smell of hot cotton filled the room. She touched the spot and burned her finger. She tried to stand the iron up on the bed but it rolled off onto the floor, and then she gave up, shoving the shirt to the bottom of the pile.

When Lilibeth appeared, she was pale and drawn.

"I'm going for coal," Violet said curtly. "And bread."

"Yes, yes," Lilibeth exhaled, crawling onto the bed. "Get me some remedy? I don't feel well. Money's up in the tin."

"When do I get to meet your Mr. Lewis?" Violet asked.

Her mother knit her brows. "Oh, soon, Vi. Real soon. You're going to like him a whole lot."

"Okay," Violet said, resolving not to ask about him again.

"I brought you something."

Violet turned to her, easily warmed.

Lilibeth reached into her drawstring pouch and pulled out a pink rose blossom, its petals bruised in transit.

"I thought we could pin it in your hair." She patted the bed for Violet to sit and reached for her hairbrush on the windowsill.

Violet closed her eyes as her mother pulled the brush through her hair. Lilibeth pulled two pins from her own hair and fastened the flower behind Violet's ear.

"Look at you," she said. "Stay still for a second. I'm going to remember you just like this. There." She pulled a small mirror from her purse and held it up. "A real young lady."

Violet blushed when she saw herself; the frilliness of the flower in her chopped hair embarrassed her. But her mother looked pleased, momentarily relieved of the groove between her eyes, and Violet was happy for that.

"You know he had a photograph taken of me at a portrait studio uptown?" Lilibeth said.

"Really?"

"I never had my photograph taken before. Bluford thought it was a waste of money whenever the traveling man brought his camera to Aberdeen. He didn't even want a wedding picture." She smiled. "I always wanted to have my photograph taken. To see what I really look like."

"You see yourself in mirrors," Violet said.

"Well, yes." Lilibeth tucked her hands under the pillow. "But you know how you can catch a glimpse of yourself in a shiny window before you know it's you?"

"I suppose," Violet said, not really understanding.

"In a photograph you can see how other people see you," she said, angling her face to look at the window.

"You always look pretty, Mama."

Lilibeth held out her hand for Violet to hold. "You are dear to me. Go on, now. My head hurts something awful."

"Will you be here when I get back?"

Lilibeth nodded. "We'll eat our breakfast together."

Outside it smelled of acrid chemical smoke from a fire at the soap factory. Violet's eyes burned. At the market, she bought bread, apples, and a slab of butter, and lifted a handful of caramels and a sack of dried apricots. She walked all over looking for Pardee's for her mother, but everywhere was out. She took the long way, swinging by the Mission, to see if the Aid Society ladies were out again, looking for kids. Maybe someone she knew was going to get on a train. But no one was there except a drunk who looked already dead.

On her way home, Violet found Nino hustling papers on Cherry Street.

"News of the world, one penny only! Three hundred twenty-six people dead in New Jersey steamship fire! Read all about it!"

Two men shoved coins in Nino's hand and took papers. When they were gone, Violet skipped across the street.

"Here," she said, handing him the apricots.

"You musta heard my belly grumbling. What's the flower for?"

She quickly pulled the rose from her hair and tossed it. "Nothing."

A large red-faced young man sauntered toward them, his blond hair buzzed close to the scalp, his hands in his pockets. Nino stood up straight, puffing out his chest.

"Eastman," he said under his breath, the name of a gang that controlled a section of the Fourth Ward.

"Top of the morning to you, young friend," the man said, in mocking cheer. "Why don't you hand over your coin pouch and whatever's in your pockets?"

Nino stood stone-faced and crossed his arms. He reached only to the man's chest.

"Fuck off," Violet said.

The man laughed and nodded. "I like this one," he said, and then threw a punch that landed in Nino's gut.

Nino doubled over onto the street, a wagon swinging out wide to avoid him. Violet jumped on the man, punching and scratching, until he swatted her off. She landed hard on her knees, the pain shooting up her legs. The man kicked the stack of papers into the gutter and pointed a meaty finger at Nino before walking away.

"*Figlio di puttana!*" Nino shouted, a vein on his temple bulging blue. He got up to his knees, his thick fists clenched.

She stood gingerly and limped over to Nino to help save some of the papers blowing about. They sat together on the curb and ate apricots.

"*E chi se ne frega*, my father says," he said. "Pfft. Who gives a damn."

She knew it was best not to say anything about it. "You seen them rounding up snipes for the train?" she asked.

He worked his jaws on the sticky fruit and squinted up at the soap-factory smoke hovering above the neighborhood.

"Think they really get families?" she asked.

"What?"

"Those kids that go on the train."

"I don't know," he said, impatient with her questions and annoyed that she was letting her neediness show.

"Maybe I could go on one," Violet said.

"They'll make you do chores and go to church. It'll be like the shitcan Home all over again."

"I don't know," she said.

"Besides, you're no orphan," Nino said.

"So? Mikey wasn't either."

He spat out a bad apricot onto the sidewalk. She knew he would want to get on the train, too, if his family would ever let him go.

"Vamoose. I got to sell at full chisel," he said. "Rent's late. They's banging on the door all the time."

"See you around," she said, punching him in the arm, wishing she could smooth the way for Nino, knowing what they all knew, that he had a year or two at most before he would have to pick a gang to fight for.

She held her parcel of food to her chest so no one could snatch it and set off toward home. Her knees ached. Above her in the tenements, women pulled in laundry because of the smoke.

When she returned to the room, coughing from the rotten air and six flights of damp-walled stairs, her mother was gone and so was the money, the open tin lying empty on the bed.

There had been a time in Kentucky, before the baby came, that Violet remembered as almost happy. Lilibeth, her belly a hard mound, had been vibrant and girlish, her hair thicker, curlier, blonder, her face full and flush, as she walked to town or gathered blackberries or accompanied Bluford to church.

"Feel it, Vi, can you feel it move?" she said, as they sat together on the banks of the stream, the cool, silty water twirling around their ankles.

Violet put her hand on her mother's stomach and felt the *whoosh* of the baby shifting positions, an elbow here, a foot there. It was funny to her, strange but exciting. A brother or a sister. Even her father seemed less angry at her, less likely to cuff her for burned lima beans or broken eggs or needing a pencil for school.

"He's sure it will be a boy," Lilibeth said, pulling apart a cattail and letting the fuzz blow away. "We'll call him William."

Maybe with a boy, Violet thought, he will be nicer to me.

The house was less suffocating then—her sour tobacco-chewing grandmother had not yet moved in—and Bluford had even stopped bothering Lilibeth at night, which meant no grunts, creaks, or sighs for Violet to wish away from her pallet on the floor in the living room.

During the warming humid days of spring, the air thick with the weedy smells of goat grass and foxtail, Lilibeth would sit on the broken-slatted chair on the porch, her dirty-soled bare feet resting up on the railing, and watch the birds, the ants, her belly, the sky.

"Get your mama some water?"

Violet, annoyed at being pulled away from catching frogs, dragged herself from the ditch, went to the water barrel, and ladled out a cool sip for herself before filling a jar for her mother.

"You looking at something?" Violet asked, handing her mother the glass.

"I'm watching it all grow," she said, smiling, setting her feet down on the floor. "Come sit on your mama's lap for a bit."

Violet, too old and too big, tried to balance in the small space not taken up by the baby, and nestled her face against her mother's neck.

"This is nice," Lilibeth said.

"It's too hot," Violet said, sitting up and jumping down to the porch.

"Always your own little pirate. Go on, now."

The blood arrived a few days later. Some spots in the bed became a rivulet down Lilibeth's leg, which became a gush of pink water as she tried to make it to the outhouse.

There wasn't a doctor in Aberdeen, not that it would have mattered. The baby, a boy, was dead before he was

born, blue and slick. Bluford, the only time Violet had seen
tenderness from him, wiped the blood from the baby's face
with a towel and wrapped him, still attached to the pla-
centa, in a blanket. Violet watched from the doorway
as her father kissed the baby's forehead and placed the
bundle in Lilibeth's arms. Bluford pushed by Violet and
was gone.

A neighbor's wife arrived with cabbage leaves to relieve
Lilibeth's milk-swollen breasts. The minister came by to
bless the baby's soul.

"He was warm," her mother would say for weeks afterward, her face confused and broken. "He was warm for a
little while."

After two days, Bluford finally had taken the swaddled
baby from Lilibeth and buried it in the backyard under the
branches of the mulberry tree, whose ripe and rotting berries had quickly stained the earth a sticky, inky purple.
Within a few weeks, the patch had been lost under a shroud
of weeds.

Violet waited for her mother for another day before setting
off again for Madam Tang's. This time she went alone, and
she was not scared. Fancy-suited men ducked in and sneaked
out of the customer entrance, and she hated them. Chinese
vendors pulled carts past, laden with chicken feet and roots
and fish. The neighborhood men wore short pants and col-
larless shirts. She saw only two women, one barely taller
than herself, hurrying along with a sack bulging with vegetables, a baby on her back. The other was young, her hair

pulled high and tight, her lips painted pink. She eyed Violet with a competitive glance before moving on.

Lilibeth emerged, her hand a visor against the sun, disheveled, in a dress Violet didn't recognize, brown velvet with puffed sleeves.

"Mama," Violet called, running over.

Lilibeth winced and then covered it with a smile.

"Well, hi, baby," she said, her drawl opium-slow. "I was on my way to get you. Have you been okay by yourself?"

"Mrs. Baker's come by a bunch for the laundry."

Her mother nodded, her face vacant. "I thought you might busy yourself with some of that ironing," she said. "I imagine your little hands would be good at that."

Violet gnawed her dirty thumbnail. "That's a new dress," she said.

"You like it?" her mother said, running her palms dreamily down the velvet. "I went to a restaurant uptown with Mr. Lewis, and I couldn't very well wear one of my old dresses. You should have seen it, Vi. White tablecloths, crystal glasses. The most delicious roast with these darling little carrots. Maybe we'll go there sometime. You and me."

They were out of Chinatown, and men now felt free to turn their heads to keep their eyes on Lilibeth, to tip their hats with leering eyes.

"There's no more coal," Violet said.

"Hmm," her mother said.

"And no food."

Lilibeth stopped, and leaned over with her hands on Violet's shoulders. Her breath was stale with smoke.

"Violet," she said. "I've been thinking. You know how

hard I'm trying. I am to see Reginald in a day or two. You remember Reginald? He will give me a little something, I'm sure. But until then, I don't know. I don't know what else to do. Give your mama a hug now. I love you so."

Violet felt a stone in her stomach. She knew what was coming, as she felt the bird-wing arms of her mother enfold her.

"It will just be for a few days this time. I promise," Lilibeth said. "Be a good girl, Vi, for your mama. Listen to the ward mistress." She smoothed her hand across Violet's forehead. "At least they won't have to cut your hair again."

Violet held her tears and bit the soft, smooth flesh of her inner cheek until blood, warm and salty, slid over her tongue. "No," she said softly.

Her mother pretended not to hear her. She held her hand on her chest and squinted against the sun.

"I'm not going back there," Violet said, stopping.

"Violet, please. Please don't make this harder for me. I'm doing the best I can." Her eyes, still dilated and heavy lidded, sparkled with tears. "I could have left you with him, and I didn't. I wanted better for us."

Violet wanted to pummel her mother, kick her in the shins, tear her luxurious dress. More than that, she wanted her mother to tuck her in and sing the song she used to sing when Violet had been fevered and was sweating it out in the old iron bed, looking up at the branches of the crooked pine tree smashed against the window.

A gypsy rover came over the hill,
down through the valley so shady.

He whistled and he sang till the green woods rang,
and he won the heart of a lady.

When she sang, Lilibeth's voice was a whispery slip of smoke that curled up and floated away. Violet wanted what her mother could never give her. She wanted something different from this.

"There's a train," Violet said, looking down at the sidewalk. "You can put me on the train."

IRIS

The roses had still been in bloom along the east split-rail fence of the yard. Armistice Day, 1940. School had been closed for the holiday, so Iris was home. She'd even been allowed to go to the movies the night before, a rare indulgence for a girl who spent innumerable hours daydreaming Hollywood scenarios with herself as the romantic lead. They'd gone all the way to Caledonia to see *His Girl Friday*, the drive a small sacrifice, as far as Iris was concerned, to see Cary Grant. Rosalind Russell was not as glamorous as Iris would have hoped, but she had still loved getting lost in the story on that huge screen and had slid the ticket stub into the mirror above her dresser. She twirled her ponytail for a moment, and then hopped up to wash out her oatmeal bowl.

Her mother had gone to town to deliver one of her famous Jenny Lind cakes to the Veterans' Home, and her father was out in the fields somewhere beyond the ridge surveying the new wheat grass shoots. Iris pulled on a cardigan and went out back to the garden, where there was still, strangely, plenty of spinach and broccoli to pick. Here it was

November and it was in the mid-sixties—it had been unseasonably warm for weeks—and even if her father was concerned that there would be too much crop growth before the land froze, she was happy about it, giddy with the reprieve from the withering cold that would last until April.

There was no warning, no weather service radio announcement, no siren. The wind started first and Iris spun around in her skirt. But all of a sudden it was very cold, and the sleet poured from the sky in freezing sheets, and wind almost knocked her over, and Iris knew something was terribly wrong. She ran to the house. Within an hour the temperature had dropped forty degrees, and it was a raging blizzard, the winds driving snow in every direction. She could see nothing but white from the windows. She didn't even see the car's headlights as it drove right up to the edge of the porch. Her mother pushed through the front door, gasping, her sweater, hair, even her eyelashes covered in snow.

Iris ran to her, relieved to see her but a little thrilled, too, by the scariness and excitement of the storm. It was like the time they'd had to huddle in the cellar during a tornado, like she was Dorothy in *The Wizard of Oz*, the winds moaning above them. They'd sung songs and eaten pickles she'd helped her mother can the previous fall.

"Where's your father?" her mother said. Her normally impassive face was tense in fear and wet with melting snow.

Iris's stomach dropped. She had not given him a thought.

"Iris, look at me," her mother said, grabbing her shoulders with her strong, cold fingers. "Didn't he come in?"

"He must have gone to the machine shed. He must have."

Her mother ran to the kitchen window, but she couldn't

even see to the chicken coop. She dashed to the catchall closet in the hall where tools mingled with cleaning supplies and winter boots. Iris knew her mother was going out to find him.

"Mother, no." She started to cry, panicking. "You can't go out there." She wanted to say, You can't leave me, but she knew it sounded selfish.

"Get my coat, Iris, and gloves and a hat. A wool blanket from the cedar chest."

Iris collected these things with her heart rattling in her chest.

Her mother tied one end of a large coil of rope around the outside of her coat and tied the blanket around her head.

"Hold on to this end," her mother said. The rope must have been a hundred feet. She gave her daughter a rare kiss. "It'll be fine, Iris." And she was gone, the door whipping open and cracking against the side of the house.

Iris gripped the rope, wrapping it around her rigid hand, shivering, as snow blew into the kitchen. She watched the loops of the rope slowly uncoil. And when the rope went taught, she held fast, offering God everything for her parents' return. A snowdrift grew on the landing as she watched, a powdery tower.

Ten minutes later, they were back, blundering through the door, dazed, her father with the blanket around him, still holding her mother's hand. He sat stiffly at the kitchen table as she bustled about filling the bathtub. She unpeeled the blanket and his sodden clothes, and helped him into the steamy bathroom.

Iris had stood dumbly by, unable to say anything, clutch-ing the end of the limp rope.

They'd closed the door and gotten in the bathtub together.

It was warmer now, the humidity rising with the morning, and Iris, her fingers quick to get cold these days, was com-fortable in the day's heat. It was difficult to conjure the feel-ing of that blizzard almost sixty years ago, but her heart still ricocheted recalling the ferocity of the storm, how close, in those minutes she sat with a rope in her hand, life was to death. The stories had trickled in for days about those who had died: duck hunters stranded on river islands, a family buried in a stalled car, a young farmer who went to get wood from the barn and got lost, ending up frozen in a field. It could have so easily included Samuel Olsen, lost half a mile out in his wheat field, who'd picked a direction and started walking, hoping his internal compass was right, and came upon his fearless and dogged wife, a tether around her waist, who'd come to bring him home.

"That was so brave, what you did," she had said to her mother the next morning.

"You do what you can for those close to you," her mother had said. "There's nothing brave about it."

Even now, Iris didn't know what to make of her parents' marriage. As a girl she had begrudged them for not holding hands or kissing or dancing to the radio. Later, she believed that neither had expected a lot from life, so they had been satisfied with mere companionship. But now it seemed their devotion was something far greater, quiet and abiding: faith that one was always looking out for the other.

Iris swung her feet off the couch and sat up wincing, her head swimming in stars, a deafening pulse in her ears. When her eyes cleared she looked around the room at the things she could clear out now so her children wouldn't have to deal with them: a bowl of conch shells she'd found on morning beach strolls, Scrabble—Henry's—and Yahtzee, a glossy book of photos of Sanibel's "Ding" Darling Wildlife Refuge, even the TV. But maybe Samantha will want to watch something while she's here, she thought.

Although it was never stated as such, Samantha was coming to care for Iris until she died. After the double mastectomy and the radiation had failed and the cancer was everywhere, Iris had asked her oncologist how much time he'd wager she had left. She had thought he'd say a year. He raised his shoulders and palms in a defeated shrug and said, "Maybe six months if you're lucky." Lucky. That wasn't how she would have put it, but here she was six months later, still ticking. But the ticking was stalling, skipping, slowing a bit more each day.

Samantha would arrive tomorrow. Iris sometimes thought of her daughter as a twittering bird, anxious and restless. Marriage and art—Samantha was an accomplished potter—had been grounding for her, but now that she was pregnant, Iris saw the nervousness come flooding back. Her son-in-law Jack was not all he could be. He was fine, Iris supposed, though she had hoped for someone with a little more oomph. Maybe she'd never gotten over his weak handshake. She knew she was being unfair, surely she was afraid that her daughter was repeating her own mistakes, her willingness to settle for just okay. And Samantha was not like Iris, it was true. Samantha ached to be a mother. She was exhilarated by each passing week of pregnancy—"Mom, she's the size of a baseball!"—and didn't see motherhood as a duty to fulfill. Iris worried about what would happen after the euphoria wore off and the grind set in, those long hours tending to a baby insatiable for food, attention, comfort. Those long hours trying to figure out if it was worth it after all.

Oh, Samantha, Iris thought. I wish I could be there for you then.

A succession of quick knocks hammered the door, startling Iris. Samantha? No, no, she was still in Wisconsin. I am here on the couch in Sanibel, Iris said to herself, trying to settle her mind. The knocks began again.

"Coming," she said weakly, wiping the drool from the corner of her mouth. She rose and teetered to the door, at the last minute realizing she was still in her robe. "Who is it?"

"Honey, it's me, Stephen. From next door."

She opened the door, the day clear now, the muggy warmth soft and heavy. Stephen was shirtless, his chest muscled and hairless and bronzed an orangish hue, and he wore his uniform pants and tasseled loafers.

"I'm so sorry to bother you," he said breathlessly. "This is super embarrassing. I'm locked out? I went to say goodbye to a friend. The door was propped open. Oh, it doesn't even matter, does it? The point is I'm going to be late for work and I can't be late for work. The convention has descended. The wacky orchid people."

What is he talking about? Iris wondered.

"Is there some way I can help you?" she finally asked.

"I need to climb over your balcony to mine. If you wouldn't mind."

"Of course not," she said pulling open the door. "Come on in."

"I love your place," he said, looking around. "So . . ."

"Old Lady Florida-ish?"

Stephen spun around.

"Hardly. It's kind of mid-century chic. White lacquer is very in these days."

Iris chuckled, indulging his flattery. He had kind eyes underneath the showy affectations, river green and clear.

Stephen bent down to pick up her book, which had fallen to the floor when she'd risen.

"Book club?" he asked, examining the cover.

"Of one," she said, pointing to herself.

"Do they get there?"

"What?"

"To the lighthouse?"

"I don't know. The young boy wants to go, but the father always has a reason not to take him."

"I know the feeling," Stephen said, handing her back the book.

All at once she wished she had made more of an effort with him over the years. Invited him for tea. Or dropped by with scones after the man of the night had left in the morning. And why had she ignored that pea-sized knot she had felt in her breast the night Henry had told her he could not leave his wife? She had felt it, and then pretended that she hadn't. Was it fear or denial or resignation? Or was it that she wanted to opt out? Even now, she couldn't really say. It wasn't until many months later, when her breast had become hot and painful, that she could no longer pretend. Now it

seemed loony that she had let it go, giving the disease an irrev-
ocable head start.

"I will owe you forever, Irene," Stephen said. "You're a
doll face. That new haircut really suits you, by the way. A
pixie Anna Wintour."

His compliment was preposterous, but still it brightened
her. It would be her last haircut, and she was pleased that
he had noticed.

As he passed the kitchen, Stephen registered the pill bottles
on the counter with the subtlest of eye flicks. Iris was about
to explain, but he moved quickly past, not wanting her to
reveal the details. Life was hard enough, she imagined him
thinking, without someone else's suffering ladled on top.

He wavered a little as he climbed over her balcony railing, his legs wobbly like a colt's.

"If you ever need anything," he said. His offer trailed off
as he slid open his glass balcony door.

Iris started to wave, but Stephen was already gone.

The encounter had worn her out. Iris went into the
kitchen and stared down her pills. She took them grudg-
ingly, each one leaving a hard, chalky path down her throat.
She stared into the refrigerator, then pulled out a bowl of
raspberries and set it on the table next to her book, before
easing into the chair.

Why did Mrs. Ramsay want everyone to get married
when her own marriage wasn't so great? Iris gingerly chewed
a berry, not biting too hard for fear of the seeds. Was marriage ever that great? Iris did miss Glenn sometimes; those
years together had bred a comforting shared history, an ease
of communication, not about their feelings for each other
maybe, but a shorthand of words and body cues with which

to navigate the world. After the divorce she was sorry she had lost the one person she could really talk to about Samantha and Theo, the one person who could understand without setup or explanation. "Theo is being Theo, isn't he?" or "I worry that Samantha is going to pull a Sally Reed." Iris hoped that Glenn missed her sometimes, too. Maybe when Marie was prattling on about dream catchers and turquoise jewelry and sagebrush incense, or whatever it was they talked about, he would think fondly of Iris. She wondered if Glenn would attend her funeral. Should there be a funeral? No. She would be dead, and that would be that.

Her mother had died of a heart attack, in her sleep, at the age of seventy-nine. She had lived alone on what was left of the farm, some chickens and two pigs in the yard, in the faded farmhouse, the porch sagging some and partially obscured by the lilacs, which Iris had watched her father plant, now a fragrant tangle of overgrown branches. Her mother had always been a hardy sort, never admitting to being sick or sore or tired, and Iris was particularly glad that she had not had to experience an insidious, hostile takeover of her body by disease. Her mother had died without having to think about death, and that surely beat worrying about it.

It was eleven o'clock. Iris needed to shower, to get dressed, to mimic the routine of normalcy.

"Soldier on another day, dear," Henry would have said. And she would have hopped to it, his warm, quiet voice a trigger. She missed him terribly.

He was tall and rangy, his shoulders a little stooped, with full white hair and a roman nose, on the bridge of which rested a pair of horn-rimmed glasses. How perfectly professorial, Iris had thought, given he had been the chair of the

history department at a small New England college. She had
known he was married from the beginning. But even after
they'd met twice for coffee and spent a languid afternoon
strolling the Indigo Trail in the wildlife preserve, pointing
out different species of birds, Iris didn't realize it was the
beginning of an affair. On the way home, after driving past
the low scrub pines and palms and sea oats, the sand creep-
ing onto the road along the edges, the sky an infinite blue
haze, he reached for her, his hand knowing and soft around
her fingers.

"You are lovely," he said.

She blushed so fiercely she had to turn toward her window to hide her face. She felt her heart thunder ahead. She
had never considered she would date again after Glenn,
never thought she would feel the melting heat of a man's
attention.

A trio of pelicans arrowed low across the road.

"I suppose I should say goodbye," she said, as he pulled
up to her condo.

They looked at each other and then broke into giddy
laughter.

"I know this situation is not ideal," he said, "but I'm
afraid you have made me weak in the knees."

"I'm guessing your knees were not so sturdy to begin
with," she said.

"I've only had one replaced."

"Would you like to come in?"

"I would like that very much."

They didn't sleep together that day, or even very many
times in the months that followed. Sex was almost beside the
point. But what developed was an intimacy that Iris had

never experienced. It was as if they had known each other long ago and had come back together without all the silly cares of youth or the anxieties of middle age. They were old, he even older than she, and that was part of the beauty of it. She didn't have to play a role or worry what she looked like or wonder if she was making him happy. She could just be, and that had been a revelation.

Sometimes she tried to make herself feel better about Henry leaving by telling herself she was spared his witnessing the wrath of her illness and her grueling, humiliating physical descent. That's some silver lining, she thought dryly.

Get yourself together, Iris. She stripped off her robe and her nightgown—the seagulls surely wouldn't mind her nakedness—and stretched her arms over her head with as deep a breath as she could muster. She walked to the bathroom and turned on the shower.

She needed to figure out how to see Henry one last time.

SAM

Sam would never get over the feeling that had rushed to the surface when she'd reached down and felt the top of the baby's head emerging. She'd almost laughed, it was so alien, so absurd. Ella was two weeks late, surprisingly unwrinkled and clean, her hair full and dark, her pink body more than nine pounds and long, her legs immediately folding back up like wings. And when the midwife placed the still-attached little body on her chest, and Ella looked up with blind baby-bird confusion, Sam felt, in her euphoria, that she had stepped into the continuous stream of history and humanity from which she hadn't even known she'd been excluded. Did all mothers feel this? Did her own? Sam remembered thinking that nothing would ever measure up—no experience, no achievement, no hope—to giving birth. All the stupid things she had worried about before! Even her career. Who cared if she sold another vase? How quotidian. She was a mother, and everything else was a mere subcategory.

There had been dark moments, too, that she didn't want to remember, those haunted late nights when Ella wouldn't

sleep or be put down after hours of nursing, rocking, bouncing, pleading, crying, even praying in a glassy-eyed stupor, a
cyclone of exhaustion and despair raging in Sam's head. She
had felt broken by her baby's will, ready to leave her in her
crib and walk away, out the front door. Jack had slept, obliv-
ious, in their big bed while Sam eventually curled up on Ella's
floor at dawn. Thankfully there had always been the morning, her mind restored by the daylight, her mother instinct
righted, the corrosive fury of the previous night chalked up
to sleep-deprived irrationality.

She stood in the doorway of her studio, a room con-
verted from the cement-floored basement. For most of the
year, a row of glass-block windows in the house's foundation let in a steady flow of light. It still smelled like clay dust
despite the room's year of disuse. Sam moved her eyes from
her wheel to her array of tools, like a medieval surgeon's,
crude and sharp and strange, and her fingerbowl of chamois
strips—now desiccated and brittle—for smoothing edges.
Above them, her bulletin board was pegged with images of
pots that moved her, that made her sigh with longing, from
ancient Japanese to mid-century Scandinavian to Brother
Thomas. Sam quickly looked away. Once this room had
seemed like the answer to everything. She shut the door and
went upstairs.

The box Theo had sent was on the table where she'd left
it. She slid her keys through the packing tape, pulled open
the cardboard flaps, and called Theo.

"Hey. Did you get the box?" he asked.

"Yeah. Thanks. Did you even go through the stuff in it?
Or did you just send it?"

"I went through it. A little."

"I just opened it, and there's mouse shit on top of the wooden box inside."

"No. Really?"

"Theo."

"Okay. I was too tired. I looked in but then taped the whole thing up again."

Sam shook her head. Through the kitchen window, a large, furry, stump-legged animal waddled across the back patio and into the side yard. A badger? A hedgehog?

"Where was this from, anyway?" she asked. "The condo was bare when I left."

"Dad's basement. He said he must have taken it with him by accident."

"He didn't notice it for eight years? Fucking Dad." Sam knew she sounded like a bratty teenager. Theo brought it out in her.

"Come on, Sammy."

Sam rarely spoke with her father. He and his second wife, Marie, twenty years his junior, lived in a tract home in a suburb of Las Vegas. When Glenn had been married to Iris in Chicago, he had been an estate lawyer, conservative and dignified. Now Marie had turned him into a parody: a golf-shirt-wearing, country-music-loving retiree. He even wore sandals. It smacked of life crisis to Sam, and she found it insulting to her mother. She missed him, but she couldn't bring herself to smooth it over just yet.

"No wonder it took him so long to find it. They've been so busy traveling around to NASCAR events," she said.

"They happen to be in Canada at the moment," Theo said. "Don't be such a snob."

"I'm sure Cindy would be thrilled if they pulled the RV into Georgetown."

"Cindy likes Dad."

"That's not the point."

"What is the point? That you're still angry at him for leaving a loveless marriage and finding happiness with someone else? Mom liked her life after Dad. He did her a favor."

"You don't know shit about Mom," she said, with melodramatic flourish.

"Here we go. You were the martyr who took care of her for a month so now you have proprietary insight. Let's not forget I had ten more years with her than you did."

"That's mature."

"I have to go. I have a meeting."

"Ella's up anyway," she lied. "Say hi to Cindy for me."

"Tell me what you find in the box."

"You wish."

Whatever was in the box had waited this long so it could wait a little longer, Sam thought, jittery with hunger. From the refrigerator she pulled what was left from last night's roast chicken and set it on the kitchen table, then returned for the orange juice. But she knew she had to pump first. The bovine indignity of milking herself was yet another reason to leave Ella as infrequently as possible. How did women do this at work? She took off her shirt and bra and sat at the table, strapping the funnellike attachments to her breasts. The motor whirred and thwunked, and her milk dribbled into the bottles as she tore off a chicken wing and gnawed at the skin. She ate and ate, pulling every last piece of meat from the bones with her fingers, digging underneath the carcass for anything she had missed, and chased it with orange juice straight from the carton, her greasy fingers slipping as she set it down, spilling some into her lap. She hoped that the mailman would not come early. What have I become? she thought.

When the first breast had produced four ounces—the left always outperforming the right—Sam wiped her hands on her already juice-splattered jeans and detached one side from the pump. The clock on the coffeemaker read 12:19. She still had four hours before she had to pick up Ella, which gave her plenty of time to start throwing. But this was a specious pep talk. She felt scattered, her mind pinging with worries that had nothing to do with clay. Talking to Theo had unsettled her, and there was the mouse-turded box sitting on the other side of the table. Maybe it was the prostitute who had made her feel like she was frivolous for worrying about her creativity, when the girl had to degrade herself to pay for a shitty motel. Or maybe it was that, out of sight, Sam didn't think about Ella as much as she thought she would.

And there was always the first baby, the boy they would have named Charlie, the son who would have been three years old. She had wanted to forget—she and Jack never talked about it—but of course she found herself fondling the what-ifs, wondering what he would have been like, rooting out her tamped-down guilt. At the twelve-week ultrasound, the test to assess the amount of fluid behind the neck of the fetus had given the radiologist pause, but the measurement was on the edge of normal, and the hormone markers had been reassuring. She hadn't even been worried about it when the large needle went into her abdomen for the amniocentesis. The results—delayed by a lab error—were delivered over the phone two weeks later by a doctor filling in while her own doctor learned to surf in Costa Rica.

Trisomy 21, an extra twenty-first chromosome. Down syndrome. Sam was the one in seven hundred. "Oh, and it's a boy," the doctor added.

Before she'd gotten pregnant, she and Jack had both been sure and emphatic about what they would do if she were carrying a Down's baby, but of course they really had never considered that it might happen to them. When it did, she no longer felt such certainty. She had already felt the baby kick, though she tried to convince herself that the flutter was indigestion. Sam willed a miscarriage that didn't happen. She'd had to go to an abortion clinic near campus—the hospital did not perform them—sitting with Jack among the college girls and their boyfriends in the waiting room, not allowing herself to look at her belly, not allowing any second-guessing, any recognition of the wavering, of the thorny moral brambles that surrounded her on all sides.

She had banked on that great myth of closure, but almost four years later she still came up short.

Her left breast was empty. Sam switched off the pump, eager for the silence. She put her bra and shirt back on. The refrigerator trickled and hummed. Squirrels skittered across the roof. The furnace switched on with a click and a ramp-up of blowing air. The sun warmed her back through the window. She wished she were already at her wheel, her left elbow braced against her hip bone, her wet hands forcing a hunk of spinning clay into a centered cylinder, that hypnotic physicality that took her out of her thoughts. But she couldn't bring

herself to get up, walk the six steps to the door of the basement, go down a flight of stairs, and dig her hands into the
clay. Getting started seemed too high a hurdle.

Instead, she grabbed the opened cardboard box and
dumped the mouse droppings and old wadded newspaper
into the garbage can. She eased out the bulky wooden box
from inside and set it on the table. It was quite beautiful,
really, made of maple, she guessed, with a darkened patina
of wear and oil. Sam admired its well-made, solid construction, with its close-fitting top and brass hinges. The underside of the lid was lined with fraying red silk, three rusty
needles still threaded through the fabric. Iris had never been
a sewer, but maybe she'd just liked the box.

Sam took a breath. Here she was with things her mother
had saved and purposely packaged up to keep, yet had not
realized, or had not cared, that they had been lost. Inside
was a series of envelopes. Iris had always liked things to be
contained. After the divorce, she had said that one of the
things she liked best was living in an order that no one would
mess up. At the condo, her sweaters were individually
bagged, her coins were sorted by denomination in bowls—
made by Sam—her refrigerator was a neat grid of Tupper-
ware, and even the remote control for the TV had its own
little basket. Sam picked up a manila envelope from the top
of the box, bent the metal clip straight, teased open the flap,
and spilled the contents onto the table.

Out came a rubber-banded set of yellowed index cards,
recipes, written in a female hand, the loops long and fluid.
Sam fanned through the cards—Charlotte Russe, Molasses
Bread, Butterscotch Pudding, Tennessee Silver Cake, Jenny
Lind Cake, the last a strange confection with brandy and

raisins and strawberry jelly. The desserts were a peculiar bunch, dated and unrefined and very unlike Iris, whose signature dessert had been a flourless bittersweet-chocolate cake. Sam was intrigued by the antiquated formality of one of the names, Conserve of Roses, and pulled out the card to read the recipe:

> *Gather petals from bloomed (but not wilted) roses.*
> *Weigh them and set aside. Put an equal weight*
> *of sugar in a bowl and add only enough water to*
> *moisten, set in the sun until sugar is dissolved, then*
> *place over low heat. As soon as the syrup boils add*
> *the petals. Stir gently for ten minutes, then remove*
> *from heat. Cool and pack into jars.*

Were these from Iris's mother? Sam knew little about her, other than that she had been a farm wife in Minnesota, who'd grown up, coincidentally, somewhere in Wisconsin. It was hard to imagine the no-nonsense countrywoman she'd seen in photos bringing Conserve of Roses to church potlucks.

In another envelope Sam found a pocket calendar from 1965, a program from a middle school production of *Cheaper by the Dozen* with Theo playing the part of Frank Gilbreth (efficiency expert and father of twelve), purple marker scribbles on a piece of faded red construction paper (assumedly by Sam), some sheet music of Christmas hymns, a sow's-ear purse losing its beading.

A tattered movie ticket stub from 1940 fell to the table: *His Girl Friday*, starring Cary Grant and Rosalind Russell. She tried to envision her mother at thirteen staring dreamily at the big screen. Iris had kept this reminder for almost sixty years. What did it really mean? Sam wondered. An artifact without context begged more questions than it answered. She used to think she understood her mother, but the truth was, in the end, Iris had become more of a mystery. It was as if when she had gotten divorced and then moved away, she had turned back into who she'd been before becoming a mother, a woman Sam never knew, or maybe she had become someone altogether different.

In Sanibel, Sam would sit her mother in the sun on the balcony on a chaise, a blanket around her fragile legs, and they would have tea and scones from the nearby bakery each morning, and they would talk as if she weren't dying.

"You don't know that I've become a reader in my old age," Iris said. This woman whom Sam had only ever known to read magazines was reading *To the Lighthouse*, the plastic-covered book in her lap. "I never had the patience before, but it's as close to meditating as I'll ever get."

"What made you choose Virginia Woolf?"

Her mother pursed her lips. "I suppose I should have solicited advice from your husband. But a nice young man in the library recommended this book. And I liked the idea of a family at a summerhouse, even if the initial cheeriness is deceptive. I hope I finish it before I kick the bucket."

"Mom."

"Have you read it?"

"In college, I think."

"Well, it's wonderful. Maybe you should take it with you. I don't think the library will track you back to Wisconsin." She laughed and then had to rest a little to regain her breath.

Sam found herself unable to tell her mother those things that she thought impending death would spur, like admitting that she had aborted the first baby. Why couldn't she tell her? Now, of all times. If her mother said it was okay, that Sam had made the right decision, she might feel absolved. But Sam could not trust postdivorce Iris to say what would make her feel better. She could not trust that Iris would act as her mother.

"You're looking at me like you want something," Iris said. "I've got nothing for you. No platitudes. No great wisdom. You don't need anything more from me, Samantha."

She opened her book then as the sea air lifted her dark hair a little from her face, now gaunt and bluish but smoothed with an unfamiliar contentedness. The baby had rolled over and Sam had felt utterly unequipped for both the birth and death that were coming.

"You know what my mother used to say?" Iris had asked. "People think too much. And I've come to agree with her."

"Mom?"

"Why don't you pick yourself out something to read. There are some home décor magazines on the coffee table in the living room."

Sam's neighbor Ted, who lived next door in a tottering Victorian with a chicken coop in the back, approached the front door with his usual springy jog, and she was glad she'd put her shirt back on. Ted wore his white hair in a bowl cut and favored flannel shirts and bleached-out jeans. He'd gone to college at the university during the smoldering late sixties and never left Madison, now teaching math at the local junior college. Raking and shoveling were the usual occasions for conversation—Ted was an obsessive shoveler who made sure his sidewalks were iceless and perfectly edged—and Jack particularly loved to get him going about October 18, 1967, when Ted was one of hundreds of students who protested recruiters from Dow Chemical, the makers of napalm.

"We blocked the Commerce Building and then the cops rolled in. Motherfuckers whacked us with clubs. It was a bloodbath," Ted had said, waving his hands in the air, the first time they'd met him. "Have you ever been tear-gassed? Well, avoid it if you can. It's really scary. Awful. You can't open your eyes, and it feels like you're choking. Fucking cops."

One of the things Jack liked most about Madison was living next door to Ted. He'd go out to shovel, and an hour later, when he came back in raw-cheeked and sniffling, he'd impart some new nugget of information, some new shading to the portrait of his neighbor.

"Did you know that Ted used to be a Teamster?"

"Did you know that Ted has a twenty-seven-year-old daughter who lives in Poughkeepsie?"

"Did you know that Ted's hair went from brown to white in one year?"

Ted was a never-ending source of mystery. Why did he keep his TV on all day and all night? What happened to Mrs. Ted? What did he do with all that space in his large house? Sam and Jack loved to fill in their narrative about him, speculate, hypothesize, and always they would laugh, not out of mockery but of a shared mirth about Ted's curious humanity. This was when Sam and Jack were good together. They didn't laugh much anymore, or she didn't anyway. Sam imagined Jack at work, charming it up in the English Department, relieved to be away from her. How could she blame him?

Ted cupped his hands to the window and, when he saw Sam, gave an animated wave, his eyebrows raised and his mouth smiling wide and open.

"Hi, Ted," she said, opening the door.

"Howdy. Can you believe it's fall already? Man, I swear it was just the Fourth of July. Where's the kiddo?"

"She's at a friend's house."

"That's good, that's good. Sorry to interrupt."

"Oh, don't be silly. Come on in," Sam said, meaning it, happy to see him.

"Just for a second. Just for a second," he said stepping inside the door. "I just wanted to tell you that you're parked on the street-cleaning side. Didn't want you to get a ticket."

"I totally forgot. Thanks so much. I really appreciate it," she said.

"Sure, sure, no problem. I don't want anyone to fall victim to those overzealous parking nazis. I circulated a petition a few years back to change the signs since it's not clear in the winter when you're allowed to park where. Got twenty-one hundred signatures."

"Wow. Whatever happened with it?"

"Nothing much. But I got to meet the mayor." Ted danced a bit in exuberance, his white hair flopping. "You look like you're in the midst of a project."

"I was going through a box of my mother's things from years ago."

Ted puffed out his cheeks and shook his head. "When did she pass?"

What a funny euphemism, Sam thought, as if her mother merely walked by the window, out of sight.

"A year ago," she said.

"It's an adult rite of passage, isn't it? My father was a hoarder, can you imagine? He had twenty years of *Sunset* magazines stacked from floor to ceiling. And a whole room full of coffee cans. I'm not joking."

"What did you do with all of it?" she asked.

"At first I went through it, piece by piece, looking for clues, you know, something to help me make sense of the man." He laughed. "But after two days I realized there was nothing there for me to find. I wouldn't know if I came across something important without him to explain it and give it meaning, right?" He gave an exaggerated shrug, with bent elbows, his palms up to the ceiling. "So I rented a Dumpster."

"Where was that, where your dad lived?" Sam asked.

"Los Alamos, New Mexico. Where I grew up. He worked on the H-bomb, but I didn't know about it until years later. You can imagine we never quite saw eye to eye." He clapped his hands once. "Okay then. I'll let you get back to your business. It sure is a random collection, isn't it? The stuff that remains after a life." Ted pulled open the door and stepped onto the porch. "Just wacky," he said, shaking his mop-top head. "Okay then, see you! I'm off to teach."

Sam waved and smiled. Some gems for the Ted file. She was warmed by the idea of presenting her new findings to Jack over dinner. Maybe she would make linguini carbonara and arugula salad and act like things were as they used to be. But then she remembered he was getting takeout and there was the looming commission for his colleague that she couldn't start, and she wasn't sure what being normal was anymore. She used to think she knew herself, but in the past year her certainty had fallen away.

The tree-roots guy. She'd forgotten. While she had been staking out the Sunrise Inn, he had come and gone.

How many opportunities there must have been to detect her mother's cancer. It was already metastatic stage four when Iris was diagnosed. Cancer cells had spread from the original tumor in a milk duct to the axillary lymph nodes to what the doctor referred to as *distant organs*, in this case her bones, where they continued to grow and multiply, eventually taking over her liver and lungs. Months, years even, when she could have noticed a lump, gone to the doctor, taken care of it with a straightforward lumpectomy. Sam tried to block the persistent insidious thought that Iris had waited too long on purpose.

She shoved the laundry into the washing machine, making sure Ella's tiny socks were at the bottom so one wouldn't float out and clog the drainage tube again. She started the wash and then surveyed the basement.

One thing, she told herself, just do one thing, and the will to create will self-perpetuate. The clay trap she'd installed on the utility sink was full and black, the caught particles from rinsing her tools and sponges had turned into moldy sludge, so she squatted and unscrewed the plastic jar. But she'd forgotten to empty the spigot, so water and ooze splashed down all over her hands, a fetid pool that trickled toward the floor drain with the rank smell of organic decomposition. She had to laugh. After a cursory mop up, she emptied the trap of old clay and washed her hands.

The ring of the phone jolted her into panicked mother mode—Ella, Ella, Ella—and she ran upstairs to get it.

"Hello?"

"Everything's fine, don't worry," Melanie said.

"Ella—"

"Is asleep in the Pack 'n' Play like you were sure would never happen. I checked in with Sarah ten minutes ago, and she had nothing to report, other than Rosalee saying *shit* when she spilled applesauce into her lap."

"That's great," Sam said, trying to sound convincing. "I mean about Ella." Part of her had wanted this babysitter experiment to fail, she realized. She had wanted Ella to miss her too much. Sam had wanted to be summoned, to swoop in, to prove to everyone that she wasn't crazy for not wanting to be apart from her daughter.

"You don't fool me, Samantha. I know you were hoping you would *have* to come get her. But that's the rub, isn't it? They can actually exist without us."

Sam could hear the *click click* of Melanie's laptop keyboard. She wedged the phone between ear and shoulder, and looked into the refrigerator, grabbing a half bottle of Riesling—where it had come from she couldn't say—and then a glass from the drying rack. She took them both to the kitchen table.

"I'm glad it's working out," Sam said. "I am. I mean, okay. I wanted to be missed. But now I'm glad. I swear."

"How's it going over there?"

"I couldn't even manage to open a bag of clay."

"That's okay. I spent the whole morning reading celebrity gossip blogs and playing online Scrabble with my mother."

"I'm stuck, Mel."

"I know. The first year kicks all our asses. Go get a massage or something. Today is not the day to launch back into making stuff."

Sam was thankful, then, for her friend, to whom she never gave enough credit. She pulled her favorite mug—a large egg shape glazed in a lustrous celadon—from the cupboard and poured herself a glass of wine.

"So the real reason I'm calling: we want to have you guys over for dinner next week. With Kelly and Michael. You met them at that barbecue we had over the summer. Thursday?"

"That sounds great. Let me check with Jack—"

"He's clear. Doug already asked."

"Oh. Okay."

"But with one caveat," Melanie said. "You can't bring the baby. You have to get a sitter. If you don't have one I'll get you one. I mean it. If you bring Ella, she'll be spending the evening on the front porch."

"It's a deal," Sam said, hoping she could actually follow through.

"Okay, I'm going to try to write something. See you in three hours."

Sam had forgone alcohol for a year and a half of pregnancy and breast-feeding, which had not been much of a sacrifice, but sipping the cold sweet wine now, in daylight no less, was an unexpected thrill. She closed her eyes and let her shoulders drop, and then she remembered that she'd forgotten to move the car, even after Ted's reminder.

There was no ticket tucked under the leaves on her windshield, to her relief. She U-turned and parked on the other side of the street. Looking back at the empty car seat, she felt a ribbon of ache encircle her chest. She missed her rose-lipped baby, that open-mouthed smile, that extra-large head, those elbow creases and fat knees, that dimple on her torso, that outie belly button on a balloon-shaped tummy. It was going to be a lifetime of Ella slipping away, of her not needing Sam a little more each day.

Jack was calling, but she let it go. She couldn't admit to him that she hadn't gotten started yet.

The day had turned beautiful, the sky a high light blue, the sun deceptively strong, though the emptying trees were a clear enough reminder that winter wouldn't be forestalled. Through her windshield she could see that Ted's TV was on—*Judge Judy*—even though he wasn't home. The old man in a red windbreaker from one street over—a row of bowling balls on posts in his front yard—walked his Corgi dog as he did at the same time and on the same route twice a day. He had always seemed like a lonely soul to Sam, and she had tried to be extra friendly, but he had let his dog shit on their yard once as Sam watched from the window, and she had yanked back her compassion for him. A young woman she didn't recognize pushed a baby in a $400 stroller along the sidewalk. A nanny, most likely, maybe for the new people that built the mishmash of a Tudor mansion—nicknamed the Castle by the neighborhood—on Lake Monona. As the woman neared, talking on a cell phone, Sam could see that she was pretty, with a pouty mouth and cheeks with Slavic angularity.

And then Sam thought of the prostitute eating her Skittles, waiting to walk over to the Lotus House or, worse, heading off to see who would pay at one of the gas stations near 51 or 94 or the Admiral or the parking lot of Red Light Entertainment.

"Hi," Jack said. "I know you're working. I just wanted to say thanks. For doing the thing for Franklin. And don't be too hard on yourself. It doesn't have to be perfect. See you tonight."

She didn't want to go back in the house. The one place that came to mind was illogical, even worrisome, but she wanted another look. She restarted the car. And headed back to the Sunrise Inn.

VIOLET

Nino coughed and spat and stuck his head under the pump for a drink. The late afternoon was warm and damp as spring slid toward summer. Slaughter Alley had a rotting ripeness.

"Charlie says I could work at the boiler," Nino said. "When I'm too old for the papers."

"You could come with me," Violet said. "Work on a farm. It's got to be better than smelling like Charlie."

He smiled. "You know that kid Bobo? He's got those bruises all the time from some kind of sickness?"

She nodded. She'd seen the boy around Nino's building, his skinny legs blotched yellow and purple.

"He tried," Nino said. "No Italians they said. No Chineses, Negroes, Jews, Spanish, Turks. No Russians, neither."

"So? You could hop the train anyway."

"I never even seen a alive cow," he said. "What would I do on a farm?"

"I don't know. Same as me. Eat good. Run around. It can't be that hard to pick corn."

He shook his head in dismissal.

With Nino she could leave her mother. How could she leave them both? She kicked a bag of ash, which spewed coal dust in the courtyard, eliciting a string of Italian screams from the women pounding on their washboards. Violet and Nino ran out to the street, leaping over the sewer channel into the last of the afternoon sunshine.

"How much they give your mama?" Nino asked.

"Nothing."

"She's giving you for nothing?" His face crinkled in contrition for what he'd said.

Violet shrugged. "She was putting me in the Home anyways."

A hunched and mangy woman used a stick to rifle through a heap of garbage outside of the mercantile. She didn't bother wiping the flies from her face.

"Your grandma'am die yet?" Violet asked.

"Yesterday I thought for sure she was cold as a wagon tire, her mouth all hanging open. But she's still breathing up there," he said, nodding his head at their apartment. "It's a wonder he hasn't tossed her out the window."

"Come to the station tomorrow," she said. He rubbed the back of his neck. They didn't usually talk like this, direct and serious, and she knew he didn't like it. "We'll leave together."

The older Dugan boy ran by, a flash of copper hair.

"I'll tell them you're my brother," she said.

Nino looked at her straight on, and Violet saw him weigh the possibility of escape. She pictured them next to each other on the train, watching the city get small behind them. It would be their greatest adventure.

"You'll come then?" She bit her lip to clamp down her smile.

"Can't," he said.

Violet felt cold and prickly. She didn't speak for fear of what her voice would reveal. She wanted to punch Nino square in the face, and she wanted to cry about the unfairness of it all, and she wanted him to know things she could never tell him.

"I'm going to find Jimmy," Nino said. "Want to come?"

"Can't," she said.

"Okay," he said, looking at the space above her head.

She already felt the sickening lightness of his loss, air in her bones where the marrow used to be.

"Bye, I guess," he said, hitching up his pants.

"Yeah," she said.

She saluted him, and he was gone.

"This is just for a short time, Vi. It's not like I'm giving you up, you know that. I'm your mother."

Lilibeth placed her shawl, along with a small hairbrush and comb, on top of Violet's meager clothes in her beloved carpetbag. From a small pouch she pulled the silk sachet bedizened with an owl, the pre-wedding gift from Bluford. The embroidery around the owl's eyes was frayed, the silk water-stained and mildewed. Lilibeth ran her finger over the owl with a wistful reverence.

"It was lovely once," she said. "Here."

Violet took it and ran the silk against her cheek.

"Heavens," Lilibeth said suddenly, her hands fluttering up around her. "I almost forgot."

From her coat pocket she pulled a small silver case and held it out to Violet. Lilibeth tried to smile, but it forced a tear to spill over onto her cheek. Opposite a red velvet cushion was the photograph Mr. Lewis had commissioned, sepia-toned and striking in its clarity. In it, Lilibeth looked serious, her eyes almost sleepy, her hair pulled back in a softly piled bun with a spit curl on each side of her forehead. She wore a dark taffeta dress with a high-necked collar of white lace, her body angled away, her face turned to the camera. Her eyes looked dark, unlike their usual blue, and her gaze was straight on, impermeable, almost challenging.

"They have dresses there for you to wear," Lilibeth said, breathlessly. "I felt like I was trying on one of my mother's when I was a girl. I wanted to smile. I thought it would be nicer to smile. But the man told me not to. He said people don't do that."

Violet was mesmerized by the image of her mother. The woman in the photograph looked substantial and knowing, even strong. She did not look like the woman who'd cried when a May storm washed out a robin's nest in the crabapple tree—"Three perfect blue eggs, Violet, can you imagine"—or the one who'd stared out the window as Bluford thwacked Violet's legs with a broom handle for leaving the chicken coop door open. Or the same one who'd slept with the body of her dead baby boy for two days.

I don't want to go, Violet thought.

"I got to choose between three of them," Lilibeth said. "I hope I picked the best one. I don't know about my hair. I look old. Do you think I look pretty?"

Violet nodded, feeling like the floor had begun to tilt

beneath her. I will do as I'm told, I won't eat much, I'll be better, she wanted to say. Don't let me go.

"You'll remember me, won't you, Vi?"

Violet felt like her mouth had been filled with dirt.

Nino did not see Violet off, nor did any of the other boys. She knew she would fade quickly into a story, like Sammy who drowned in the river or George who left to find gold in California, and then be forgotten altogether.

She was to be at the Children's Aid Society by four o'clock. Lilibeth powdered her face and tied a green ribbon around Violet's hair. They did not talk about where they were going, where Violet would be going. They took a streetcar—Violet's first paid trip—up to East 22nd Street. She felt a seed of fear. This neighborhood might as well have been in a different city, the buildings tall, the streets wide and clean. Lilibeth clutched the card she was given at the Mission and checked the address again. They walked west, to the last building before Park Avenue, a tall brownstone with arched windows, two gas lamps ablaze on either side of the entrance.

"Oh, I don't know, Vi. Maybe we should come back tomorrow," Lillibeth said, fanning her face. "I'm not sure about this." She grabbed Violet's hand. "What do you think? You really want to go?"

I want to stay with you, Violet thought. But she knew this wasn't what was being offered.

"Come on, Mama," she said.

They were greeted by a smiling, plump-faced woman with volelike eyes in head-to-toe black. Lilibeth handed her the card, her hand quivering.

"God bless you," the woman said. "What is the child's name?"

"Violet," Lilibeth said softly. She cleared her throat. "Violet Elaine White."

Violet looked around at the dark wood trim of the foyer, a vase of cream-colored roses on a side table. She tried to pick somewhere to look, something to focus on, to maintain her tough veneer. She found a divot in the marble floor.

The woman pulled out a piece of paper from a folder.

"Sign here, please, Mrs. White. It's just a formality. No need to worry yourself over the particulars."

This is to certify that I am the mother and only legal guardian of Violet White. I hereby freely and of my own will agree for the Children's Aid Society to provide a home until she is of age. I hereby promise not to interfere in any arrangements they may make.

Lilibeth struggled over the words, her eyes jumping all around the sheet of paper, before she picked up the pen in what looked like defeat.

"If things were different," Lilibeth said, her voice faltering. "I wish things were different."

Take me home, Violet thought.

Lilibeth signed the paper and at once covered her mouth with her hand.

"Here, my baby," she said. She handed Violet the bag. "Be good. Don't let them take you back to Kentucky." She forced a small laugh that quickly died and hung in the air.

"Mama," Violet said. This couldn't be all there was. This quick cut. She clung to the idea of the train and how it would take her to the wide-open Middle West, someplace on the map she couldn't remember. "I'll write you a letter," she said, even though she'd never written a letter and wouldn't know where to send it.

"I will come get you," Lilibeth said, looking trapped, her eyes wide and frightened. "I will come when I can."

"We'll take her from here," the woman said. "It's for the best." She separated Violet from her mother with an ushering arm around her shoulders.

"How will I know where she is?" Lilibeth said, her voice rising. "How will I find her?"

"She will get a good home," the woman said, quietly but firmly, her authority now firmly in place. "It is better for the child. Say your goodbyes now."

Lilibeth wavered for the briefest of moments, but then she pulled her daughter into her fragile chest.

"Forgive me," she whispered, into Violet's hair.

Violet watched the silhouette of her mother's willowy figure floating out the door, lost in the evening's descent. She knew she would see Lilibeth again, because she couldn't conceive of the alternative.

I can go now, she thought. *I'm on my way.*

"Through this door," the woman said. "I'll take your bag."

Their feet tap-tapped along a shiny black-and-white-squared floor.

"I'll keep it with me," Violet said, sensing a shift in the woman's tone now that Lilibeth was gone. "It's no trouble."

"You won't be needing anything in there anymore," the

woman said, pulling it from Violet's hand. "You are going to a new Christian life. To start clean."

Violet's mind flashed, and she thought, *run*, but then she thought about the train and how it made her pulse quicken to imagine it delivering her somewhere new.

"Can I have the photograph that's in there?" she asked, trying to keep her voice even and polite. "My mother's photograph. That's all I want."

"Shhh, now," the woman said. "It will all be fine. God is looking after you."

Violet swallowed, disoriented by it all, her heart skittering as her resolve gave way. She followed.

The woman led her up a staircase, through another door, down a hall, and into a large room where children of different ages—girls and boys, some in orphanage-issued uniforms, others in tattered, street-worn clothes—stood in various lines. None of them talked. There was only the scuffing of boots, the shuffling of papers, and the murmurs of Aid Society women.

"Here is Mrs. Pettigrew. She'll get you freshened up and fit you with a brand-new dress for the trip. Supper will be at five. You have a big day tomorrow."

Violet looked down at her mother's bag in the woman's hand, a relic to which she no longer had claim.

"You'll be reunited. When things are better," the woman said. "You can pick up your things then."

"This way," Mrs. Pettigrew said, her old fingers curled like claws. "You are a lovely girl. You should have no trouble getting chosen."

Violet scanned the crowd for anyone she might recognize.

Some of the younger children cried, others merely stared. Two twin boys around the age of five, their hair cut in a line high on their foreheads, held hands and squatted in the corner. Across the room she saw Buck, the newsboy from her neighborhood, biting his bottom lip.

"Buck," she called.

Everyone turned to look. He scowled back at her and turned away.

"Hush, child," Mrs. Pettigrew said. "Let's let Dr. Smith have a look at you. To make sure you're fit for the country."

They told the children very little about where they were going. Each was pinned with a square of paper with a number on it. Each was given a Bible. Each was given a new birth date because, they were told, that's what their new families wanted. The girls wore white ruffled dresses and black bows in their hair. The boys wore dark blue suits and ties.

Violet did not know much about geography, about which state was where, other than what she remembered from sporadic school attendance. She knew that Indiana and Ohio were above Kentucky. She knew that President Lincoln—the teacher barely masking her contempt—had been born in Illinois. West was a bright, gauzy place that was never loud or crowded or dirty. The farms there were not like the dusty, broken-down farms of Barren County, where chickens scratched at dried-mud yards, cornstalks sagged, worms chewed through cabbages, and squirrels took out whole strawberry patches in one night. The farms out west were huge and green and abundant.

At dawn the children were gathered and grouped into

"little companies" of thirty or so, for trains heading out in a fan across the country. Buck—his number was on yellow paper—was headed to Texas, or so he boasted to Violet during the wagon ride to the station. She had snorted when she'd first seen him in a suit, his hair cut high over his ears so his teeth were more noticeable than ever.

"I'm going to ride horses and carry a gun," he said, squirming in his new clothes. "I'm going to come back a outlaw and shoot my pa."

Violet laughed at him. "No, you ain't," she said.

The paper pinned to her dress was light blue. She didn't know where her train was going.

It was festive at the station, a flurry of commotion. An audience of benefactors, church supporters, and politicians stood off to the side, smiling and pointing, exclaiming how lucky the children were, how darling in their little outfits that their own contributions had helped supply. The Aid Society women pushed the children together, and they recited the Lord's Prayer and the Ten Commandments and sang a feeble "Amazing Grace," which they had rehearsed the previous night. And then the audience quickly disbanded with waves and *Bon voyage!* and *Godspeed.*

Violet took her Bible and found the other light blues— girls and boys of mixed ages, plus a group of young ones from the Foundling Hospital. Mrs. Comstock, a gray-haired, soft-bodied woman with crepey pockets of skin below her eyes, was to be their handler, and also traveling with them was a nurse, wiry Miss Bodean, a white bonnet on her small ginger-haired head perched on a giraffean neck, who would accompany the babies. A few of the younger children clung to Mrs. Comstock's skirt. The institution kids stood blankly, waiting for orders. Violet, wary, hung back, her stance wide and defiant, as she surveyed her fellow travelers.

"Hey, twelve," she said to a teenage boy, who slouched near her. He glanced down at his tag. "Where we going?"

He shrugged. "Twenty-five dollars a month farm wage, they told me. All's I know."

His face had the yellow-gray pallor of having grown up indoors. His shoulders were lost in his ill-fitting suit jacket.

"They make us all work?" she asked.

"I don't know. Maybe the younger ones get taken in like they say. This boy Nicholas," he said, "from my ward. Thirteen about. Went to Iowas. He ran away, took freight trains back, and tried to break back into the asylum."

"How come?" Violet asked.

The boy shrugged again and worked his toe against a dried spot of chewing gum. "Missed it, I guess. He wouldn't talk nothing about it."

"You," Mrs. Comstock said, looking down at her manifest. "Violet, is it? Go on over with the other girls, now. We're getting ready to board."

IRIS

Breasts. All the hoopla over breasts.

From her top drawer Iris pulled the mastectomy bra and silicone breast forms—her explants. The prosthetics were a peachy flesh color (there had been three skin tones from which to choose) with surprising heft; they looked like chicken cutlets with nipples. Nipples! She had laughed, aghast, when she'd first pulled them from their case. Good Lord, she'd spent a lifetime trying to hide her own. She'd gone with the forms that slipped into the bra instead of the ones that rode against her skin. Her scars had been fresh at the time, and it had been hard to imagine anything rubbing against them, particularly in the unseemly August heat. Not to mention she hadn't exactly seen the point.

Iris slipped the explants into the pockets of the bra and strapped the whole thing on. She felt armored, her wasting body less vulnerable. When the long-haired girls had thrown their bras in the trash can at the 1968 Miss America pageant, Iris had been chasing after a newly toddling Samantha, driving Theo to band practice, picking up dry cleaning, planning a dinner party for Glenn's golfing friends and their wives. What women had time for this theater? she had wondered. She understood the meaning of the protest and agreed that, in theory, yes, women should be valued for their whole selves, not just their looks. But at the time Iris didn't feel the need for liberation. She didn't even mind wearing a bra, she thought snidely. She'd known what she was getting into when she married Glenn, and she'd wanted to be a mother. She had chosen her life, hadn't she?

The blinds lifted away from the window in the breeze and then clacked back down, again and again, a somnolent rhythm. Maybe she would need to turn on the air conditioning after all. The humidity was making her bangs curl up and out into little wings. Outside the seagulls cried their *why, why, why, why,* Sanibel's background noise. She pulled a white cotton tunic over her head, its neck high enough to hide both bones and scars. It had been a gift from Samantha last year after the surgery. She had always been a thoughtful girl. Of course she is coming down here to be with me, Iris thought. She chose a pair of black capris and then found a belt—cinched tighter by the week—and slipped on her sandals. Getting ready depleted her, but she was glad to prepare for her daughter's arrival. It was time to go to the market.

What would Samantha like? As a girl she'd loved blueberries, shortbread, grape juice, fried chicken. As a teenager, Diet Coke. But maybe she didn't drink that stuff anymore, so overly cautious, hysterical even, women were these days when they were pregnant. Coffee, wine, Brie, even cigarettes then—and her children had turned out just fine. Iris strolled through the produce aisle. Bananas. Avocados. Cantaloupe. Strawberries. Lemons. Radishes. Artichokes. She wanted to provide abundance. It was the least she could do.

She felt a wave of nausea as she passed the meat section. It was like morning sickness, this aversion to different foods she had now, this lack of hunger. At forty, pregnant with Samantha, she had felt an unbearable weight of exhaustion, her joints aching from the beginning, and for months she'd been unable to stomach much more than lemonade and salty potatoes. She'd resented being at the mercy of her body, resented the baby—she sensed it would be a girl—and, after dropping Theo off at school, had often gone home and hauled herself back into bed and hadn't risen until it was time to pick him up. She had never admitted any of this to Glenn. Glenn had thought another baby was what she wanted—didn't all women?

Iris could not recall hearing her mother say "I love you." She hadn't felt unloved, but she had often felt she could never get quite enough of what she needed from her mother, who doled out affection in frugal portions. Her mother had offered gruff hugs and the occasional kiss on the top of the head as comfort, usually accompanied by "Buck up, Iris. It's not that bad." Nothing, in her mother's eye, had ever been that bad. Not the chickenpox, or cod liver oil, or a sprained ankle, or a dead bird, or a broken heart.

As much as Iris had wanted to be a different kind of

mother, she, too, had been stingy in telling her children she loved them. It had felt forced and vaguely embarrassing to utter those words, and then it became something they just didn't say to each other, not part of the family currency. How repressed, she thought now, how inexcusable.

Iris wheeled her cart to the checkout line. When she looked up, the woman in front of her made her catch her breath. It was Henry's wife. Iris had seen her once before, had noticed the beauty in the one-shouldered white gown, the night she'd met Henry, at a fund-raiser for the Friends of "Ding" Darling Wildlife Refuge. She, Kathleen, had been his research assistant in the early sixties and had dropped out of her graduate program to marry him and mother their three boys. Iris knew little more about her—Kathleen was a subject they had spoken around most of the time—but she felt intimidated, bested. Henry had made his choice. Iris devoured the details of this woman, her slightly tanned skin, her muscular calves—tennis, probably—her champagne-colored hair pulled sleekly back. She had quick, feminine movements, an air of quiet confidence and sophistication. She was tall and slender and wore a French-blue shirtdress and leather thong sandals that looked like they'd been picked up in Saint-Tropez. As she stowed her credit card, she smiled politely at Iris, without recognition, and left with her purchases tucked neatly into a single bag.

"Buck up," Iris said to herself. "It's not that bad."

She remembered an evening she and Henry had spent in her condo. Kathleen was away visiting one of their sons in Boston. He'd cooked a porcini risotto in her kitchen, the sight of which, along with the fine Cabernet they were drinking, made Iris feel radiant. She had never been cooked for by a man—Glenn hadn't even known where the pans were—and here Henry was completely at ease, joyful even, as he stood stirring, ladling warm stock into the pot.

"My daughter-in-law's latest round of fertility treatments didn't take," she said.

"I'm sorry to hear that. She must have been devastated. How did Theo sound?"

"Oh, he was fine. He sounded more upset at failing than the actual not getting pregnant part. Besides, I think Theo is secretly pleased."

"You don't think he wants kids?"

"I think he's scared, like everyone is. But it's the selfish streak. The sacrifice seems too great for him for so little a perceived reward."

"Not everyone should be a parent."

"I know. But I think it would be good for him. I fear he's veering down a hardened path. I'm sorry to say he's become a cynic, my son."

"It's the generation, I think. Benjamin is like that. Golf and the office are his priorities. His wife is a distant third."

"You said he's the most like you."

Henry laughed. "So he is. Eighteenth-century British texts were my golf. Here, taste this. More salt?" He blew on the rice in the wooden spoon and held it out to her.

"Oh, boy. Delicious. I just melted."

"I've got you right where I want you," he said.

Iris retrieved their bowls from the table.

"Go on with what you were saying," he said.

"I just think being a father would bring Theo back to his essential goodness."

"How you remember him as a boy."

"Maybe that's it. At least he'd be closer allied with the human race. It would be humbling for him."

"That it is. Think of how big my ego would be if I hadn't had kids." He smiled. She laughed. He stopped stirring to refill her glass. He held her cheeks in his hands and kissed her nose.

"This is wonderful, isn't it?" he said. "I feel I am home."

After dinner, they sat on the couch drinking ginger tea, talking about what they rarely talked about.

"At some point it got too late to make changes. Or to question. To talk about the things I found lacking in our marriage after we'd been together thirty, forty, fifty years? I felt that if I went pecking around, the exposure would be too much and we'd lose what had been pretty good for a long time."

"Couldn't it have gotten better? If you'd been honest with her?"

"It's true, I suppose. But I'm not much for taking risks. Aside from this"—he pointed to her and back to himself— "I'm a bit of a coward. Why do you think I went into academia?"

"Good old tenure," she said.

"I guess I liked having tenure with Kathleen, too."

Iris grabbed his hand with a passion new to her, roused by this man whom she loved. "Henry, we're too old for pretty good, aren't we?"

"'Guilt . . . 'tis the fiend, th' avenging fiend, that follows us behind with whips and stings,'" he said, his mock baritone a weak attempt to conceal his sorrow. "So said by one Nicholas Rowe three hundred years ago. It's aptly poetic and savage, I think."

She tucked her feet under herself and did not ask again about his wife. She must have felt it already, knew what she could never unknow, that she would not be with him in the end, that he was not hers. Iris was the raft in the water, but Kathleen was the riverbank. No matter how he clung to Iris now, how warm and safe they felt together, swirling about, their arrangement was temporary. Eventually he'd have to swim ashore.

"Iris, is that you?"

Iris looked up from loading her groceries in the car. It was Susan Harrison, her realtor—brassy hair, French manicure, tinkling gold bangles on her wrists—clacking on tiny heels in her direction.

"Susan. How nice to see you."

Susan pushed her big sunglasses up to the top of her head. Her face froze when she saw how much Iris had deteriorated since she'd seen her a month before. She smiled too broadly, her teeth bleached inhumanly bright.

"Here, let me help you with that." She swooped the bag from Iris's hands and set it in the trunk.

"I'm not dead yet," Iris said.

"Oh, Iris, I didn't mean to imply anything," she said, her palm pressed to her tanned and freckled cleavage.

"Sorry. It was a joke. I've been meaning to call you, actually. My daughter arrives tomorrow. I'll leave her your name."

A blank smile bisected Susan's face.

"About selling the condo."

"Yes, yes, for sure!" she said too eagerly. "Whatever I can do."

She thinks death might be contagious. "Happy shopping," Iris said.

"You take care of yourself," Susan said, hustling away.

Iris sighed, worn out from the minefield of a trip. Her body felt floppy and rigid at the same time. She sank into the hot front seat and slid her hand under her bra to scratch her scars. She wished dying weren't so damn tiring.

The phone was ringing as she walked in the apartment with the last bag of groceries, but she stopped to click on the air-conditioning anyway—of course it wouldn't be the last time. What was she thinking this morning? This was Florida.

"Hello?" She breathed heavily.

"Mom? Are you okay? You took so long to answer."

Iris rolled her eyes at Samantha's echoing of her brother.

"I just walked in the door," she said, but then regretted her curtness. "I'm fine, honey. I was at the store. Getting ready for your visit."

Visit. Well, what am I supposed to call it, Iris replied to herself in her head, as she slumped into the glider chair.

"My flight's coming in a little earlier than I told you. Three o'clock. Are you sure you're okay to drive to Fort

Myers? I can take a shuttle or cab or something. I wouldn't mind at all."

"Samantha. I can pick you up. I would like to pick you up."

"Okay."

"Okay. Do you still drink that Diet Coke?"

Iris felt her weakness lift a little in the cool air.

"Yeah," Samantha said. "I'm not supposed to. I told Jack I quit but I still do."

"Good. I got some for you, just in case. I won't tell on you."

"The baby is crazy today. Rolling around. Jabbing me with her elbows."

"Theo was like that. I'm convinced his personality was set by the time he came screaming out, butt first."

"You know they don't deliver breech anymore. Automatic C-section. God, I really don't want a C-section."

"You'll be fine. I'm sorry I won't be there, though."

"You might? You don't know." Samantha's voice grew shrill.

Unspoken was how long Samantha would be staying, how long Iris would live. Iris did not want her daughter's martyrdom.

"I'm sorry to pull you away from your work," Iris said.

She was astounded, sometimes, by what her daughter could make with her hands and raw clay. Where did talent come from? Iris wondered if she herself had some latent ability that was never activated. Gardening or chess or watercolors or poetry. She couldn't even knit, though her mother had tried to teach her again and again.

"I had to stop the wheel," Samantha said. "My belly made it too awkward."

"You'll start up again soon after the baby. You must make yourself get back to it. Remember that. The longer you wait, the harder it will be. Before Theo I was a whiz at the harmonica."

Samantha laughed. "I'm not worried," she said. "I'm already anxious to get back to work."

Iris closed her eyes against a headache that pressed behind her eyes.

"You don't know what you'll be like. You can't know."

She could sense her daughter chafe. It seemed they always reached this point, this brittle place.

"You'll be fine," Iris said again.

Iris's mother had been an orphan who'd never known her parents. It had not been a secret, but neither had it been openly discussed.

"Do you think about who your parents might have been?" Iris had asked her once, as they had fished for rock bass on a late summer Sunday afternoon. The sun burned their arms and faces, while their feet were numb in the river water. Iris didn't care much if her line got a nibble, but she loved to sit next to her mother, listening to the rush of water over the smooth stones in the shallows, relishing the moments of cool and clarity when clouds obscured the sun's glare. And her mother, here, with her.

"Why, sure," her mother said. Her hair was gray and pulled back in a ponytail. She only wore it down when she went to bed. "About my mother sometimes. But there's not a lot of use in it, is there?"

"Maybe she was a movie star," Iris said.

Her mother laughed. "I don't think so. They didn't have movies in the eighteen hundreds."

Iris wanted to know what the orphanage had been like— she imagined white rooms with tall windows and nuns floating down quiet hallways—but her mother was vague and deflective. "I don't remember much about it," she would say. "That was a long time ago." At age eleven she'd been taken on as kitchen help at a small private hospital in Wisconsin, where she had learned how to make all those fussy desserts. She'd lived and worked there until she was eighteen, married Samuel Olsen, and moved across the border to Minnesota.

"There's no way of finding out?" Iris pressed. "You could write to the orphanage maybe and ask about who she was."

"We should get going," her mother said, winding the reel of her fishing rod. "It must be well past two. I need you to shell that batch of peas."

"Just a little longer. Please? I haven't even caught one yet."

Her mother laughed. "Your worm's been off your hook for an hour."

Iris could feel time moving on, her mother already going over what needed to be done back at the house. There wouldn't be time for this again for a long time with fall closing in.

"You have ten more minutes," her mother said. "I mean it. Don't be late."

"Do you think Bobby Bergesen will ask me to the dance?" Iris asked, in a transparent attempt to forestall her mother, who had already picked up her basket of fish and was dusting off her skirt.

"Iris," she said. "All my information on the matter comes from you. Do you think he's going to ask you to the dance?"

"No. Maybe," Iris had stuttered. "I don't know. He waved to me in town the other day."

Her mother shook her head, always flummoxed by Iris's theatrics.

"I wouldn't worry so much about it."

"But I like him," Iris had said, putting her palms to her cheeks.

"Boys will come and go," her mother had said, less to Iris than the river.

Iris remembered even now how there had been no conviction in her voice, no weary "mother knows best" authority, only opaque wistfulness, a window into which Iris was not privy. She wondered if on some level all mothers were ciphers to their children. She wondered if having children was a way to try and understand one's own mother, to bridge the unknowability. How she wished she could know her mother now. Iris didn't believe in heaven, but lately she indulged a childish notion of seeing her mother again. She liked the idea of the two of them being old women together.

Iris unhooked her bra and shimmied her arms out of the straps. It fell heavy into her lap.

Outside on the landing was the familiar trudge of the mailman—redheaded Albert, who never wore a hat in the sun and never thanked her for the check she left for him every Christmas—the clang of her metal mailbox closing, and then his retreat.

Iris wondered what her mother would have thought about Samantha's now living in Wisconsin. It was a return of sorts. Her mother would have liked that her granddaughter made things, that she was an artisan.

Iris picked herself up to retrieve the mail—a sad little stack—and went to the kitchen. Could it be that she actually felt hungry? She wanted peanut butter and jelly. She pulled the jars from one of the grocery bags, still on the floor where she'd left them, and slathered peanut butter, then strawberry jelly on two pieces of soft white bread. Salty, sweet, soft, creamy comfort. Why hadn't she been eating this for every meal?

She flipped the bank statement, credit card offers, and Planned Parenthood donation solicitation into the trash— she'd have to pretend to recycle when Samantha was there—and slid open the Lively Arts calendar of upcoming events.

Community theater performance of *West Side Story*. Pass. Children's chorus. Pass. The Ying Quartet: Tchaikovsky. Almost three weeks away, just before her birthday. Surely she could make it that long, now that she'd rediscovered peanut butter. Henry was a sucker for Tchaikovsky. It would be her opportunity to see him again. She dialed the box office and reserved two tickets. Samantha would be her date.

Iris picked up her book from the counter where she'd placed it earlier. Her run-in with Stephen seemed like days ago. She had noticed in the last week that she was losing control of her sense of time, stretching here, warping there, a gradual meandering off the track. She would have to write herself a note about Samantha's arrival, just in case. She slid open the door to the balcony and stepped from the dry cool air into a blanket of humid warmth. She eased into a chaise and joined Mrs. Ramsay, knitting a stocking for the lighthouse keeper's son, after the children were in bed.

> *She could be herself, by herself. And that was what now she often felt the need of—to think; well, not even to think. To be silent; to be alone. All the being and the doing, expansive, glittering, vocal evaporated; and one shrunk, with a sense of solemnity, to being oneself, a wedge-shaped core of darkness, something invisible to others.*

Yes. Iris thought of her mother and believed now that she had welcomed some time alone before she died. And here Iris was, in Sanibel after marriage and motherhood and a last-minute affair, at home in a quiet loneliness. It was not happiness, no. But it was humility. It was acceptance.

Her eyes were heavy with narcotics, and she set the book down. Her energy had fizzled. Her limbs felt limp, her bones like lead, bearing down on her muscles and skin with each movement. Her head was throbbing again, blurring the edge of her vision with each pulse. Even her lungs ached. As a child she had sometimes fantasized about being bedridden with some serious sickness, her face rosy with fever, her mother and father fussing over her, talking in hushed tones, nursing her back to health.

How foolish. Illness was so inelegant, she thought, so messy and ugly, so unromantic. Getting to death was going to be awful. This slipping away, this erosion of body and, finally, mind.

She pulled herself out of the chair to go take her pills. In the kitchen she shook the colorful tablets in her palm. How many would it take to get the job done?

SAM

Iris had once said, "You will be a good mother because you want to be a mother."

Sam pulled her car into the parking lot behind the Sunrise Inn. She wondered now if her mother's cryptic pronouncement had meant *she* had not wanted to be a mother. Or maybe ten years after Theo, Iris had not wanted to be a mother again. But she hadn't been a bad mother, had she? Distant, perhaps, preoccupied. It's true that Sam had often felt lonesome as a child. Iris had seemed much more comfortable with Sam as an adult than Sam as a little girl, whom she had looked at with perplexity, as if to say, How did you get here?

Up close, the beige bricks of the motel were dirt- and water-stained in the exposing light of the afternoon sun. Grim, Sam thought. A young father in low-slung jeans, a tank top under an open North Face parka, herded two little boys, also in puffy jackets, inside a bottom-floor room, and she wondered if the Sunrise, like many of the cheap motels in the area, was used as backup for an inadequate shelter system.

She couldn't say why she had returned to this place. Maybe the starkness of the life she imagined for the girl was the dark draw. The fragility of our trajectories, Sam thought, the downward momentum of a few bad breaks. She made fists with her hands to warm her fingertips.

Unlike other pregnant women she had known, Sam had not felt overheated, had not thrown off covers at night or walked around in shirtsleeves as temperatures dipped. Her hands had often been cold. This made her nervous that there was something wrong with this pregnancy, too, despite the fact that the chorionic villus sampling test done at twelve weeks— she would not wait for an amnio—had shown that the baby, a girl, was genetically fine. So she was glad for the soft heat and the blurry humidity of Florida after the early mean freeze she had left in Wisconsin. Despite the circumstances, she was glad to be warm.

When she and Iris drove from the airport en route to Sanibel Island, they passed a small billboard on I-75 with the smiling moon face of a Down syndrome baby, his almond eyes with the characteristic epicanthic eyelid folds. In child-like writing it said, "I deserve to live!"

Sam—driving so her mother could rest—shook her head faintly and felt a cold wave creep down to her toes. She had hoped that when she became pregnant again the first preg-nancy would somehow reshape in her mind, fading into the miscarriage everyone else thought it had been. She hated that she felt guilt about a choice she had defended the right to make her entire adult life. But it had not been an unwanted pregnancy, and eighteen weeks was not five weeks, and when

it came down to it, she had put herself first. She had not
wanted the life of taking care of a special needs child, whatever that entailed. She'd immediately thrown out the packet
of information on Down syndrome given to her by the nurse,
not wanting to know anything. She was selfish and shallow,
a coward. Was it really more important to be able to make
another set of dinner plates?

Sam had read an article about a woman who gave her
adopted son back after a month because she didn't feel any
bond with the eighteen-month-old and thought it would be
best for everyone if he went to a different home. She and her
husband had tried for years to have their own child, and
what they really wanted was a child formed from their
genetic material, a reflection of them. The public outrage had
been swift and damning—Sam and Jack had even discussed
how traumatic it must have been for the toddler—but quietly she had wondered if this was any more reprehensible
than what she had done.

Jack would say it had been a five-inch fetus, an organ-
ism that couldn't live outside the body. And even if they had
had the child, there was a chance he might have been
severely disabled, never able to dress or feed himself. She
knew all these things, agreed with them, and yet, and yet.
Jack might also say she could not let it go because it gave
her something to hate herself for, a wound to poke at. That
is, he might say these things if she ever talked about it with
him, which she didn't.

"How are you feeling these days?" her mother asked,
eyes closed. "You barely look pregnant."

"I don't?" Sam immediately leaped to worry.

"Oh, not in a bad way, honey," Iris said, opening her eyes and perking her head up. "Like you haven't gained too much weight. I gained fifty pounds with you. I ate donuts and hot fudge sundaes. It took me a whole year to lose it. But boy, was it fun."

Sam smiled, looking quickly at her mother, and turned onto the causeway. She didn't know how long her mother would live. Iris was cagey about what the doctor had said, calling any estimate maudlin and unnecessary. "I'll die when I die," she had said. But would it be days, weeks, months?

"Tell Jack you'll be home well before Christmas," Iris had said.

When Sam had heard this—it was already mid-October—she'd backpedaled, wanting to un-know the time frame.

"Let's not talk about it," she had said.

If her mother had dated or had a relationship since the divorce, she never shared it with Sam or, as far as she knew, with Theo. And other than an occasional bridge game, she didn't seem to socialize much in Florida. It was as if after all the years of dinner parties and tennis groups and being a wife and mother in the suburbs, Iris had slipped out the back door.

"It's so weird you live here," Sam said.

"The shell collecting was a big draw," Iris said, wryly. "It's warm. It felt new. After your father, I wanted something different. To be away from all that."

Sam wondered if her mother wanted not just to be away but to be disconnected. Freed. Even from me and Theo, she thought. To Sam, such buoyancy seemed frightening.

"You know, the island itself is only six thousand years

old? I like the feeling of newness. It feels accidental," Iris said.

They drove over the bridge to Sanibel. Sam had visited a few times over the years, but it still felt as though her mother was on vacation. The island was twelve miles long and four miles wide, with over half of it a protected wildlife reserve. Iris rarely left it.

"I've already talked to Susan, my realtor, about selling the condo. You should get a decent price for it. It'll be a good time of year to sell. The snowbirds will be arriving soon."

Sam turned to look at Iris and then back at the road.

"We're going to have to talk about the details, Samantha."

"I don't want to."

"You shouldn't worry so much," Iris said.

Sam, irked, had wanted to say that you really can't tell someone not to worry. It doesn't work like that.

Sam pulled the keys from the ignition and tried to focus on what she was doing at this forlorn motel. Maybe the young prostitute's mother had been unfit, and the girl had drifted without anyone to help her, a dirty and deflated balloon whose string finally got caught on a dead branch. How easily we can be lost, Sam thought. But maybe it didn't take a lot—kindness from a stranger even—to pull someone back from that vast aloneness. Sam imagined herself knocking on the door, introducing herself, offering her help finding a job, a little money, a call to social services—something. Why was that such a big deal? Because, she said to herself, you are you.

But she got out of the car anyway, not ready to give up—
she'd made this crazy return here after all—wanting one
more glimpse into a life that was not hers, to get outside
herself and do something decent for someone else. It was
too cold to be without a jacket. She'd been fooled by the
sun, now on the down slope, already having slid clear of the
parking lot. She tucked her hands under her arms, her shoulders raised up toward her ears in an effort to block the wind
that was rattling the straggling leaves on the stunted walnut
tree saplings at the edge of the motel. She walked around the
outside of the indoor pool, empty and swamp green, its glass
fogged with condensation and soot from the exhaust of the
cars roaring past on East Washington.

In the front parking lot, Sam looked around and, seeing
no one, cupped her hands against the driver's side window
of the girl's car. The blue vinyl seats were cracked and sun-
faded, and electrical tape mummied the steering wheel. On
the floor was a Green Bay Packers ice scraper, a torn map of
Wisconsin, and a half-empty two-liter bottle of Mountain
Dew peeking out from under the passenger seat. A garbage
bag of clothes filled the floor of the backseat, a dirty pink
towel obscenely spilling out the top. The girl was living out
of her car. Sam wondered if she longed to be settled or if
settled was what she was running from.

"Hey!" the girl yelled from the balcony.

"Oh," Sam said, startled. She felt wobbly after seeing the
girl's scant possessions, artifacts of impermanence and dis-
connection. And now the girl was here, looking like a child
dressed up as a hooker, her knees knobby, her shoes too big.
Sam backed away, with her hands ridiculously in the air.

"What the fuck? That's my car, lady."

"I know. I mean, I'm sorry."

"What?" She tilted her head like a puppy. "Wait, I've seen you before."

"I don't think so."

"The drugstore," the girl said, her voice rising. "Did you follow me?"

"No. Well, yes, sort of," Sam stuttered.

"What the hell do you want?"

Sam felt her face flush, her scalp prickle with heat. Say it, she said to herself, do this one thing. "I thought—I don't know. When I saw you at the store I thought, You're so young. Maybe I could help you out."

"What?" The girl shook her head and crossed her arms in defiance.

"Okay," Sam said. "It was a misunderstanding. A mistake. I'm going."

The girl slammed the motel door behind her.

Sam bumbled her way back to her own car, tripping off the curb, and fell heavily into the front seat. What had happened to her? How had she so misjudged? She felt like a lunatic. Why don't you get your own house in order? she said to herself.

Just before Sam and Jack had moved in, a house on their street had blown up. The man who'd lived there, in his sixties, had opened all the gas valves in order to asphyxiate himself, and then his house exploded, taking out half the house next to it, cracking windows, plaster walls, and ceilings all down the street. He'd managed to make it through the grueling winter, only to give up once spring had arrived—the tree flush, the crocuses and daffodils pushed up, the last patches of snow in the shadows. How lonely he must have been. Three years later the lot was still empty, a now-grassy plot that kids had claimed as a makeshift playing field, orange traffic cones marking the goal posts. Ted had told them that the man had bouts of depression and rarely slept, often taking walks in the middle of the night. He was a high school art teacher but retired early, and since then had never left the neighborhood. He walked to the market a few blocks away, and he occasionally ate a hamburger at the bar around the corner. He didn't have a car and didn't take the bus, because, he'd told Ted, there was nowhere he wanted to go. Ted had wondered why someone who'd kept to himself wanted to go out with a literal bang. To Sam it had made sense. The man had been angry about the emptiness, and he'd wanted everyone to know it.

She turned away from the kitchen window. On the counter was one of her large lidded jars with a milky robin's-egg glaze. She pulled off the lid with the familiar emery-board scrape of its unglazed flange, impressed anew by the closeness of its fit, and pulled out a tin of roasted almonds. The anticipation of their smoky-salty bite made her salivate. And then it occurred to her that she had no idea what held her mother's ashes. A cheesy funeral parlor urn? A box? A bag? Theo had picked them up after the cremation, and they had yet to decide what to do with them. She had made a jar for nuts, but she hadn't even thought to make something to contain her mother's remains.

It was two o'clock. Ella was supposed to be napping. Sam missed the sumptuous weight of a baby asleep against her. She never missed Jack anymore, though. And that was the fear, wasn't it? That she had fallen in love with Ella and the feeling had eclipsed what she felt for Jack. The love was different, of course, it didn't have to be one or the other, but what she felt for Ella seemed richer, dizzying, and undiminishable.

Out the window a squirrel sat balanced on the fence, nibbling away the soft green peel of a walnut. Every fall the squirrels encamped in the walnut trees and stripped them bare of fruit, chirping and squeaking, littering the ground below with shells and meat that stained the sidewalks a deep red ocher. The squirrels gorged themselves for a week, and then the feast was over and the trees were bare. Looking into Ted's yard, she guessed it was still a little early for the squirrel bacchanalia.

I'll make the pound cake and give it to Ted, Sam thought. She had made a fool of herself with the prostitute, but she could redeem the day by doing something nice for her neighbor. There would be no one more appreciative. She dumped a handful of almonds into her palm and poured some of them into her mouth, the salt puckering her tongue. But as she crunched, she knew the box of Iris's wasn't going away. She switched tack and sat down at the table again, steering herself to at least get something done today, something to show for the baby-less hours.

Her cell phone rang, startling her. Theo again, and, despite her peevishness toward him today, she was glad to see the familiar number.

"Hi," she said.

"Hey, sorry to bother you," he said.

"You're not. What's up?"

"I keep thinking about that box of stuff. I should have looked through it. That was really lame of me."

"I never knew you had dramatic aspirations."

"What do you mean?"

"*Cheaper by the Dozen.*"

Theo laughed. "Seventh grade. I had to wear a fake mustache, and for a week I had a mustache-shaped rash from the glue."

"I'll send you the program."

"What else did you find?"

"No jewels or anything. Stuff from both of us as kids. Recipes. Random scrapbook-type stuff. I haven't gone through it all yet. It's both overwhelming and utterly mundane."

"It's depressing to see the remnants of a life in a box. The ticket stubs and report cards. Snapshots. I don't know. I think I'm feeling my age."

Sam felt emboldened. "You and Cindy should adopt a baby."

"What?" he asked, annoyed. "No."

"Come on, Theo. If you want a kid, have a kid."

Theo was quiet for a moment and then exhaled.

"Are you smoking?" she asked.

"I started back up again. Just a few a day."

"I won't bring it up again. About adopting. "

"No, it's okay."

"I think you'd be good as a dad."

"Thanks, Sammy," he said quietly. "Oh, so Dad and Marie are coming your way. Clear out a big parking space."

"To Madison?"

"In the RV. After Canada. In a couple weeks. He's going to call you."

"No way."

"He wants to meet Ella, Sammy. Give him a break."

She wanted her dad to come. Why was it so hard for her to admit?

"I'll call him."

"Sure you will," Theo said.

"What'd we put Mom in?"

"What?"

"Her ashes. What did we put them in?"

"That's so weird. I have no idea. I think the funeral home just took care of it. Something standard."

"We're terrible," she said.

"Come on, it was an emotional time. It doesn't matter really, does it?"

Of course it matters, she thought. I should be making something in honor of my mother instead of dithering about, stalking prostitutes.

"You have them, right?" she asked.

"I think they're in the downstairs closet."

"You think?"

"I have them, Sam, relax. But we need to deal with them soon, okay?"

With the watershed of Ella's arrival, Sam had forgotten that they had not buried the ashes, and now here it was, a whole year later. Theo was right.

She pulled out the next envelope in the box. Inside were some sixties-era photographs of people she didn't know, a dinner party with an empty seat—Iris must have been holding the camera—couples holding piña coladas and cigarettes at a lake house, identities forever lost. There was a picture of Chicago in a blizzard. There were also some outtakes of her parents' wedding not included in the official album—a candid of Iris standing alone, watching the reception, her hair poofed up behind a white satin bow, a shot of her being fed cake by Glenn, her eyes closed, a fleck of opaque pink lipstick on her tooth, Glenn laughing, showing his gums. Sam wondered if her mother had kept these because she couldn't bear to throw them out, or if they'd held some secret meaning for her, something she'd wanted to remember of her wedding day that was not staged. And what would Sam do with them now? Stick them back in the box for Ella to discover in fifty years?

She unfolded a yellowed plastic bag. Inside wrapped in tissue paper was a square coaster from someplace in Chicago called the Coq d'Or, with an image of a rooster on it, flecked with the remains of gold paint. The cardboard was deteriorating and furry around the edges. Really, Mom? A coaster from a bar?

There was a book in the box, a small Bible, with a battered black cover bent in around the pages, the gold lettering rubbed away. Her staunchly atheist mother had kept a Bible. Sam cracked open the musty cover, but the nameplate was blank. Only the date was filled in: June 10, 1900. In the top corner, a black stamp:

Children's Aid Society
105 East Twenty-Second Street
New York City, New York

Her grandmother's, surely, given the date—she would have been about eleven then—but it was a strange notation. New York was a long way from Wisconsin. Maybe she picked it up at a church bazaar, Sam thought, and there was no more to it than that.

Sticking out of the pages was a photograph of Sam's grandparents on the sagging porch of their old southern Minnesota farmhouse, its white paint flaking off from the battering seasons, the snaking branches of the overgrown lilac trees obscuring the edge of the house. The Olsens were an impassive-looking pair, probably in their sixties here, she without makeup, her white hair pulled back in a low pony-tail, without any attempt to pretty herself. She had been a farm wife, after all, not fancy or vain. In the photograph her grandfather sat straight on a rough-hewn wooden bench with the newspaper on his lap, his bifocals on the end of his nose. Sam's grandmother, nestled in a frayed wingback chair, was knitting. Neither of them smiled, though they didn't look unhappy either, just separate, as if they didn't live with each other as much as next to each other, and they were ready to get back to what they were doing before the pho-tographer had asked them to please look up.

Her grandfather looked unmistakably Scandinavian, his hair, even in old age, blond and wispy, too soft-looking for his heavily creased face. He was quiet, Iris had said, though sometimes funny and often kind, a farmer who, later in life, became the manager of a feed mill. Iris's mother was, she'd said, infinitely capable, a fixer and a coper.

Sam didn't even know where in Wisconsin her grand-mother had grown up. Not asking her mother about her family in those final weeks seemed an egregious lapse. Iris had been an only child, and now there was no one left. But then again, it might have seemed to Iris a forced and senti-mental exercise. Sam was, she realized, intimidated by her mother to the end.

Although Iris had claimed she couldn't get away from her rural, provincial background fast enough, she had at times, over the years, spoken lovingly of the south branch of the Root River, along whose banks she'd spent many childhood afternoons fishing for channel catfish, rock bass, and sunfish. In rare moments her mother had gotten wistful and spoken of the land near the farm, the limestone bluffs topped with oak and hickory, the egrets and wood ducks on the river's edge, the otters and beavers. My mother! Sam thought now. The woman who'd gotten a manicure every two weeks and ironed the sheets and had pesticide sprayed on the lawn so it would be perfectly green. Sam had been in Madison for years and not driven the three hours to see the river. Why have I not gone there yet? she thought.

Through the front window she could see that Ted was back from campus and was now raking his yard, even though the leaf drop had barely begun, his hair bouncing with each comb of the rake. He wore his seventies maroon leather jacket and a turtleneck underneath. She admired his vigor and optimism.

The pound cake. She went to the kitchen and turned on the oven. Her mother used to make a pound cake on occa-sion, though a more delicate version than the original Sam was going for. "Always use vanilla, even if the recipe doesn't call for it," Iris had said. And what was that odd spice she'd used? Mace, Sam remembered. Who had ever used mace? On a whim she rummaged around her spice drawer and found a small, faded canister unopened, wedged into the back corner. She must have acquired it long before she met Jack—no doubt on advice from Iris on outfitting her kitchen—and it had accompanied her all the way here.

Sam knifed open the seal. However old it was, it had the mellow nutmeggy smell she recalled from her childhood. She scooped a quarter teaspoon into a bowl and pulled down the vanilla.

"I never considered getting a divorce," her mother had said, pushing away a plate of salmon she couldn't eat. "Even when I would have preferred it. Now it seems so obvious. But then I thought I needed some kind of permission. I didn't think I could do something so big."

Sam had never heard her mother talk like this, and she wanted both more and less of it. It was welcoming after all the years of her policing the fortress of her interior life, but she feared Iris would unveil a stranger and then up and die.

"Did you know about Marie?" Sam asked.

"Oh, sure," she said. "That wasn't anything really. It stung my ego, I guess. But your father and I . . ." She waved her hand and then closed her eyes, leaning back in her chair, too exhausted to go on.

As Iris withered, she actually looked younger, the refined bone structure of her face pronounced and delicate, her dark bob wispy and girlish, her feet now too big for her body.

"I genuinely hope Glenn is happy," she said quietly, her eyes still closed, "in the RV."

They laughed together, and Sam was thankful for the

warm and briny breeze through the open balcony doors, incongruously pleasant given Iris's deterioration. The baby lodged her foot under Sam's ribs. Iris could no longer walk unaided and it hurt her to sit for long. The multitudinous pills were becoming more difficult for her to get down by the day. Sam had been in Sanibel for two weeks, and although they'd talked about the practical matters of death—her will, her accounts, her wishes—they had not discussed the death itself. Iris had seemed to have no interest in talking about it, and Sam hadn't had the guts to bring it up.

"Let's go see the birds," Iris said.

They drove to the "Ding" Darling National Wildlife Refuge, less than a half mile from the condo. Iris had hoped she would have the energy to walk a little way to see the alligators and get close to the herons, but the day was warm and hazy, and she felt too sick to get out of the car.

"Oh, well," she said. "The mosquitoes are terrible anyway. And they find pregnant women particularly irresistible."

So Sam drove slowly, stopping at viewing platforms, signs, and observation towers, trying to coax her mother from the car.

"Park up here," Iris said.

Sam stopped next to a phalanx of mangrove trees, their rust-red roots like tentacles holding fast to the swampland beneath.

"Read me what that sign says," Iris said.

"Estuarine Ecosystem. The process of passing nutrients from one animal to another through feeding is called a food web."

"I thought it would talk about the birds. Ibises, egrets, dunlins, hawks. Where are all the birds? I've only seen two

pelicans. It was right around here we used to see the spoon-
bills."

We? Sam opened her mouth but closed it again, unable
to ask.

"Have you ever seen a spoonbill?"

Sam shook her head.

"They look prehistoric with these weird rounded beaks.
Like a forgotten species. I don't think there are many left.
Maybe there aren't any left now."

Sam drove a little farther and pulled over again next to
a ropy branched gumbo-limbo tree—she'd read about them
in the brochure—its crazy orange bark cracked and peeling
like dead skin.

"We should have brought binoculars," Sam said. "I'm
sure the birds are just blending in."

"It's okay, honey. I don't feel the need to check anything
off the list."

They'd come in the late afternoon at low tide—best to
catch the wading birds—and as they rounded the fourth
mile, the sun was lowering, its reflection painting the lagoon
pink.

"It's time for me to go, Samantha."

"We're at the exit." Sam turned out onto Sanibel-Captiva
Road, pointing at the hawk circling above.

"There's no point in dragging it out," her mother said.
"One's body shutting down is no fun, believe me."

It shouldn't have been much of a surprise.

"Mom. Stop it. Please." She'd pushed thoughts of her
mother's death into the sand, and now she was unprepared
for their barb and weight. She felt the baby kick her bladder,
and she had to strain not to wet her pants.

"It's undignified. This rot. I'd rather have some say in it," Iris said.

"Why are you telling me this? I don't want to know," Sam said, her voice pinched and high.

"Because I need your help."

"No. No. I'm not doing that. I can't do that."

"Yes, you can."

"What about Theo—"

"Theo. No. You're stronger than you think you are. Most women are. I should have done it earlier and spared you, I know. But I waited too long and got too weak." Iris closed her eyes, scowling in pain. "When the baby comes you'll forget all about it."

It's not right, Sam screamed to herself. To ask this of a daughter. She wanted to yell in protest at the barbarous request, to get on the next plane back to Madison. She felt a lick of anger flare, its heat shooting up to her head before fizzling to a simmer.

"You might have months," Sam said weakly.

"It's merciful, Samantha. I have had enough."

Sam had eased her mother's car into the garage below the condo and stared ahead at the neat shelves of household supplies in labeled plastic containers.

"I was thinking on my birthday," Iris had said. "There's a pleasing symmetry to that, don't you think?"

Sam retrieved the packet of her grandmother's recipes from the pile on the table, just to see if there might be one for pound cake. The rubber band was dried out and cracked, and when she went to slide it off, it broke. A tissue-thin piece of lavender paper, folded in thirds, slipped out and fluttered into her lap. A letter. The ink was faded, the handwriting, shaky. Dated December 10, 1910.

"Dear Mrs. Olsen," it began. "It was with great expectation that I read your letter."

VIOLET

The train was loud, the horsehair seat uncomfortable. Violet sat behind the nurse, Miss Bodean, barely older than some of the girls, who held an infant in her lap and was flanked by two toddler girls on one side, a boy on the other. One of the babies was invariably crying, but the sounds were covered by the clattering windows, the roaring engine, the scrape and scream of metal wheels against the rails. After the train had rocketed out of the city, the buildings became lower, sparser, and the landscape turned green and rolling.

The company had the car to itself. A tiny German boy with straw-colored hair did cartwheels in the aisles for laughs until he was ordered to sit.

"Save the performing for Indiana, Joseph," Mrs. Comstock said.

"What's Indiana?" he said.

"It's where the parents are."

Violet sat next to a brother and sister with the same wide-set brown eyes, who held hands and looked straight ahead.

"You want to sit by the window for a while?" Violet asked the boy.

He shook his head.

"What's your name?"

"Elmer."

"This your sister?" Violet said, pointing.

"Yeah. I think she pooped her pants."

"Did not," the girl said.

"Shut up, Elsie," he said.

"I don't smell nothing," Violet said.

Mrs. Comstock moved down the aisle, turning sideways to make her large bottom half fit, and addressed the group.

"Remember, children, labor is elevating, and idleness is sinful. You are fortunate to get this opportunity, to be delivered from poverty and sin. Your new parents might want to give you a new name. Accept it with dignity."

Violet scowled. She didn't want to be Sarah or Mary or Helen.

"Is there a problem, Violet?" Mrs. Comstock asked, stopping next to her row.

"No, ma'am," she said, already having dismissed Mrs. Comstock as a potential ally.

In the seat ahead, Miss Bodean stuck a bottle in the infant's mouth and rocked him back and forth to coax him to sleep.

"Those of you who were raised Catholic are now Protestant. Do not talk about rites and saints to your new families. And this goes for all of you; don't talk about your old lives in the city. Try to forget. That is the past." Mrs. Comstock took a deep breath and exhaled, as if, in solidarity, she were letting go of her past, too. "Riding an orphan train is not something you will want to discuss, either."

"Why not?" asked a consumptive-looking girl with thin, grayish skin.

Mrs. Comstock paused. "Because it will be better for you if you don't."

The girl blinked blank eyes, unsatisfied by the answer. "But whoever picks me will know where I came from."

"Of course, dear. But they will not want to be reminded of it," Mrs. Comstock said.

Soon Violet saw nothing but trees, a steady blur of trunks and bushy leaves. She daydreamed about having a room of her own, a brother to go fishing with, a mother who would teach her how to knit, a father who would sweep her up at the end of the day and swing her around. She dozed, Elmer's head leaning against her arm.

Mrs. Comstock passed out mustard sandwiches and apples, the same as they had had for lunch, and small cups of condensed milk. Joseph, the cartwheeling German boy, knelt on his seat, facing back, pulling his ears wide and rolling his eyes for the little ones behind him. He yodeled.

"Quite an entertainer," Mrs. Comstock said, patting his head, but she did not make him face forward. As they had gotten farther from the city, she had relaxed some, even taking off her bonnet. Joseph smiled and hopped into her lap.

Violet thought about Nino and tried to remember what he'd looked like when she'd first seen him kicking along on Water Street, gangly limbs, a nose too big for his face. She had filched an orange in front of him to get his attention. He had corrected her technique.

"Help me, please?" Miss Bodean said, turning around in her seat. "I need you to hold the baby. So I can change Frederick's soiled nappy."

Violet had never held a baby and didn't want to start now. "I never held one before."

"There's nothing to it. Just sit there and don't move." The nurse placed the wrapped bundle across Violet's lap. Elmer peered over.

"What's wrong with it?" he asked. "The face looks like a dried-up apple."

Violet felt a bolt of anger toward the infant, its needy, milk-wet mouth, its tiny useless fists, the ugly rash on its cheeks, bumpy and pink.

They received blankets to sleep in their seats. The car had no lights, so when darkness fell, they curled every which way to get comfortable. Some of the boys gave up and stretched out on the floor. The train jerked around a sharp curve and Violet felt Elmer go rigid beside her before he fell back to sleep, Elsie's head in his lap. She leaned against the window frame, her head jostling, and tried to contain her fierce hope for a real family that would take her in. She imagined milking a cow in the peachy dawn, her cheek against the warm flank, the steaming cream thick at the top of the pail. She imagined her bed, reaching out her arms and legs under a pile of soft quilts. She tried not to think of her mother, alone in their old attic room. In the last of the sun, she marveled at the flat, flat world where the sky rolled on forever, until it was too dark to see, and her lids fell over her eyes.

Two days after they left New York City, they got off the train in Sheridan, Indiana. It was windy on the platform, the sun high, and the children in their wrinkled, dusty clothes, clutching their Bibles, blinked and bumped around one another like moles. The train pulled away in a rush of screeching metal and chugging steam and left them in a dazed huddle around Mrs. Comstock. The wind whipped against Violet's ears, and she felt a stinging, unfamiliar loneliness. She had half expected a cheering crowd when the train arrived, parents waving, scooping up their new children. Streamers and music. Cakes and punch, even. But it was empty, save for a railroad worker stacking crates and a Mr. Drummond, the local coordinator.

Handbills skidded by their feet and flapped against the posts of the depot:

HOMES WANTED FOR CHILDREN

A Mercy Train of Orphan Children will arrive at
Sheridan, Indiana, Friday, June 15, 1900.

The Distribution will take place at the Opera House at 1:00 pm. The object of the coming of these children is to find homes in your midst, especially among farmers, where they may enjoy a happy and wholesome family life, where kind care, good example and moral training will fit them for a life of self-support and usefulness. They come under the auspices of the New York Children's Aid Society,

by whom they have been tested and found to be
well-meaning and willing boys and girls.

Remember the time and place. All are invited.

The children held hands as they were told and followed
Mrs. Comstock and Mr. Drummond, who carried the
trunk—Miss Bodean followed behind the group—across the
mostly empty town square. A man in a wagon stopped to
watch. A woman on the courthouse steps held the hand of a
young girl and pointed. Violet wondered if this was to be
where she would call home. She looked around for things to
make her feel better about it. It was quiet. It didn't smell bad.
There wasn't manure all over the street. She told herself these
things, but it only made her feel more out of place.

At the Sheridan Hotel, the boys were shuttled into one
room, the girls into another, where their hands and faces
were wiped and their hair brushed. They were each given a
glass of fresh milk.

"Smile for the people," Mrs. Comstock said. "Answer
their questions. Act ladylike and proper. Do as you're told."

The girls twittered and licked their lips, readying themselves for the audition. Miss Bodean dabbed the noses of
the babies with a damp rag and dug at their crusty eyes.

"What if we don't like where we go?" Violet asked.

The other girls sat up, quiet, and turned their heads
toward her, fear taking hold of their features.

Mrs. Comstock inhaled and exhaled through her nose
and narrowed stern eyes at Violet.

"Be grateful for this opportunity, young lady. If there is
a problem, you can write to the Aid Society. The address is

in your Bible. But it must be serious, mind you. Try to make the best of your situation. Say your prayers at night."

Violet stopped listening. She smoothed the paper pinned to her chest and watched the raggedy clouds skitter by through the slit in the curtains. She had always known in some sense, even back in Aberdeen, that she was on her own. She slipped down a little further into herself, and touched the dark core no one could reach.

"Girls, let scripture be your guide," Mrs. Comstock said. "Repeat after me: *I will sing of loyalty and of justice; to Thee, O Lord, I will sing.*"

The girls repeated the words in a grave monotone.

"I will give heed to the way that is blameless. Oh, when wilt Thou come to me?"

Elsie, Elmer's little sister, started to cry and held her hands over her eyes.

"Quiet now, little one," Miss Bodean shushed.

"I will walk with integrity of heart within my house."

"I will walk with integrity of heart within my house," Violet mumbled, not caring about the words.

She tried to remember what the moment she'd been baptized in the Barren River had felt like, the tips of the willow branches dipping in and out of the water, the July sun beaming down on her wet head, the white gown her mother had kept in her carved cedar chest floating around her legs. She had not felt reborn. But she had felt hopeful.

"Line up for the toilet, girls. We leave in one half hour."

One long row of chairs was set up on the stage. The curtain, a heavy green velvet, was drawn so they could not see who had gathered, but they could hear the rustling of an audience on the other side.

"Boys first, oldest to youngest, then girls, then Miss Bodean and the babies."

Violet sat next to Eileen, a skinny Irish girl who was missing a front tooth, and Maryanne, a half-orphan who said her mother would come for her in a couple of months. No one spoke. Elsie clung to Elmer's hand and cried as Mrs. Comstock pulled her away to a chair near the end. Elmer held his trembling chin up and looked straight ahead.

"Let us say together the Twenty-third Psalm," Mrs. Comstock said, facing them and bowing her head. *"The Lord is my shepherd; I shall not want."*

Some of the children joined in, others halfheartedly mouthed the words. Violet closed her eyes and thought, *Pick me, pick me, pick me, pick me.*

"Surely goodness and mercy shall follow me all the days of my life; and I will dwell in the house of the Lord for ever. Amen."

The older orphan boy, number twelve, coughed into his fist, trying to clear his throat. Eileen, next to Violet, tapped her foot. The infant hiccuped.

Mr. Drummond peeked his head through the curtain. "Mrs. Comstock? We have quite a crowd gathered. I think it's going to be a very good day."

Mrs. Comstock clapped her hands together and held them in front of her chest, smiling from face to face. "Children," she said, "it is time."

When the curtains swept apart, all Violet could see were eyes shining back at her, reflecting the electric lights of the windowless opera house. The floor had been cleared of chairs, and curious sightseers and potential applicants milled about, gawking at the children, waving, smiling. Some of the little ones waved back. Violet didn't know what to do with her hands or where to look, if she should seek out a friendly face or if she should wait to be noticed.

The first group approached the stage, pencils and paper in hand. A woman ran to the end, to Miss Bodean, and swept the infant up into her arms.

"Andrew, look," she said to her husband, a large farmer who was trying to scoot around the others. "We'll take this one," she said to Miss Bodean. "Can we take him now?"

"Fill out an application over here with me, madam" Mr. Drummond said. "It's number twenty-three you want?" He checked his list. "Edward Leperdoff, aged six months."

"We will call him Thomas," the woman said quickly into the baby's face. "He will be Thomas Pugh. Fill out the paper-work, Andrew. I'll hold our son."

Another couple eyed the woman with envy and anger. They moved to one of the toddlers.

"How old is he?" the husband asked.

Violet felt her chances slip. The younger ones will run out eventually, she told herself, straightening in her chair. Her smile tightened.

"Almost three years," Miss Bodean said. "Very agreeable and docile. Not a mischief maker."

The woman sighed but knelt down in front of the boy. "Hello, little fellow," she said. "Do you want to come home with us?"

The child seemed to weigh her words, eyes squinting, head atilt. "Ice cream?" he asked.

"I don't see why not," she said, patting his head. He took hold of her hand and hopped down from the chair.

"Sally, can we talk about this?" the husband asked. He called to Mr. Drummond. "Sir, can we bring him back if change our minds?"

Mr. Drummond jogged over, glancing at the boy, who looked up in fright.

"Should the child prove unsatisfactory, he will be taken back by the Society," Mr. Drummond said quietly.

"Eighty-seven percent of the children we place do well and grow up to be useful men and women," Mrs. Comstock added.

The little boy pulled his hand from the woman and backed away.

"Now, now," the woman said.

"Frederick," Mrs. Comstock said. "Go with your new mother now."

It was not as Violet had imagined. People weren't nicer in the country, and they didn't want her here anymore than they had in the city.

Down at the other end, men inspected the older boys like horses.

"Weak hands."

"Fine leg muscles."

"Let me see your arms."

"Ever done farm work?"

"You won't do me any good."

"Too short."

"I'll take him."

It had become clear to Violet that the little ones would be adopted and the older ones would be put to work. She hovered somewhere in the middle. She felt the slow burn of shame bloom under her skin for thinking that she would be chosen as a daughter, for skidding past all this to the part where she was laughing and eating custard in a warm dining room with her new family.

When she looked up there was an old man in front of her smelling of beer and manure.

"How old are you?"

"Eleven," she said.

He looked her up and down and sniffed. "I need a girl to do the washing and cooking. For your keep."

Violet took quick shallow breaths, unable to get enough air, unable to accept that this might be it.

"Well, speak up, girl."

She wobbled her head. The man moved on to Irish Eileen. Down the row, Elsie screamed and kicked the man who'd chosen her.

"I can't feed two," he explained to Mrs. Comstock. "I would if I could, but I just come to replace what I lost."

The German boy, Joseph, did a handstand on his chair to the delight of his potential adopters and the remaining crowd, who waited for the next spectacle, the next hug and happy ending.

A late-arriving middle-aged couple stopped and smiled at Violet.

"What's your name?" the woman asked, her face soft like rising dough.

"Violet."

"You have lovely eyes, Violet," she said.

"Thank you, ma'am," Violet said, her palms sweating against her knees.

"Our children are grown," the husband said. "We would like to take in a needy child."

Violet's hope gurgled up to the surface. She sat up, ready to go.

"How old are you?" the man asked.

"Eleven," she said, smiling. Relief washed through her, swift and sweet.

"I'm afraid we were wanting a boy," the woman said. "We need someone to do some work around the place."

"I can work," Violet said, confused by the sudden shift.

"I don't doubt it," the man said, "but it's a boy we're after."

"It was nice to meet you. Good luck, dear," the woman said. "I'm sure you will get a nice family."

Violet looked away, unable to let them see her face fall, tears of anger pushing at her eyes. She had let herself be fooled. She had thought she deserved it and then had been justly rewarded. She felt like a sucker, but underneath she felt something worse. Her father had been right all along. She was not worth what it cost to feed her.

At the end of the showing, sixteen of them were taken. Fourteen were getting back on the train.

Since the young ones all found homes, Miss Bodean was taking a train back to New York. Violet saw it as a chance. The Fourth Ward was better than an orphanage. As the group ate their peanut butter sandwiches on the lawn of the courthouse, she found Mrs. Comstock shining an apple with a handkerchief.

"Can I go with the nurse?" Violet asked. "I can work to pay you back for the ticket."

Mrs. Comstock busied herself with her apple, her hair in a crooked bun.

"Ma'am?"

"I'm sorry, but that's not possible," Mrs. Comstock said, in a weary but not unkind voice.

"I don't want to go on." She felt a new helplessness, and she could barely get the words out.

"It's not up to you now, is it? Besides, the eastbound train has already left," Mrs. Comstock said. "Violet, it's best not to look backward."

"What happens if no one takes us?"

"We'll talk about that when the time comes."

Violet stood, her feet rooted. But she didn't protest because, she realized, she didn't really want to go back to New York anyway. That would be giving up, and she knew, without yet knowing, that returning was impossible.

"Here," Mrs. Comstock said, handing Violet the apple. "You have it."

After a night with the other four girls who were left—one Violet thought meek and not worth the effort, another ugly and irksome, one older girl who turned away when Violet asked her name, and one Polish girl who didn't speak English—she was on a train heading farther west to Illinois, Elmer back beside her, kicking the seat in front of them.

"I thought I saw you with the man in the muddy boots," Violet said.

"He stank and I said so. He said I was incorrigible and handed me back over," Elmer said.

"I thought it would be different, too."

"I hope they's nice to Elsie," he said. "She don't like to sleep by herself."

"She can tell them that," Violet said. "She's not yours to worry about anymore."

From the window she watched a blur of fields in every direction, the land cleared of trees, a patchwork of squares and lines, new cornstalks like green fountains. She wished Nino could see how much space there was, how much bigger the sky looked out here. She wished her mother had never met Reginald Smith. She wished her brother hadn't been stillborn.

Mrs. Comstock stood in the aisle. Now that her little Joseph had been adopted away, she had to face the dreary rest of them.

"Children," she said hoarsely. She cleared her throat and tried again. "Children. Your attention."

The Polish girl mouthed words to her lap and crossed herself. One of the rough older boys laughed like a donkey and said something to his friend—Violet could only make out *old biddy*. The older girl turned around and shushed them, which only inspired them to make faces behind her head.

"William. Patrick," Mrs. Comstock said. "Enough."

Violet felt sorry for her, for her droopy face and her wrinkled dress slightly askew. Mrs. Comstock looked bewildered, as if she'd awakened to find herself on the train without any idea of how to shepherd this ragtag bunch. Violet reached over to quiet Elmer's kicks.

"Do not feel dispirited," Mrs. Comstock said, chin held high, not meeting their eyes. She wasn't a good bluffer. Even the younger ones looked at the floor, embarrassed by her poor acting and their dim chances. "There will be plenty of opportunities for you yet."

One of the older boys elbowed his friend and nodded toward the ugly girl, Nettie, her face coarse and red, her eyes too far apart.

"Plenty of opportunities for you, mate," he said.

"Fuck all, Patrick," the friend said, ramming him with his shoulder. He got up and threw himself into a different seat.

Nettie shoved out her bottom lip and turned fully to face the window. Violet refused to feel sorry for her because she'd hogged the bedcovers the previous night and smelled like turnips. Mrs. Comstock stood with her lips apart as if waiting to answer a question.

"Dignity, children," she said, finally, wagging her head. "You are in control of your dignity."

A boy named Frank who sat alone started to cry. The sun glowed through his large translucent ears. Elmer's lip trembled at the sight of the other boy's tears.

"Hey, cut it out," Violet said. She pinched Elmer's pudgy leg until he hit her hand away, angry, and the tears had passed.

"Ma'am?" A young boy in back of the car raised his hand. He had a spray of freckles across his nose that matched his chestnut hair.

Mrs. Comstock walked down the aisle toward him, her skirt swishing against the benches.

"Yes, Herbert."

"Is it true we got to pick cotton like we's slaves?"

"Who told you that?"

"The boys have been saying."

Mrs. Comstock flicked her gaze to each of the boys in the seats around his. They kept their eyes on their laps.

"Boys should not be talking of what they do not know," she said, regaining some composure, a sternness returning to her voice. "You will have a chance to have a normal life. Remember you are in God's hands."

Herbert smiled in relief, too young to know better. "Ma'am?"

"Yes, Herbert."

"Can I come up and sit next to you?"

Mrs. Comstock's shoulders softened, and her mouth turned up in a dolorous smile.

"Yes, Herbert," she said. "Bring your Bible and come along."

The boy scampered up to the front, and Mrs. Comstock made her way behind him, jostled as the train lurched.

"Illinois is next," she said to them. "Your new home."

Violet turned back to face forward in her seat and balled her hands into fists. She closed her eyes and said to herself, *I am ready.*

IRIS

A palm frond tapped against the kitchen window. Iris knew she should take a walk. It would do her good to move around, to breathe in the fresh ocean air. But the phone rang, and she picked it up. Theo.

"Don't drive all the way to Fort Myers to pick up Samantha tomorrow. She can take a cab."

Theo had always criticized his sister—a tree isn't blue, that's not how you throw a baseball, you can't major in anthropology—but becoming a lawyer had made it worse, solidified the tendency into habit.

"Yes, she can. But I insisted," Iris said.

"Mom, you have cancer."

"Ha," Iris laughed. "Honey." She knew it irritated him when she called him this, reminding him that she was his mother, that she knew him, was in essence saying, You came out of me. "It may shock you to learn that I am still of sound mind."

For the first time Iris admitted to herself that her allegiance had shifted, that she favored Samantha now. Could she even say she loved her more? It was different from when they were children. As adults they were no longer blameless. Was it fair, then, to end her life with Samantha here? It was not fair, maybe, but she had not asked a lot of her children.

"I know, I know," Theo said.

"At least that means you and Samantha have talked. That's something."

That her children were not close wasn't surprising, given their ten-year age separation, but it was still a disappointment.

"Yeah," he said, sighing. "I suppose."

She decided she would indulge in a small glass of wine, and walk over to the beach as the sky turned colorful and dark, to mark her last night of solitude.

"Mom?"

"Hmm?"

"I think your phone cut out for a second."

"You better get back to work," she said. "We'll talk tomorrow."

"You need a cell phone."

"I need a lot of things," she said, and then added hurriedly, "I love you."

The words came out more rushed than she would have liked, but they didn't sound strained, and for that she was pleased.

"You too," he said quietly. "Okay, then. Bye."

Iris closed her eyes, and breathed in as deeply as her damaged lungs would allow.

Samantha had sent her a card for her birthday years ago, just after the divorce, with a reproduction of a painting on the front: *The Bay* by Helen Frankenthaler, 1963. The picture had moved something in Iris, opened her up. Those saturated blues and watery violets, a top-heavy stain on a flat earth of sage. And that small wedge of orange. What was it doing there? It was so strange and compelling, a splinter that seemed to hold the whole thing in place. She immediately went to the library to learn more about the painter. Frankenthaler was an abstract expressionist, more precisely, a field painter, married to—and overshadowed by—Robert Motherwell. But the most striking thing was that she was the same age as Iris. In 1963, while Iris was dropping Theo off at kindergarten, getting the carpets cleaned, dusting the chandelier, Helen Frankenthaler was living her bohemian life, diluting her oil paint with turpentine and creating the fluid other world of *The Bay*. She hadn't been saddened by the comparison as much as impressed by the other woman's self-possession, which had taken Iris a lifetime to cobble together.

This is my sky, Iris thought, as she sat hugging her knees on the edge of the small dunes, with the tide high, the waves calm and even. It reminded her of the painting, how the gray-purple clouds seemed to have more heft than the water beneath. She supposed the chardonnay-and-painkiller mix might have something to do with it, but she didn't find it any less wondrous. It would be a relief to let go, she thought now. A handful of morphine pills. When the time was right.

The day's beach crowd had mostly cleared. An older couple—probably her age, she thought, abashed by this recognition—walked by her holding hands, he carrying a camera, she swinging a bucket of shells. A little girl in a pink bathing suit, her hair a fountain on her head, made a break for the water but was quickly scooped up by her father, who carried her over his sunburned shoulder. Iris was glad for all of this, or maybe she was grateful.

She and Henry had come to this beach only once together. It had been dusk then, too, but winter, blustery, the sky gunmetal gray. The sand was cold against her feet. Other than the sandpipers and seagulls, they were alone. His hand was warm around hers. They talked about aging ("I still haven't gotten used to the fact that I'm older than almost everyone in the world," Henry said), about their kids pushing them to get e-mail ("What would I write that I couldn't say to them over the phone?" Iris said), about how the invasive Brazilian pepper and Australian pine were degrading the wildlife habitat at the refuge.

Iris had felt good then, her health issues—osteoporosis, high cholesterol, a back that gave her trouble—were commonplace and unthreatening. She no longer cared about who she was supposed to be. With Henry, she was more comfortable than she'd been her whole life. They had walked until darkness took hold and they could hear the waves but no longer see them.

And then he'd said, "She knows, my dear."

Iris filled her hand with the warm white sand and funneled it over her feet. She knew she should get up while she still could muster the strength, but she was lulled by the warm breeze on the now dark, empty beach. If she stayed very still, she could pretend she wasn't sick, pretend she would be here for another spring, pretend she was fearless.

≫

"Mother?"

"Yes, Iris."

"Can you hear the bees?"

"Yes, Iris. I can hear them," she'd said, sitting on the bed.

A crawling, humming mass of bees—all piled on the queen—had swathed a branch of the maple tree outside of Iris's window.

"It's almost as big as me," she said, burrowing deeper into the bed and clutching her doll.

"They won't stay for long," her mother said, pulling the sheet up over Iris's shoulders. "They're visitors. The colony is migrating. Father says they're getting ready to leave."

"Where are they going?"

"Don't know."

"Why'd they leave their house in the first place?"

"Maybe their hive got too small. Or it got damaged in the hailstorm last week. Remember how it sounded like rocks were hitting the hog-pen roof?"

Iris nodded.

"Or maybe the bees just felt like a change." Her mother shrugged and smiled. "It's a mystery, isn't it?"

"Will they come back?"

"I don't think so."

Iris wondered how they knew when to go, where to go, how they communicated, and how the ones in the middle could breathe, smothered by all those other bees, but she couldn't keep her thoughts straight as she neared sleep.

"I can still hear them."

"Close your eyes, Iris . . ."

At dawn, her mother swooshed into her room. "Wake up, sleepyhead. The bees are moving."

Iris groggily clambered to the window, her mother behind her. The colony looked to be in a frenzy, crawling and shaking, the bodies shiny in the rising sun. Some of the bees were flying off and orbiting the cluster. And then all at once, as if some giant hand had bounced the branch, the swarm was airborne, a black buzzing cloud, swirling, up and up and then away, west over the farm until she could no longer see it.

"Oh," her mother said, a small plaintive sound, and Iris looked up to see that her eyes were full of tears.

"Mother?"

"I will miss them," she had said. "Isn't that a funny thing?"

For days Iris had looked for the bees in the sky, hoping they would return for her mother. But they had gone for good.

Iris had read that fake smiling could make something more enjoyable, that facial movement could influence emotional experience. What if she could fake wellness? She could go through the motions as if it were any other day, and maybe it would make her feel better. So she passed on the peanut butter and jelly—sadly—and warmed up a bowl of carrot soup, and tossed a small salad of spinach, goat cheese, and walnuts. She even pulled a cloth napkin from the drawer and set out silverware, a glass of sparkling water.

But she kept thinking about the bees, and how she'd never seen anything like them for the rest of her life, the wild and magical beauty of them, and how her mother had cried, and how she thought she finally understood why her mother had cried when the bees had flown away.

Loud voices echoed on the landing, her neighbor Stephen and another man, in some kind of quarrel. Iris went to her door and strained to see through the peephole. Stephen was in a towel, his hair wet from a shower. The other man was barely more than a boy, skinny, his jeans low and tight. He stood with his arms crossed, his head cocked: petulant, Iris thought, hateful.

"I didn't take it!" he yelled. "Like I'd want your shitty watch."

"Give it back, and that will be that."

"Whatever," he said.

"I'll call the cops," Stephen said, one hand holding his towel.

The boy laughed, a mirthless *ha-ha-ha*.

Iris wondered if she should call the police, but something in Stephen's weak posture, his furtive glances, told her not to.

"Go on, big boy, call them. I'll be waiting right here."

Stephen grabbed his arm, but the boy spun out of his grip and ran. Stephen slipped back into his apartment and slammed the door.

Poor Stephen, she thought. How unseemly, how embarrassing the encounter must have been for him. To be shamed so because someone sniffed out your weakness. Will he change? Does he want to? Maybe he doesn't aspire to settle down, she thought, or he feels he isn't worthy of someone who would choose him. Maybe the thrill of possibility each night brings gets him through the day of forced cheer at the hotel desk. Samantha had once accused her of imposing her feelings on others, and Iris decided she would try in the next three weeks to do less of that.

She sipped her soup, tasting the carrot and ginger and cream on her tongue, and felt nourished. She had made it through another day, and she felt satisfied by the very passing of day into night.

She'd still been single at twenty-eight, and Glenn had been the quiet new associate at the Chicago firm where she was a secretary. Eligible, all the girls said with hungry eyes. Iris decided that it was time. Her girlhood romanticism had gotten her nowhere, and it was time to pack it away. Glenn was not exciting to her, but he was a decent man—handsome, polite, and successful—who thought she was pretty and wanted her to be his wife. Waiting around for passion surely wouldn't afford her a life on the North Shore. After the engagement was announced, she promptly quit her job, knowing she would never work again. In those newlywed days she used to greet him at the door in full makeup, dressed up in heels and wasp-waist dresses, dinner on the table. She'd have spent hours preparing some dish she'd seen in a magazine: beef Wellington, tomato aspic, baked Alaska. It was, she had thought, her end of the bargain, and Glenn had been ever appreciative.

How different her life might have looked from here had she married a saxophone player instead of Glenn, or if she'd become a teacher instead of a secretary, or if she'd turned left instead of right on any given day. It was a futile, wistful game with infinite variations and outcomes, an ideal pastime for someone with regrets and the long view.

But there had been one moment, one day, when Iris, at thirty-seven, had decided that she could bend her course off its rails, to begin again. She didn't know what that change looked like, but she wanted to make herself available to it. There had been no big argument with Glenn. In fact, everything was fine. He'd just given her an Hermès scarf for their ninth wedding anniversary. Theo had started second grade. She had recently begun tennis lessons. She had a pork roast defrosting in the refrigerator.

After dropping Theo off at school, she returned to a clean and quiet house, put on her pale-rose wool suit from Bonwit's, her most flattering and sophisticated outfit, the belt of the dress cinched tight around her slim waist above an A-line knife-pleated skirt. A cropped little jacket over it. White square-heeled pumps. She wore her hair in a modified flip, the ends curled up and set twice a month at the hairdresser's, which she now brushed and smoothed. She didn't know where she was going, but she got in the car and drove south. When she hit Chicago she drove along Lake Shore, the lake a wind-whipped blue, the sun's reflection making it too bright to look at straight on. She felt both numb and exuberant, her freedom a secret no one yet knew, as she veered into the city at Michigan Avenue. And there it was, the Drake Hotel, just to the left on East Walton, and Iris felt as if it were what she had been looking for.

The Drake was where those with means stayed in Chicago. Iris had attended wedding receptions here, and she and Glenn had eaten at the Cape Cod Room many times,

big nights out when they still lived in the city. She'd even
taken her mother to the Drake to give her the full Chicago
experience. Her mother had declared the hotel a little snooty
and the tea weak, and she had not seemed awed by the
grand scale and excitement of the city. Iris had been surprised, even a little hurt. She'd always had the silly inclina-
tion to impress her mother by the trappings of her life, as if
she needed to show off why she'd left Minnesota.

As the valet took her car, Iris straightened her skirt,
pressed her lips together to even her pale pink lipstick,
wiggled off her engagement and wedding rings, and pretended she was someone else. The hotel bar, the Coq d'Or,
had a dark, clubby feel, with butternut paneling, swanky
lantern lamps that hung low from the ceiling over the tables,
and a quilted turquoise leather banquette against the back
wall. The bow-tied piano player, an older man with sparse
gray hair slicked back from his forehead, smiled as she
glanced over. The heavy bar was lined with red leather
seats, a large crystal ashtray at each. It being midday, there
were groups of suited men at a few tables, even a group
of women laughing and smoking, but the bar itself was
empty, save for an old man at the end nursing a watery
scotch.

Iris perched on a seat at the bar, crossing her legs a little
to the side, and pulled out a cigarette from a small silver
case in her purse. She didn't smoke a lot, but it calmed her
nerves, and she thought it made her look alluring. The bartender was instantly in front of her with a lighter. She felt
conspicuous—a woman drinking alone was uncouth—but
in the role she was playing, she didn't mind. She rubbed the
absence of her rings with her thumb.

"Gin and tonic please," she said to the bartender. "And a cucumber sandwich."

The room's sounds enveloped her in a warm cocoon: ice tinkling in thick bar glasses, martinis being shaken, the low tones of professional men's conversations, the occasional roar of a man's laugh, the magpie cackle of one of the women, and, in the lulls, the soothing piano to smooth over any moments of fearful silence. She sipped her cold and bitter drink, the green ribbon of lime peel clinging to the edge of the glass, and stubbed out her half-smoked cigarette. The bartender whisked away her ashtray and replaced it with a clean one. She crunched her dainty sandwich and dabbed at her mouth, careful not to wipe away her lipstick. The part up until now had been fun—she'd felt uncharacteristically nervy—but the reality of sitting here now started to feel desperate. What did she have to complain about, really? And Theo. As if she could ever leave her brown-eyed little boy who loved trains and still held her hand when they walked down the sidewalk.

"Excuse me," a man said, suddenly beside her. "Are you waiting for someone?"

She furrowed her brow a little to stifle the laugh she felt gurgle in her throat.

"No. Having lunch," was all she could get out.

"May I join you?" He was younger than she was, confident. She guessed he was in advertising from his slim little black suit and flamboyant paisley tie.

"That would be fine," she said.

"Richard."

He held out his small hand and she shook it. It was damp, unappealing.

"Iris." This does not feel exciting or romantic, she thought. She felt foolish.

"You are one pretty lady, Iris."

She cleared her throat. "Thank you."

"What're you drinking?" he asked, leaning in.

"Gin. And tonic."

Richard held up two fingers to the bartender and pointed to Iris's glass.

This is ridiculous, she thought. What was she going to do? Have an affair with this man in one of the upstairs rooms? She was not a movie heroine. She was Iris, wife and mother.

She caught the bartender's eye. "My bill, please."

"Oh, come on now." Richard placed a proprietary hand on her wrist. "We were just getting acquainted. Stay for one more drink."

Iris smiled and pulled her arm free. "It was nice to meet you, Richard."

She retrieved more money than was necessary from her billfold and stacked it on her check.

Richard sighed loudly and lit a cigarette as she left. As she swung past the curve of the bar, she slipped a gold-rooster coaster in her purse.

She drove home. She didn't feel embarrassed by what she'd done or disappointed that nothing came of it. In fact, the excursion had made her feel powerful, and she would think back on it on occasion, in the months and years that followed, to remind herself of how easy it had been, momentarily at least, to walk away. And somehow that had made it more palatable to stay.

≫

Out on her balcony, swallowed up by the dark, soft air, Iris sat and sipped her water and listened to the sounds that had become a backdrop to her aloneness: the crickets, the frogs, faint calypso music from the bar near the beach, the thudding of Stephen jumping rope for the second time today, the mosquito zapper from the pink house encrusted with seashells, and always the seagulls. The wind carried with it the soft sticky sea with a tangy endnote from the orange and lemon trees below. Sanibel had been a good home for her. It had let her be and, most importantly, she had chosen it.

SAM

Dear Mrs. Olsen,

It was with great expectation that I read your letter. A flood of emotion overtook me when I realized who you were. Has it really been ten years already? Where does the time go? Here I am, an old woman, a grandmother many times over.

As for your request, I am afraid I came up sorely short. I inquired at the Aid Society of one Joseph Sewell, bookkeeper, but after an exhaustive examination, as he characterized it, he was unable to find anything that might assist you in your search. Adequate records, I'm afraid, have never been the Society's strong suit. I took it upon myself to check the most recent Manhattan directory, but found no one by the name you provided.

You were my last group of children. I have fond memories of our journey together, though certainly there is sadness in remembering our farewell. I will always believe that the Lord's hand steered us, and that He keeps watch over us all.

I am pleased to hear of your health, and hope soon you will be blessed with a child of your own.

Faithfully yours,
Mrs. Harriet Comstock

While the pound cake baked, Sam tried to tease out meaning from the letter to her grandmother. Where had she come from? Who was she looking for?

The buzzer sounded and she lifted the butter-glistening brick out of the oven. It landed with a *thwunk* as she over-turned it on a wire cooling rack, a rich and delicious mess. She pulled out the aluminum foil, tearing off a sheet against the tiny metal teeth of the box, and encased the still-warm cake. Maybe her brother would know something.

"What's up?" Theo answered.

"I found this letter to Grandmother Olsen in the box. From 1910."

"And?"

"I can't figure it out. The woman mentions the Aid Society. And there was a Bible in the box with the address of the Children's Aid Society in it. Is there any way Grandmother could have been an orphan? In New York City?"

"All I know about her is that she grew up in Ohio or somewhere before Minnesota."

"Wisconsin."

"Whatever. The Midwest. And that she knit. A lot. And made a kickass butterscotch pudding. The letter was in

Mom's stuff. Don't you think she would have told us if her mother had been an orphan in New York? That's a pretty big detail."

"It was in with recipes Mom probably never even looked through. Maybe Grandmother never told her."

Iris had gotten tickets to a concert to be held at the Presbyterian church, a performance by the Ying Quartet, precocious Chinese-American siblings from Iowa, and despite her inability to walk, her morphine flooded nod-offs, and her shallow, wheezy breaths, she had been insistent that she and Sam attend. Sam blow-dried her mother's hair, helped apply mascara, blush, and lipstick to her hollow, gray-skinned face, and dressed her in a navy silk caftan that swathed her ravaged body.

"Are you sure you want to go?" Sam asked again.

"I want to go out with Tchaikovsky in my head," she said.

The wheelchair was heavier than Iris was to load into the car.

The church had a dated island feel, the stained glass panels too modern and bright, the pew cushions, like everything in Florida, sea-foam green. Sam rolled Iris up to the front row, the wheelchair parked on the end of the pew.

"Let's move back some," Iris said. "I'd like to be able to see everyone."

It was a strange request, given that Iris always wanted to sit close—for movies, for weddings even—but Sam complied.

Iris hungrily watched the arriving audience walk up the aisle and fill the seats, her eyes hot and foggy. She was not here for the music after all. She was looking for someone. In her periphery, Sam watched her mother's eyes roam and seek.

"Are you okay?" Sam whispered as the church quieted.

"Ha ha," Iris rasped, her feathery hands momentarily aloft.

As the four young musicians took to the stage wielding their stringed instruments behind the pulpit, an older couple hustled up the center aisle. The man was tall and white-haired and wore horn-rimmed glasses and a well-tailored gray pinstripe suit—he was the only man there so dressed—and the woman wore a crisp white shirt and black trousers, a blond chignon at the nape of her neck. Iris lifted her chin and dropped her shoulders. Her gaze softened. The music began—Tchaikovsky's String Quartet No. 3 in E-flat minor, Sam read in the program—and then Iris dozed off, her head cocked awkwardly toward her shoulder. Sam allowed her mind to wander. She and Jack had had a mild argument on the phone the night before over baby names; she liked Charlotte, Helen, and Louise, while Jack was pushing for Flannery.

"It's too literary," she said.

"Why is that bad?" he asked.

"Because she's a baby. Not a footnote on your CV."

She had said this in jest, and he had chuckled—"at least I'm not proposing Salman"—but she had the unsettling realization that Jack's career would always mean more to him than she'd like it to.

At intermission, roused by the applause, Iris tried to adjust herself in the wheelchair. She swallowed, an effort, and pressed her lips together to even her lipstick.

"How do I look?" she said.

Sam smiled and wiped a fleck of mascara from her mother's cheek.

As the distinguished couple passed by on the way to the lobby, the man glanced at Iris with the slightest shift of his eyes. His face tightened on sight, his mouth a grim line. Sam tried to look elsewhere, to afford her mother the privacy of the moment. A minute later the man returned alone.

"Hello, Iris," he said, crouching down beside her.

"Hello, Henry."

"How are you?" His voice was quiet and grave.

"This is my daughter, Samantha."

Sam shook his soft hand and smiled, and he squeezed hers in return.

"It is wonderful to meet you," he said. "Tchaikovsky," he said to Iris.

"Tchaikovsky," she replied.

Henry leaned in to Iris and said hoarsely, "I have missed you, dear."

There was something in Iris's face then, a spark of heat, a knowingness, and it seemed that whatever it was she had been after, she'd found it.

"I will miss you," she said to him with a faint smile, and it seemed he understood the finality.

He cleared his throat and straightened up just as his wife appeared, a lovely woman with slim hands and regal cheekbones. The lights flickered, signaling the end of intermission, and he placed his hand on his wife's back and led her to their seats without turning around.

Sam felt a dart of sorrow for her mother then, for the banality of having loved a married man, for the affair that had happened or had not, for Iris wanting to see him, or to be seen by him, one last time.

"Now we can go," Iris had said. Inside the car, she didn't volunteer anything further.

"Mom?"

She didn't respond.

"Did you love him?"

Iris waved her hand dismissively, as if in the face of death, there wasn't any point in discussing it.

"I'm thankful to have known him," she said, closing her eyes.

You're not going to tell me anything? You're going to die and I won't know you at all, Sam said to herself. She drove slowly under a heavy moon that paled the sky, her hands clenching the top of the steering wheel. Frantic bugs danced in the headlights.

"He didn't choose you," Sam said softly, her anger honed to a fine, sharp point.

Iris's head lolled against the seat belt. She was asleep.

The following day, at her weekly hospital visit, Iris, dehydrated, her weight plummeting, her heart skittish, had been outfitted with a feeding tube. She refused hospice. Sam fed her with nutrition shakes and crushed pills every four hours, a varying mix of Roxanol, Ketamine, Clodronate, Colace, Haldol, and Ambien.

"Bottoms up," Sam would say, her mother most of the time too sick to smile.

Iris had amassed the morphine pills to kill herself, but she needed Sam to administer them.

"I won't," Sam said again and again, but she knew she would do what her mother asked of her. She would be the approval-seeking daughter to the end.

In the evening, the smell of hibiscus and orange trees mixed with the sea air. Sam parked Iris's wheelchair in front of the open French doors so she could watch the colors of the sky change; she said it was one of the things she loved about her life in Sanibel. Sam sat next to her and placed her mother's hand on her belly to feel the baby's quick pitter-patter of hiccups.

"How much do I give you?" Sam asked.

"I have a pill box in my nightstand."

"What will happen?"

"I'll fall asleep. And then you'll call Dr. Jones."

"He'll know."

"I was supposed to die three weeks ago, honey."

Sam spoke to Jack each night after Iris went down for the night. But she hadn't told him of her mother's request. Somehow it felt like her burden, her responsibility, and she didn't want to talk it out, didn't want to hear his level-headed wisdom, didn't want to share it. He was her husband, but Iris was her mother.

"Mom, please. Can't you just wait?" Sam asked, fear and frustration leaking into her voice.

The bougainvillea that wrapped around the edge of the balcony rustled quietly in the breeze.

"Samantha. I have lived a life. Two days or two weeks more in this ruined body won't matter much to anyone. I'm still an atheist, you know. I haven't had one of those last-minute conversions." She shrugged. "Death is death. I'm ready."

Who was this woman? She was her mother, who'd driven her to and from ballet and tennis, never made a cake from a box, always driven the speed limit, bargained hawkishly with antique dealers, been cool with her maternal affection, stayed in an unfulfilling marriage for a lifetime, and, in the end, moved away to be alone. And yet here Sam was. Part of her was glad she'd been chosen. She would take what she could get.

It would be tomorrow, then, in the morning. Sam felt there was everything to say and nothing. She had been a little relieved. She had wanted to go home, to hear the baby's heartbeat, to let her mother go.

The TV was on in Ted's house—*Oprah*—but he wasn't in the front room. Sam knocked, holding the pound cake like a football, the letter in her back pocket.

Ted came bouncing out from the kitchen in an apron with a giant lobster on it.

"Hiya, Sam. Come on in."

Sam had never been inside his house. It was dark but not unpleasant. A stack of logs near the fireplace. An old plaid couch. A burnished tree-stump coffee table. A carved wooden cuckoo clock on the wall.

"Nice apron."

"I just put a meat loaf in for supper." He rubbed his hands together. "What brings you over?"

"I made you a pound cake," she said, handing it to him.

"Really?"

"Yeah. I wanted to make it, to see if a pound each of butter, sugar, flour, and eggs would actually work."

"Did it?" He unpeeled a corner.

"You tell me."

"Oh, this smells wonderful. We'll have some now."

"No, no."

"I insist. The baker has to sample her work."

He bounded into the kitchen and came back with a knife, forks, and plates.

"That reminds me, I need to give you guys some eggs. The girls are on a roll. A man can only eat so many omelets."

The cake was divine. Sam ate it fast and took a second slab.

"How's it going over there with your mother's things?"

Sam raised her hands and let them fall.

"I know, I know," he said.

"I did find something intriguing, though. A letter."

"Yeah?"

"Would you mind taking a look?"

She smoothed the letter against the coffee table in front of him. He pulled off his thick plastic glasses and rubbed his eyes—bare-faced, his eyes looked smaller and younger—before replacing them and fixing his gaze on the thin, pale paper.

"Mrs. Olsen is your mother's mother?"

Sam nodded.

Ted looked again at the letter and scrunched his face. "How old would she have been in 1910?" he asked.

"Twenty-one. I don't know a lot about her, but I thought she grew up here."

"She probably did," Ted said, rubbing his chin. "After age eleven. But I'm afraid I'm a little stumped by the rest of it."

"No one's alive who would know anything about it," she said.

He glanced over at the clock on the wall. "It's too late tonight, but I bet they could help you out at the Historical Society. They're real detectives over there. I found an eighty-year-old postcard behind my refrigerator once. They told me everything about it. Written to the original owner of my house, a doctor of dubious reputation. He supposedly kept the Eastside in liquor during Prohibition."

"What was on the postcard?" Sam asked.

"A painted scene of New Orleans. The sender's name was illegible. But it said in part, *Happy days. I'll be home soon.*

"Do you still have it?"

"I sent it to one of the doctor's great-grandchildren. A guy just over here on Morrison."

"Sorry I ate half the cake I made for you," she said.

"Nonsense! Everything is better with company."

She and Iris had spent the early morning side by side in the rising sun, Sam on a chaise, Iris wrapped in a comforter in her wheelchair, the seagulls' piercing cries overhead as they flew from one side of the island to the other. Between dread and the baby kicking, Sam hadn't slept. She nursed her cup of coffee as Iris drifted in and out of a stupor, her breathing irregular and sharp. A neighbor dumped a bag of bottles into a recycling bin, and the clanging finally roused her.

"Happy Birthday, Mom," Sam said.

Iris rolled her head toward Sam and smiled with the corner of her mouth.

"I'm glad you'll get to go home," she said, her tongue thick.

Sam looked away then, without any idea how to talk on this last day of her mother's life. Everything seemed trifling or melodramatic or false.

"You make beautiful things, Samantha. I don't know if I have told you that."

"Thank you," Sam said, willing the rawness from her voice. She fretted, picking at her fingernails.

"You will never know how I love you until you have your baby." Iris dozed again, her face in drugged serenity.

Sam touched her mother's limp hand and thought, I have waited for that my whole life. She let out a whispered "no"—a useless protest.

The appointed hour was noon. At 11:30, Sam pulled the box of pills out of her mother's nightstand and placed it on the kitchen table. And then she threw up in the kitchen sink. Her hands shook as she crushed the pills with her usual implement, a stainless steel cup measure, and brushed the white dust into a glass, careful to wash her hands afterward, lest her unborn child be delivered a dose of morphine.

When Theo called, she tried to sound normal.

"How is she?" he asked.

"How do you think she is?" she clipped.

"I know it's stressful taking care of her, okay?"

"Sorry. She's really sick. This is it for her, Theo."

"What does the doctor say?"

"He thought she would die weeks ago."

"Jesus," he said. "Should we come down there?"

"Yes." Her anger was steadying. She felt, at last, that she could do this.

"We'll be there tomorrow. I'll call you with our flight stuff. Can I talk to her?"

Sam walked out to the balcony and gently squeezed her mother's frail shoulder, placed the phone at her ear, and closed the door behind her.

She went into Iris's bedroom and lay back on the bed, her belly heavy against her back, taking in her mother's view: a watercolor of sea oats and sand dunes, a beveled mirror above the white wicker dresser, the sky out toward the sea. Next to the bed was *To the Lighthouse*, which Sam would not bother returning to the library. There were no photographs, no tchotchkes. There would be little to clean out when she was gone.

Sam heaved herself off the bed and went back to her mother, who held the phone on her lap.

"It's time," Iris said, almost dreamily.

"Theo will be here tomorrow."

"I said goodbye."

"You didn't tell him."

"No."

Iris turned and stared off into the white sky, the wind warm and strong, the sun high and taunting overhead.

"It was beautiful, where I grew up," she said. "The river was so cold. Even in summer it would numb my feet." She smiled. "I used to lie in the sun on this one smooth boulder and watch the treetops and the sky. The rushing water blocked out all the other sounds. I'd pretend the earth had dropped away."

It was as if she were already gone, nostalgic for when she was alive.

"Okay, Samantha," she said.

Sam did not cry. She wheeled her mother into the house, into the kitchen, and attached the feeding tube. She filled the glass of crushed pills with water and stirred the thick and cloudy poison. It was a series of steps, tasks to complete. She held the funnel and, without waiting for a final signal from her mother, she poured.

Once she got Iris on the bed, she pulled the covers up and got in with her, spooning the wasted frame, the baby between them. They did not say goodbye. Sam placed her hand on her mother's and waited. Death was not silent and swift, and in those terrible moments when Iris's body bucked, unable to get air, Sam held fast and closed her eyes and screamed.

Outside it was close to dusk, the sky a bruised purple beyond the scuttling clouds, and Sam's tears began before she could get next door. She cried for her grandmother and for her mother, for their loss, and for all the stories they didn't tell.

She thought back on the year since her mother's death. She didn't like who she had become. The petty grievances against her husband were mere diversions. It was her own shame she couldn't face and couldn't share with him.

Her breath eased out of her lungs in one long lugubrious hiss. She'd never told Jack about how Iris died. At the time she'd felt confused, twisted with grief, and she had told herself it was something no one needed to know. She convinced herself that she and Jack didn't see things, life itself, in the same way—that was the ultimate fear in a marriage, wasn't it?—and she wanted to let it lie. But the shame for what she had done—the first baby, her mother—had slowly dug a trench around her, cutting herself off from him. She had been hiding alone, deep within the silence. And she was tired of it.

She needed her baby. Sam's heart lurched at the thought of Ella. And she needed to talk to Jack.

VIOLET

Fairbury didn't look much different from Sheridan: a small town square, low buildings, empty sidewalks. The sky was swollen with rain, the clouds dense and dark overhead, casting a light that made the fields look an eerily bright shade of green, the buildings like cardboard cutouts. The children were tired and bedraggled. What had been anticipation in Sheridan had turned to toe-dragging defeat as they shuffled over to the meeting hall under the first plump drops of rain.

The proceedings weren't as heavily attended as they had been in Indiana, and the townspeople who did show up were disgruntled by the lack of selection. The children stood in the center of the room, and viewers circled around them. Some quickly left. Two of the older boys, number twelve included, Violet noticed, were nabbed by a farmer and his son. Elmer went happily with a well-dressed couple—a judge and his wife—and another boy of eight was taken by a kindly looking older widow who waddled in her calico dress.

"Are you good with babies?" a woman asked the meek girl, who looked down and nodded. The girl was fourteen, with a heavy bosom and a high forehead, and Violet had not yet heard her speak.

"Okay, then," the woman said. "I'll fill out the application for you. Number seventeen." She had not asked the girl's name.

"Illinois will not be a dumping ground for the filth of New York City!" a man in a suit yelled from the crowd. "Go back where you came from!"

The kids looked up, but they had all heard much worse as immigrants or orphans or street urchins. Mrs. Comstock bustled among the visitors, making assurances. As the man was escorted out of the hall he looked back, and Violet stuck out her tongue at him.

"Ain't you a picture," a man said to her. His face was sunburned and creased, his hair greasy. "Open your mouth."

"Pardon?"

"I said, open your mouth. I need to make sure you ain't sickly. I got a farm to run. Let me see your teeth."

Violet went to speak, and he jammed his sour tobacco-stained fingers in her mouth to feel around.

She gagged and then bit down as hard as she could, grinding his knuckle between her teeth before he could get his hand out, screaming. He hit her face with the back of his other hand and knocked her to the floor. Mrs. Comstock ran over, waving her hands.

"How dare you hit this child?" she said. "I must ask you to leave, sir."

"She bit me," he said, holding up a bloody finger.

"Violet?" she asked.

Violet stared at the man with a razor blade of hatred and then kicked him in the shin as hard as she could. She

ran to the door, pushing her way through the people, not
thinking about where she would go or how, just that she had
to get away and she was better off alone. She flung the door
open and leaped out of the hall. But once outside, she was
shocked by rain like she had never before seen, hitting her
head like pebbles, the wind slapping her wet dress around
her legs. The sky was tinged a menacing tornado yellow.

She retreated and sat along the wall of the building
under the overhang of the roof, which did little to shield her
from the pelting rain. No one would care if the earth opened
up and she fell in. There was nowhere for her to go.

A while later the door to the meeting hall creaked open.
Expecting Mrs. Comstock, Violet looked away. But it was
the boy Frank, his ears too big, his jacket too small. He sat
down next to her and tucked his knees to his chest.

"It's over?" she asked.

He nodded. "There's a bunch of us left. No one even
talked to me."

"How old are you?" she asked.

"Eleven," he said.

"Yeah, me too. I guess we're too old for out here."

"Too young for everything else."

"Where'd you live before?"

"Five Points."

"Fourth."

He nodded. "Miss it?"

"A little. You?"

"I didn't want to go. I got parents. They's in the poor-
house. That's why I went on the train. This whole business
is for the birds."

They sat without talking, watching the rain. She couldn't tell him about her mother, because then she'd have to admit that Lilibeth could have kept her but chose to give her away. Instead, she thought about the night before she'd gone into the Home, running around with Nino and the other boys. Before she'd ever heard of the orphan trains.

They had jumped off the back of the streetcar before it stopped, before the conductor could come after them, the electric lights of the theater signs hazy beacons above them. They had whooped and darted out of the street, one behind the other.

"Hey," Violet said, pointing up, as they stopped to catch their breaths. "Look."

"What I tell you?" Buck said, bobbing his small head, his teeth resting on his bottom lip. "I know the way. I told you I know it."

In front of them the Moorish tower rose up to a colonnade and niche arches, topped by a magnificent dome, with the word CASINO a collar of winking lights at its base. Violet had never seen anything like it, had never even been uptown. She felt something expand in her chest, a warm balloon pushing against her ribs.

"Every man for himself, fellas," Jimmy said, skirting down 39th Street.

Violet worked her fingers, sore from gripping the ledge of the streetcar, and breathed in the foggy air, redolent with the scent of hay and manure from the Horse Exchange a few blocks north. Despite the carnival lights all around

them, there was a quiet pent-up stillness—the night's shows
had already begun, and patrons were packed snugly inside
the theaters.

Charlie stood next to her on the sidewalk and rocked on
his heels. He smelled fishy, like putrid fat.

"Any ideas?" he asked.

Nino's large hands hung down at his sides like sacks of
flour. He made fists and unclenched them as he thought.

"I ain't waiting around for you dillydalliers," Buck said.
"I aim to see maidens."

He was scrawny, with a mouselike quickness, and Violet
wouldn't have been surprised if he nibbled his way inside
with those teeth.

"Go on, then," Violet said.

"Who made you the biggest toad in the puddle?" Buck
asked, looking for backup from any of the others.

"*Ribbit*," she said, planting her hands on her hips.

"Screw you and your mother," Buck said.

Charlie laughed, crinkling his chubby face. "You wish,"
he said.

Buck wagged his head and skittered off down Broadway
in a huff.

It had been Violet's idea for them to come up here, her
mother having talked about *Florodora* with breathless delight
since Reginald Smith had taken her to see it. But everyone
knew about the Florodora girls anyway, a sextet of beauties
exactly the same height and weight with the same glamorous pile of dark hair. Violet touched her own unruly mane,
thick and long, held back from her face with a blue satin
ribbon she had found that morning tied around her mother's wrist.

"I don't know," Nino said. "I never been inside one of these places."

"What if we end up on the stage or something," Charlie said.

Violet laughed. "Maybe you'd get a girlfriend out of it," she said. "If she doesn't faint from a whiff of you."

"Shut up, Kentucky. What do you know about anything?" Charlie said.

They could hear drums and cymbals from the orchestra, the serpentine cry of a violin.

They walked down 39th Street to the end of the theater, where it was darker, where the fire escape made a lightning bolt down the side of the building.

"Get up here," Nino said to Violet. "Try to grab the ladder."

Violet climbed up, planting her feet on Nino's muscled shoulders. He held her calves next to his ears. She reached a hand for the bottom rung, bobbling to maintain her balance, her fingers grazing the cold metal. Her dress hiked up above her knees as she stretched, the night cold against her legs.

"Higher," she said, the bar just out of reach. "Push me up."

"I can't grow none," Nino said.

She stood for a moment longer and then jumped. Her hands landed squarely on the pigeon-shit-crusted lowest bar, and the ladder groaned and rolled out with her weight until it stopped with a jolt, dangling her just above the sidewalk. She hopped down, wiping her palms on the front of her coat.

"You could have told me," Nino said, rubbing his shoulders. "Your head would have split open like a watermelon if you missed."

"I got it, didn't I?" Violet asked, punching his arm.

Nino went up first, then Violet, then Charlie, who pulled the ladder up behind them.

"O tell me, pretty maiden, are there any more at home like
   you?"
"There are a few, kind sir, but simple girls, and proper too."

The song from the theater was tinny but recognizable as they reached the last stairwell. Violet and Nino cracked open the door—they'd lost Charlie somewhere on the way down—and found themselves in a room of gold. Intricate inlaid patterns covered the walls, from the marble floor all the way across the span of the high arched ceiling, shimmering in the low orange light of the filigreed wall sconces.

Violet gasped. The room glowed. Nino flicked his eyes around, uncertain. The opulence made them momentarily shy with each other. They were both trying to pretend they weren't in awe, but neither could think of what to say to deflate the otherworldliness of the vestibule. Finally, Nino motioned toward the empty ticket booth and the entrance.

There was no one to keep them out of the theater. The ushers were all watching the show, the biggest thing to hit New York since the century turned a few months before. Violet and Nino squeezed through a door and then stepped around purple velvet curtains. She held her breath as they slipped in behind hundreds of people shoulder-to-shoulder in their seats. Ahead of them in a blaze of light was the magnificent stage. There they were, the six perfectly sized Florodora girls with their ruffled white dresses and black sashes and large befeathered hats, each of them with a man in a morning suit and top hat on her arm.

"On bended knee, if I lov'd you, would you tell me what I ought to do?" the ladies sang, their voices like tinkling bells.

"Then why not me?" the men answered.

"Yes, I must love someone, really, and it might as well be you!"

The audience erupted in a boom of laughter and applause. A group of sailors near the back whistled through their fingers.

Music from the orchestra pit swelled up into the theater, as the Florodora girls opened white parasols and spun away from the men, their skirts lifting just enough to see their ankles.

Violet glanced at Nino, who stared, rapt, at the stage. The theater was warm with bodies and lights, the smell of tobacco mixed with something dry and clean like her mother's face powder.

"What's it about?" Nino whispered, nodding toward the stage.

"My mama said something about perfume. I don't know," Violet said. "They're on an island."

"Let's go there," he said.

Violet did not want the night to end, could not tell Nino that, come daybreak, her mother would deliver her to the Home.

"I don't know what else to do with you, Vi," her mother had said, her gaze darting around as if looking for a place to hide.

Violet had quickly tried to suture the hurt with a thread of defiance, stomping her foot. But when she'd looked at her mother's ashamed face, she couldn't say any of the mean things she'd wanted to.

They sat out the rest of the storm in the empty hall. Fourteen were now six: the ugly girl Nettie; the two teenage boys, Patrick and William—ruffians that no one seemed fooled by; big-eared Frank; Hans, a younger German boy who was sullen and pouty and spoke little English; and Violet.

The Lutherans had provided lunch for them, and the children, worn and spent, ate the pickles and ham sandwiches on the floor. Mrs. Comstock left them to attend to particulars with the local agent. One of the older boys leaned against the wall and picked his teeth.

"This here is crap," Patrick said, his Irish accent coming through in his *r*s. "You think we're stuck out here if no one takes us?"

"They got to take us back," William said. "Drop us off where they got us with a kick in the ass."

Violet, her dress still damp, watched the boys, weighing whether she should place her lot with theirs.

"I heard of a boy who ran off from out here and hitched back on the freights," Violet said.

"You going to lead the way?" Patrick challenged.

Violet shrugged.

"They won't take us back," Nettie said. "You think they pay for our passage? They dump us in orphanages out here. Or jails."

Frank stopped chewing. "I got a ma and a pa," he said.

"We all got something," Nettie said.

The older boys snickered.

"You sure do, Rosie," Patrick said.

"My name ain't Rosie. It's Nettie."

"Whatever you say, Rosie," Violet said, making the boys laugh.

Mrs. Comstock returned, carrying bottles of milk.

"Wisconsin," she said. "We're going on to Wisconsin."

None of them knew where that was, and they no longer cared.

"The tornado didn't touch down so the trains are running again."

Mrs. Comstock looked older and muddled, in disarray. The blossoms of blood vessels on her face were more pronounced, the skin under her eyes puffy and gray.

She looks like a crushed hat, Violet thought.

"You got young ones, ma'am?" Nettie asked.

"Oh, no," she said, laughing a little. "They're grown. But I think of you all as mine in a way, you know." She dabbed at the inside corners of her eyes with her handkerchief. "I have faith that you will all find families."

Violet clutched her Bible, because it was all she had. It felt better to have something than nothing at all.

"I have a family," Frank said, picking up where he'd left off.

"They couldn't care for you, dear," Mrs. Comstock said quietly. "They did what was best."

"But no one's picked me," Frank said. "They wouldn't have done it if they knew no one'd pick me."

The others looked at the floor, the ceiling, or their hands.

"They didn't have a choice," Mrs. Comstock said firmly.

"They're condemned to the almshouse. You know they don't take children there." Her voice lost its resolve, and she knew she should not have pursued the point. The trip, her third for the Aid Society, she had told them, had eroded her. "Come, come, everyone. Gather yourselves."

She went to the door and looked out, squinting at the new sun.

"The rain has stopped. We'd best make our way while we can."

As they neared Wisconsin, there were more hills and more trees, fewer towns, and fewer people on the train. As travelers got off in Chicago and Rockford, only a smattering of new passengers took their places. The orphan train riders spread out in the empty car, and Mrs. Comstock slept with her bonnet atilt, her arm hugging her suitcase.

Violet was restless and anxious. She smoothed the rumpled number 8 on her chest and then tried to scrape the dirt from underneath her fingernails. She leaned up to Patrick in the seat in front of her.

"You think this will be the last stop?"

He turned to her and shifted in his seat. "I heard the agent lady talking to one of the locals back at the hall. She said she'd be on her way home tonight. Alone."

"They don't take us back," Violet said.

He shook his head. "I got to indenture myself. Or rob a bank or something. I'm too old for no orphanage."

Violet bit her lip. She was not too old for an orphanage.

"There ain't nothing you can do about it," he said.

"What about him?" she asked, pointing to William, the other older boy. "What's he going to do?"

"Don't go sniffing up that one," he said. "Pretty girl like you."

Across from them, Nettie started to cry.

"Come on, Rosie," Patrick sneered. "It can't be that bad."

Nettie cinched her arms more tightly around her body and squared her face with the window.

He chuckled. Violet sat back in her seat, and a heavy wave of sleepiness made her eyes droop. For the first time, she thought, What will be, will be. She felt like her grandmother's old weather-beaten shack when the roof had finally caved in, like a tumbledown heap. She felt done in. There was no going back, and going forward, she was no longer who she had been.

Although they had all taken their own seats in the empty car, Frank moved up and fell in next to Violet.

"Who invited you?" she asked.

He pulled on his reddening ear and kicked the seat.

"It's okay," she said. "You can sit."

"I'll go with you. We could get back like you said on the freights."

"What good are you to me?" But she said it softly, without bite. "We're just kids," she said, to make him feel better.

He nodded and scraped at an oval mustard stain on his pants.

A few seats up, the boy Hans muttered in German.

"Shh, child," Mrs. Comstock said. "They'll be Germans in these parts. Don't you worry."

But he couldn't understand her and kept right on talking to himself.

Violet hummed the tune from *Florodora*, and Frank gave a little smile.

"I know that song," Nettie said, turning from the window. "That's the maiden song."

"No one asked you," Violet said, glad to have someone to be mean to.

The night they had stolen into the theater, Nino had nudged her and flapped his elbow—a watch dangled from the pocket of the man at the end of the last row, from their angle, perfectly backlit by the stage lights, swinging like a golden yo-yo. Violet wanted to take in every last moment of the show, but an opportunity was an opportunity.

"Next clapping," he said. "Get ready."

When the audience bellowed its applause, Nino, already crouched behind the man's seat, yanked the watch, tearing it from its clasp. Violet was out first, through the curtains and doors into the lobby, and then she shot through the front door, Nino barreling out behind her into the cold night, now alive with theatergoers whose shows had already let out. Violet ran, legs kicking behind her, hearing nothing but her breath and the snare drum of pumping blood in her ears, laughing, knocking into the flounce of skirts, Nino struggling to keep up, as they dashed across Broadway, dodging the uptown and downtown streetcars and the horse-drawn taxi carriages lined up to spirit the fancy people home.

They walked south, and the crowd thinned out, night

lamps casting murky yellow pools of light. Nino tossed the watch to Violet. It felt like a river stone in her hand, cold and worn smooth.

"Ollie'll take it," he said. His newsboy captain was a willing unloader of stolen goods.

"How much'll you get for it?"

"I don't know. A dollar. Two."

Violet held the watch up to her ear, the tick soft and insistent. Holding the chain, she swung it back to Nino.

"Maybe you should keep it," she said.

"What do I need a watch for? Someone'd just steal it off me anyways."

In the distance, the Fourth Avenue horsecar, one of the last in the city, came in and out of view between buildings. Electric streetcars and motorcars had been a baffling discovery when she and her mother had first arrived. In Kentucky, if it wasn't pulled, it wasn't moving.

Violet didn't know where they were, but as they walked east she could see the spires of the new bridge under construction. The river oriented her. She knew she could always follow it back to the neighborhood.

When they neared Pearl Street, Nino stopped. Drunken men hitched and lurched down the sidewalk, and a pair of prostitutes stood outside a tavern and squawked, their shoulders white, their mouths crooked and red.

"I got to beg off. Swing by Ollie's," Nino said.

"Yeah," she said.

Nino chewed on his blackened thumbnail and then fake-boxed a few jabs toward Violet.

"See you around," he said. "I'll buy you a root beer. With our haul."

He laughed before he jammed his fists in his pockets and trotted away.

A pack of newsboys she didn't recognize came toward her. They stopped, trying to force her off the sidewalk, but she wouldn't concede to them. The boys pushed and poked her, and Violet shoved back. An older boy, a few fine black wisps above his lip, grabbed her arm and dug his fingers in as hard as he could through her coat sleeve.

"I could cotton to you, sure," he said, close to her ear. "A girl's a girl."

She twisted away and spat at him. The boys whistled and guffawed before moving past her.

Violet smelled the river, its sour brine a comfort. She plunked herself down on the curb, rolled up the sleeves of her coat, and inched a pebble out from her boot.

Ready to run.

IRIS

The heat of summer had bloomed, and in the warm, slow evening, with the smell of wet soil and shorn wheat in the air, Iris sat with her parents drinking lemonade around the kitchen table, listening to a radio report about Amelia Earhart's disappearance. Iris was riveted. The plane had lost radio contact somewhere in the Pacific a week before, but a massive search had yet to uncover any sign of wreckage or the bodies of the aviatrix and her navigator. She imagined them on a beach, windblown and suntanned, drinking out of coconuts.

"Dead," her father said. "Of course they're dead. It's irrational to think otherwise."

"They haven't found the plane," Iris said. "The announcer said it himself. They could have landed on one of those islands."

"Maybe it was all a hoax," her mother said. "Maybe she got tired of being Amelia Earheart and changed her name and moved to Kansas."

Iris frowned at her mother. "She was famous! Why would she move to Kansas?"

"You don't think they'd recognize her?" her father asked.

"If you saw her out of her fancy clothes without a plane in sight, you wouldn't know who she was neither."

"Pfft," he said, standing creakily. Harvest had taken its yearly toll on his body.

"People disappear all the time," her mother said.

"You sure got a bee in your bonnet. Maybe the heat's got to you."

Her mother sipped her lemonade. "Maybe so."

"Going outside with my pipe," he said. After sleepless weeks of frenzied, ceaseless harvest labor, racing the weather, crop growth, and fluctuating market prices, he was spent and reflective. It had been a fine yield, better than last year's, so he allowed himself an evening without work. He would walk down their long driveway and turn off into the trees and down to the river to smoke.

"Pound cake'll be waiting," her mother said. "Strawberries from Wilson's place."

He nodded and smiled at her.

Iris walked to the edge of the field in the last of the light, a dazzling orange sun at her back. She knew Amelia Earheart wasn't dead. She was just missing. And when you were missing, there was always a chance to be found. Iris looked out on the stubbled field yet to be plowed, the vastness broken only by the machine shed and row of cottonwoods. She gathered Queen Anne's lace from the meadow near the barn. The broken stems smelled faintly like carrots in her hand. She thought she would put them in a jar for her mother's windowsill above the kitchen sink. But as she neared the house she heard a rare sound, her mother singing, and she abandoned her ragged bundle on the step. She pulled the door open quietly and found her mother in the living room, mending an apron, her wooden sewing box open at her feet.

"Oh tell me, pretty maiden, are there any more at home like you?" she sang softly, diving her needle back under the faded calico. She looked up as Iris came in, her face momentarily young and open before her cheeks colored and her face closed up. "I thought you were out back."

"I like when you sing." Iris fell into the couch next to her.

"Did you feed the chickens?"

"Do you really think she's alive somewhere?"

"Iris."

"I forgot. I'll go do it."

"Before your father gets back."

"Okay." Iris sighed.

"He's right. Her plane surely crashed into the ocean."

Iris felt then that she would cry, her eyes hot with anger.

"I'm still going to hope. I don't care what you say."

She ran outside, letting the screen door slam behind her. She ran as fast as she could, straight toward the field, and tried to imagine what it would be like to fly, like it felt in dreams, to hear nothing but the *whoosh* of wind and to see the world grow small below.

It was midnight when Iris awoke with a jolt. She had not dreamed of flying but of falling, and she was glad to be up. She could hear music next door. The song was familiar, a jazzy tune from an era that she knew. Her head felt like a soggy rag, but she focused on the music, humming along, until it came to her. Of course. "Whatever Lola wants," Iris sang, her voice a sleepy rasp, "Lola gets." She and Glenn had played the *Damn Yankees* record in their first apartment on the twentieth floor of a high-rise on Michigan Avenue. He would come home from the office—a mere associate then—in his trench coat and fedora, and she would be waiting, the ice bucket filled, the meat loaf in the oven, the table polished. He was a handsome devil, Iris thought now. Tall, with dark curly hair and quiet brown eyes. It had been seven years since the divorce. She thought of Glenn now with affection. He had given her what she'd thought she wanted.

Through the wall she heard the clink and crash of a glass breaking, and remembered poor Stephen on the landing in his towel. Iris rose—I'll be sleeping soon enough, she thought—staggering a little, and wrapped herself in her robe. She didn't want to arrive empty handed, so she settled on the bowl of raspberries (sorry, Samantha) and a half bottle of vodka she would never drink.

Iris knocked loudly, and then knocked again until the music was turned down, and she could hear footsteps and a brief pause at the door.

"Irene?" Stephen pulled open the door some. "Is it too loud? Am I keeping you up?"

He had a martini glass in his hand, though it was not his first drink by the smell of him. He was dressed in a gray sweat suit, and his hair hung flat and fine without any of the goop he usually put in it. It was the first time she had ever seen him frumpy. Here was Stephen unadorned, she thought. He might as well have been naked.

"I thought you might like some company," she said boldly. Stephen was rightly confused by the appearance of his old neighbor in her robe, barefoot, and was about to turn her down when she cut him off.

"You owe me one."

He laughed, his face red and moist, and pulled open his door with a what-the-hell shrug.

"Aren't you a sassy bird," he said, slightly slurring.

"I've never been called a bird," she said.

"No? Consider it a compliment."

She walked into the living room. She had expected— what, mirrors, animal prints, a disco ball? It was modern yet warm, in shades of blue and dark brown. A row of large white candles glowed on the coffee table. She held out the berries and vodka to him. He set down his glass on the mantel—she had not once used her fireplace—and accepted her offerings.

"What can I get you?"

"A little wine would be nice."

Stephen went into the kitchen and clanked around. Iris sat in one of the leather club chairs across from the couch. When he returned, he handed her a glass of chilled white wine and relit a candle that had blown out.

"Did you get your watch back?" she asked, taking a sip.

He scowled and squinted, swaying a little on his feet.

"The boy. On the landing," she said.

"Ah," he said, falling into the couch. "No. That's what I get, I guess. For being a lonely mess." He laughed and popped a berry into his mouth. "How old do you think I am?"

"I don't know. Thirty-two, maybe?" Iris lied.

"Forty! Forty years old. I don't even know how to process that. Sorry, is that rude? I know you're older. It's just I don't feel it. I don't feel that many years."

"One never does," Iris said.

He exhaled and shook his head. They sat for a moment without talking, the music a low murmur underneath their silence. Earlier, Iris had set aside ten tablets of Roxanol, sure it would be enough morphine to stop her heart. She was relieved to have a plan in place. It calmed her now to think of those pills.

"So," Stephen said.

"So," Iris said.

"Since I'm drunk, I'll ask you."

"What's that?"

"Are you sick or something?"

"Cancer."

"No."

"Yes."

"Is it serious?"

"A little."

"At least you still have your hair."

"At least," she said, touching the cold wineglass to her cheek. "Are you going somewhere?" She pointed to a large suitcase in the hall.

"For a few weeks. I haven't taken a vacation in years. I'm going to go see my mother in Pennsylvania. Then on up to Provincetown."

"Good for you," Iris said, knowing, sadly, that she would never see Stephen again.

"I'll send you a postcard," he said, draining his glass. "From the Poconos."

Iris smiled and pushed herself to the edge of the chair. Her body ached, her head felt swollen. "Can you believe we've shared walls for five years?" she asked as she stood.

"I'm glad to finally meet you, Irene."

She turned back. "It's Iris."

Stephen clapped his hand over his eyes. "Iris," he said. "Nice to know you, Iris."

"Happy travels, Stephen."

Back in bed, Iris opened her book, thankful to the boy in the library who had chosen it for her. What a pleasure it was to be privy to the intricate pathways of the characters' interiors, to recognize her feelings in theirs. At one time it might have been frustrating, even annoying to her, this dwelling on emotional fluctuations, but maybe this was, in the end, the stuff of life.

It was quiet next door. She hoped for better for Stephen, for contentment, for love, even. And in this newfound magnanimity, she took an Ambien and set her alarm. Samantha would arrive tomorrow, and this made her happy.

Iris couldn't say she'd made peace with her private self just yet, but she could say, This is who I am, without hedging, without second-guessing, without reservation. That's all one can really ask for, she thought. It was enough.

SAM

With her grandmother's letter still in her pocket, Sam felt a new resolve as she raced across town to get Ella. But the traffic on Regent Street was backed up all the way to Park. She hit the steering wheel. It was 4:06 already, and she was late. How could a place as small as Madison possibly need this many bicycle stores? A group of college girls in jeans, heels, and tight little tops hobbled in front of her car holding their arms. And why didn't the Coasties ever wear coats?

The traffic started to move, and Sam jammed left through the tail end of the yellow light at Monroe Street, her palms damp on the steering wheel. On Jefferson, her brakes screeched as she skidded to a stop in front of Melanie's house.

"Hi," Sarah sang, as she opened the door, Ella on her hip. "Melanie's stopping off at the wine store. She told me to tell you to hang out for a bit."

But Sam wasn't listening. She pulled Ella from Sarah's arms; the recognition in that soft, perfect face, the smile on those pincushion lips, was enough to make her feel, for just a moment, grounded, holding fast to her child.

"Dadadadada," Ella said, pulling Sam's hair.

"Thank you," Sam said to Sarah. "Here, let me pay you."

"Oh, that's okay. Melanie already covered it."

Rosalee yelled a sing-song "Sarah" from inside the house.

"Okay. Well, thanks again." Sam turned, hugging Ella against her chest.

"Come on in. Melanie will be here in a minute."

"We should go."

"Sarah! Come here right now!" the toddler called.

"I'm coming, Rosa. Wait," she said to Sam, "let me get your stuff."

She jogged to the kitchen and back with the diaper bag, her face ruddy and young.

"See you soon, little girl," Sarah said to Ella, touching her cheek.

Rosalee raced down the hall and slid in her socks into Sarah's legs.

Sam waved quickly as she headed to the car. She strapped Ella into her car seat and kissed her on the forehead and on the petal-soft mouth, as her breasts surged with milk, hard mounds on her chest. The sun was already gone from the sky, the dusk, a cold arrival in the fall, unwelcome and gray.

But she had her baby back.

"What do you think, baby," she said, "should we go home?"

As she drove, Sam looked in her rearview mirror, at the reflection of Ella, who sucked her pacifier and watched the streetlights in the pale yellow sweater Sam's grandmother had knit. Her life was coming back into view.

"I was thinking about what you said earlier," Theo said. "About adopting."

"Sorry. I shouldn't have said anything," Sam said, rounding Lake Monona, lit up by the low moon.

"It's okay. I think, when it comes down to it, I don't really want a kid that badly," he said. "Not that I've ever admitted that to Cindy."

Sam thought of her friend Mina again, who had been a surrogate for her gay brother, and felt a bite of envy for such sibling closeness. To love someone enough to give over your baby—because how could it not feel like yours?

"You won't know until you have one," she said.

How strange to imagine the time before Ella when she didn't yet know this feeling, this churning mix of worry, need, longing, joy, attachment, resentment, bewilderment, and obsession—this love that had flattened her.

"Yeah. But that seems like a pretty big risk to take. I could be like that woman who gave her adopted kid back."

"I read about her."

"And I bet you thought she was awful."

"You're right. I did," Sam said.

As she drove past the food co-op, she thought about all the things they were out of at home, and she tried not to think about the day, to parse its meaning.

"I'm going to research the letter. Try to find out about Grandmother. We should know this stuff about our family." She felt a tug on a cord deep within her, a link to a connection she hadn't known she was missing.

"Go get 'em, Sherlock."

"You're the one who did Dad's family tree. Complete with a tree drawn in colored pencils."

Theo laughed. "Did you talk to him yet?"

"No. But I'll call him. I will."

"Yeah," Theo said. "Right after you clean out the gutters."

She deserved her brother's skepticism, but despite her earlier posturing she wanted to see her father. She was finished with harboring childish judgments. They were a waste.

"Hey, what are you guys doing for Thanksgiving?" she asked.

"Cindy's brother's family's house in Arlington."

"Don't sound so thrilled."

"We should plan a visit one of these days, Sammy. It's been too long."

It happened about once a year. They would decide to be closer, and then a month later the sentiment was eclipsed.

"Let's do that," she said.

"For real this time."

"Yes. I'm in. Hey, Theo?"

"Yeah?"

"We'll bury Mom."

"We'll bury Mom," he said.

Sam felt herself righted, optimistic even, gliding on a steel track toward home. She glanced back at Ella, her curious face visible in the intermittent streetlights.

"Check your calendar. We'll talk dates."

"All right, sister of mine," Theo yawned. "I better go. A benefit Cindy's dragging me to."

"For?"

"Some children's something or other."

"Nice, Theo."

"Oh, come on, they'll get their money." He laughed.

As Sam turned onto their street she was comforted by the block of worn-in houses wedged close together, warmly lit—dinnertime—the smell of oaky smoke from her neighbor's wood-burning stove, the winking colored lights wrapped around Ted's porch, which he had yet to take down from last Christmas.

She juggled the diaper bag and hugged Ella to her, stepping carefully up the dark front steps to the house. She shoved the key in the door and kicked it open. Inside it still smelled deliciously like pound cake. They were home.

The answering machine blinked red.

"Hi, Samantha. It's your dad. Marie and I are headed your way, and we'd love to stop by and see you. If that's all right with you kids, of course. In two weeks or so? We have a few more stops up here in Canada before making our way down. Well, okay then. Give me a call when you can. Kiss my granddaughter for me."

Sam blew her cheeks out with a sigh. She had lost years with her father, for reasons that no longer held much weight. She would call him in the morning. It was a start.

After changing Ella's diaper and suiting her up in footed dinosaur pajamas, Sam placed her in a plastic rain-forest-themed monstrosity called the Jumparoo and finally took off her coat. Ella chewed on a plastic toucan and bounced up and down in the bungee-attached seat.

Jack arrived a few minutes later, his chestnut curls spilling over his ears, a stain on the front of his sweater—pea soup? His eyes were tired, but when he walked in the door they brightened at the sight of Ella jumping away. Sam felt the warmth of familiarity, but it was more than that. She had missed him.

"Sorry I'm late," he said, setting the takeout bags on the table and shaking off his coat, which he hung on the back of a chair. His lips were cold as he kissed her cheek. He went to Ella and swooped her up, tossing her in the air until she giggled. "How are my girls?"

"We survived," Sam said. "Ella did great."

"And you?"

"I couldn't do it."

Jack's eyes were dark and gentle, the way she used to see them so long ago. Her heart beat like a cornered animal as she gathered her nerve.

"I'm going to cancel Franklin's commission."

Jack dropped his chin in disappointment.

"I'll call him tomorrow and apologize," she said.

He pursed his lips but then nodded. "Okay. You got to do what you got to do."

He set Ella down on the carpet, and she crawled off to retrieve a stuffed bunny.

"I'm just not ready," she said.

"It's a process. It'll take time. You took a hiatus to make a life."

Yes, she thought, I made life. And I have also taken it away.

"Maybe that phase is over, I don't know." She didn't quite mean it, but she wanted to taste the idea, roll it around on her tongue.

"Phase?"

"Clay. Pots."

"Since when is your art a phase?"

She smiled at him, thankful. "You're right. I'm just being defeatist." Ella gave a high-pitched scream, experimenting, and smiled at Sam. "Before I forget, I talked to Ted today."

"Any morsels for me?"

"His father was a scientist at Los Alamos. The hydrogen bomb."

"Nice. Wow. Hippie Ted with a bomb-maker dad. Good one." Jack picked up Ella and put her on his lap. "Are you hungry? I couldn't remember what you wanted. So I punted. Just got a bunch of stuff."

She felt a momentary pique—she ordered the same thing every time—but, as she reminded herself, this was not the stuff of tragedy. It did not have to be symbolic or weighted or tucked away to add to a pile of resentments. It was just dinner.

"Let me put Ella to bed," she said.

"Good night, my little pumpkin." He kissed her all over her face as she smiled and squirmed. "I missed you today. Sleep well. Let Mommy sleep tonight."

The dark room was a warm cocoon, shades drawn, and the soft rush of air from the humidifier hushed out the sounds of the house and noises from outside. Sam rocked in the glider chair that had been her mother's, as Ella nursed, sleep near. As her eyes adjusted, Sam could just make out the letters of Ella's name on the wall, which Jack had bought and mounted in an arc above her crib.

"Do you want to name the baby after your mother?" he had asked quietly, in bed one night, a few weeks after Iris had died.

"No," she had said quickly. "Iris was Iris. I like our name."

"Me too."

Sam picked up Ella and switched her to the other breast. The elephants of the mobile above the crib spun aimlessly in the parched air blowing from the heating vent. She closed her eyes and listened to the faint clank of plates as Jack set the table for dinner.

"What's all this?" Jack asked, palming a clay apple she'd made in kindergarten.

"A box Theo sent. Of my mom's. My dad found it in his garage. He took it by accident after the divorce."

"Your early work?" Jack raised his eyebrow and held out the apple.

She smiled and took an edamame pod from the container, squeezing out the beans with her teeth. He put the apple on the table next to other mementos she'd looked through earlier.

"I'm almost finished going through it. I wish I could be more like Theo and just let it all go."

"No, you don't."

"No, I don't." She sopped up soy sauce with a piece of a spicy tuna roll, sucking the salty liquid from the rice. "So," she said. "Congratulations."

He smiled and shook his head. "It's nuts, isn't it? Not that it's anything yet. But I'm pleased."

"Me too."

"Unfortunately I have a huge stack of papers to grade tonight," he said, standing and stretching.

"Jack?"

"Hmm?"

"Nothing. We can talk about it later. Go do your work. It's been a long day."

He kissed the top of her head.

When he was gone and she was once again alone, Sam pushed away the Styrofoam containers of food. She opened the small Bible and ran her thumb along the edges of the gossamer pages, hoping for something else, some other clue. The pages opened to a folded square of light blue paper, stained yellow in its crease, with a piece torn out near one of its edges. She held the delicate paper up and turned it over, but all that appeared to be on it was a very faint hand-written number 8. She flipped through the Bible again but found nothing else tucked inside.

Sam gathered up her grandmother's recipes, which she'd left in a messy pile after she'd discovered the letter. She stacked the cards one by one and, sure enough, after Peach Chartreuse there it was: Pound Cake. The measurements were in cups, which would have helped, and the recipe called for ten eggs. She'd been close. A note at the bottom of the card read, *Add vanilla and pinch of mace.* From her grandmother, to her mother, to her. Sam smiled, feeling a sense of rightness in that simple continuum. She ran her finger over her grandmother's handwriting and set the card aside.

She tipped the last of Iris's keepsakes onto the table, spilling the contents in a small dusty heap. Of course she had wanted to find some talisman or diary or telling residue of her mother's life in the box, and of course she had found none of those things. But neither could she part with what remained. A few centimes and franc coins rolled and spun.

A cracked postcard from Zurich, the writing faded to an illegible shadow. A photograph of Sam—age four, she guessed—in a polka-dotted dress and saddle shoes, and an adolescent Theo, his hair feathered over his ears, in front of a Christmas tree, and another of all four of them, Iris's face turned away from the camera, and Glenn in a candy-cane-striped tie. A photograph from sometime in the fifties of her parents—they must have been newly married—in the living room of the old farmhouse Iris had grown up in, his hand on her knee. And another, from a later time, of Theo, ten or so, in brown corduroys and a turtleneck, laughing as he bent toward a pig behind a fence.

The last picture was of her grandmother standing in front of a plowed field, a swaddled infant—Sam—asleep in her arms. So I have been to Minnesota after all, she thought. She pulled the picture closer. Her grandmother's face was hardened, worn, squinting into the sun. A utilitarian woman. A farmer's wife. For almost sixty years she took care of the house, a husband, a child, the chickens, the canning. Who was she before she was Mrs. Olsen, when she was just Violet? Sam flipped the photo over: *Mother and Samantha, September 1967.* The picture warmed something in Sam. It spoke of history and continuity, of life lived and of life still to live. She pulled the letter from her pocket and slipped it under a magnet on the refrigerator along with the photograph.

"Well, you sound pretty normal," Melanie said. "From what Sarah told me I thought a madwoman had come and picked up Ella."

"Sorry. It was a big day for me, you know."

"I know. I don't really get it, but I know. God, it's frigid in here. Hold on. I'm turning the heat up to seventy-eight."

"Let me guess, Doug'll secretly turn it down and you'll turn it back up again."

"Bingo. But he'll give up first. I can't believe it's cold again. Just the thought of my neighbors' rosy-cheeked cheer while they shovel their cars out of two feet of snow is enough for me to break out the vodka."

"Thanks for today."

"Really, it's nothing. I'm selfish, remember? I'm just waiting for the right moment to order new place settings from you. So, should I tell Sarah she'll have Ella during the week or what? Sarah loved her. She said she could handle both kids, no problem."

Sam bit her cheek. "I need to think about it. Maybe one morning a week?"

Melanie laughed. "Don't go too crazy, Samantha."

"Baby steps." In the background Sam could hear Rosalee saying *Mama, Mama, Mama.* "So what can we bring to dinner?" Sam asked.

"When do they start taking care of themselves?" Melanie said. "Nothing. I'm getting food from Harvest. You didn't think I'd actually cook, did you? Okay, must go tend to child."

"See you soon," Sam said.

Sam imagined a vessel for her mother's ashes. Something simple, subtle. At first she felt the creak of effort, thinking of a familiar form, an old design. But then her synapses revved up, pushing into new territory. A small lidded jar, small enough to fit in the palm of her hand, full and round like the body of a bird. The lid, sunken and flush with a round knob handle. She would carve vertical lines through the layer of dark slip from the opening of the jar to its base, exposing the white porcelain underneath, giving the piece depth and texture. An allover stony matte glaze. She sketched and sketched until she saw on paper what she had envisioned in her head.

She slid in under the covers next to Jack, who was reading the *New Yorker*.

"I'm sorry about the gift for Franklin," she said.

He finished the paragraph he was reading before he turned to her, and she wondered if he had always done this or if it was just that now she noticed.

"It's okay. I don't think it'll bring down my academic career." He smiled and smoothed her hair off her face.

"My mom was on my mind so much today."

"Grief doesn't run in a straight line," he said, laying the magazine on his chest and lacing his fingers. "It can loop around. Come and go."

"I want to go to Minnesota," she said. "To where she grew up. Where my grandparents lived. Can we go there sometime?"

"I would like that. Our first family trip. In the spring?"

"In the spring."

She picked up her mother's library copy of *To the Lighthouse*, which had been on her bedside table for a year, and opened it to the first page.

～

Sam couldn't sleep as Jack snored beside her. She got up
and went into the bathroom for her robe; the floor, buck-
ling and losing tiles and no longer charmingly antique, was
cold against her bare feet. It was fall, after all, and despite
the pumping furnace, the heat quickly seeped out from the
ill-fitting windows and poorly insulated walls and gapped
floorboards of the old house.

The studio floor was unyieldingly cold, like the marble
floors of a cathedral in winter. She flipped on the light and
winced from the flash of brightness, blinking until her eyes
adjusted. She went to her bulletin board and tacked up her
sketch. It wasn't bad, she thought, tracing her finger along
the line of the body, but going from idea to actuality seemed
monumental.

She took a breath and worked open the knotted bag of
clay, the smell pungent, earthy, and familiar. The gray-white
porcelain had little give, but she plunged her fingers into its
surface, wet with condensation. It was smooth and malleable,
the possibility of its forms infinite. The feeling of the clay
began to jog the memory in her hands, stirring the desire to
create—that elusive fire—and she knew she would be back
in her studio again soon. She pulled her hand out and tied
the bag closed.

Ella's cry was faint from this distance. Sam felt adrenaline
speed up her heart before her ears registered the sound.
She wiped her hands on a towel and padded up the stairs
to the nursery, where she found Ella sitting up, holding on to
the crib. Sam lifted her out without a word, silently moving
to the glider chair. It must be around one thirty, she thought,

one of Ella's regular intervals of waking to be nursed back to sleep. It was a choreography of need and soothing, expectation and fulfillment, one that Sam had come to rely on for a certain satisfaction. She closed her eyes and counted to sixty in time with the rock of the chair, then switched breasts and started again. She inserted a pacifier into the sleepy mouth, carried Ella back to the crib, and laid her down. She went back to the rocker and covered herself with a blanket, a cream-and-rose-checked afghan knit by her grandmother.

In a span of months she had been present for birth and for death, the wondrous first breath and the horrible last. But wasn't it an honor to be there at the end of a life as well as the beginning? To mark the extraordinariness of a lifetime, to bear witness to its completion? Could she ever convince herself of that?

The last time she and Jack had gone to Paris, over dinner at the lively Chez Janou tucked behind the place des Vosges, they had agreed it was time to have a baby. Sam had felt the bubbly aftereffects of that giddy decision. She smiled, and he smiled back. They drank more wine.

"What's *cuisses de grenouille*?" he asked, pronouncing it badly and pointing.

"Frog legs," she said. "Or, I guess, more precisely, frog thighs. *Ribbit ribbit*."

He stuck out his bottom lip and shook his head in disgust. "Don't say they taste like chicken."

She laughed, feeling light and lucky. "Hey, what's it called when a word is used that's related to the thing to represent the thing." She lowered her voice. "Like calling the French *frogs*."

"Isn't that an epithet?"

"No. I mean, I guess it's derogatory. But like they eat frogs so they're called frogs."

"Metonymy?"

"Yeah, metonymy."

"Like *the crown* for royalty."

"Or *suits* for executives," she countered.

"Madison Avenue."

"The White House."

"Mother tongue."

"Wall Street."

"Houston, we have a problem."

"Whoa. That's advanced," she said.

They drank more and ordered, he the seven-hour lamb, she the confit de canard. They held hands across the table.

"Roof," she said, which took him a moment to realize she was back at it. "As in *a roof over our head*."

"If you want to get technical," he said, "I think that's synecdoche. The same idea, but when you use a part of something to represent the whole."

"Okay, smarty pants. *Ivories* for piano," she said.

"*Threads* for clothes."

"Mouths to feed."

"All hands on deck," he said.

"White-collar criminals."

Jack spun his wine and bit his cheek, not ready to lose a language game.

"Give us this day our daily bread." He raised his hands in triumph.

"No. Really? *Merde*. I'm out."

The *escargots bourguignonnes* arrived, shiny with butter in their delicate spiral shells.

"It's weird you'll eat snails but not frogs," she said.

"I guess there's no accounting for taste." He had popped his tiny fork into the rubbery meat.

"I like the name Charlie," she said. "If we have a boy let's name him Charlie."

The memory felt like fireplace warmth to her now. It didn't make her long for what had been lost. The first baby, her mother, a blithe marriage, a steadfast desire to create, a life before Ella when her fears were containable—she had fingered those worry beads enough for one day. Instead it was synecdoche that stuck with her, how a part might stand for a whole, how it might, in fact, let you tap into something larger. How a day could represent a lifetime, a snapshot of humanity that wouldn't exist without all that came before it. It comforted her to think this way. Sam dozed in the chair, awash in the humidifier's lulling hum. But then she thought, Enough of this, and forced herself to get up.

She slipped back into the cold sheets beside her sleeping husband and tried to hold on to her newfound clarity. She scooted her body next to Jack's, molding to his familiar curve.

"Jack," she said, shaking his shoulder. "Wake up."

VIOLET

"I'll do it," Violet said to Frank. "We'll hop out at the next stop."

Frank looked terrified. "Do you think they'll come after us?"

"What do they care? Two less to worry about." She relaced her boots and shoved her Bible under the seat.

Mrs. Comstock dozed at the front of the car, her head cocked against her shoulder.

"We got to get lost from the rest. Go up to a different car."

"You mean now?" Frank asked.

"I'll go. You follow in a minute." Violet jumped up.

Patrick grabbed her arm as she passed. "Where you off to, huh?"

She jutted her chin toward the front of the car.

He laughed. "Well, ain't you the adventurer." But he didn't offer to come along, resignation having deflated his bravado.

She slipped by Mrs. Comstock, and all of a sudden she was outside in the deafening space between cars, a new quickness in her feet. She pushed through the door into the next car, sparsely filled with riders who didn't turn to look at her as she made her way up the aisle, running her hand along the backs of the seats. Frank finally appeared, nervous and shifty, hunched over, with his hands hiding in his pockets.

"Wait up," he said.

"Beloit!" a porter called. "Next stop, Beloit!"

"What're we going to do for food?" Frank asked. "I'm hungry."

"I don't know. Swipe something from the station. Or a store in town. Every place has a store, don't it?"

He followed her to the top of the car, and they stood at the door watching the world slow down. Frank didn't offer her much, but being with him was better than being alone. She would keep running until she got back to New York. She could find Nino again, she could even find her mother. Lilibeth would have to take her back, wouldn't she?

The train groaned to a stop. She jumped down the steps.

"Now!" she called to Frank, who hung back in the doorway. "Come on!"

But he wouldn't move.

"You go on," he said, tugging his cap down low. He took a step back into the shadow of the vestibule, like he was worried she would try to pull him off.

Violet looked at the people milling about on the platform, and through the windows of the station she could see the waiting wagons and carriages. Did freights even come through here? A man with a thin mustache and dark close-set eyes leaned against the depot wall and watched her. He ran his hand over his mouth and stared. She didn't know what to do next, and she felt frightened by her smallness in this strange wide-open place. The whistle shrieked.

She heaved herself up the ladder and shoved Frank out of the way. She was back on the train.

The conductor came through and punched their tickets, alerting Mrs. Comstock to their approaching destination. She sat up and shook her head to clear it.

"Children," she said. "Wake up now. We are almost at Stoughton."

Violet retrieved her Bible from underneath the seat where she'd left it.

They were herded down Main Street, through the small town of brick-and-stone buildings, and crossed over the Yahara River, its water green and placid.

"What a lovely little place," Mrs. Comstock said to the attendant rolling the trunk and bags.

"Yes, ma'am," he said, through a thick Norwegian accent. "The church is just up ahead."

"Look at the ducks," she said to Frank. "You ever see ducks before?"

He leaned over the railing for a better look.

"Wouldn't you like to live in a place where ducks swim about, no one bothering them?"

He smiled a little. He wouldn't look at Violet, who'd been scowling at him since Beloit. The group walked on.

She wondered if this river went south and met up with a bigger river, which might connect to the Ohio, which might snake all the way to the Kentucky border, back to where she had started. Her boots pinched her toes. Her dress was no longer white, its hem ruffle was torn, and she smelled of coal ash and sweat.

They were greeted by a somber group of women with weathered country faces who served them fried fish, boiled potatoes, and cabbage on the lawn in back of the church alongside the cemetery.

"Grace, children," Mrs. Comstock said, eyeing Nettie, who'd already picked up the fish with her fingers. "*O Lord, we pray thy blessings, upon this food and upon our souls. Guide us through life and save us through Christ. Amen.*"

"Amen," the kids mumbled.

"They're setting up a platform out in front," one of the women said to Mrs. Comstock. "Bring them around when you finish eating."

Soon Violet could hear wagons and carriages, horse hooves against the gravel, as the curious and the interested arrived. Amidst the chittering of birds and the rustling of the heavy-leafed towering oak came the low murmur of voices.

The children ate and ate, forestalling the terrible auction to follow.

"William, Patrick, Nettie, Violet, Frank, Hans." Mrs. Comstock knelt before them. "Give your best smiles. Stay cheerful. Be polite. Patrick, speak slowly and hide your accent. Hans, nod, even if you don't understand what someone says to you." The boy looked down and smashed an ant with the tip of his finger. "The past is the past. Remember that."

Mrs. Comstock rose and rummaged in the trunk for a comb, which she used on each of their heads. Even the older ones didn't resist. They were all too fearful that this was their last chance.

"We are all God's children," she said, straightening jackets and dresses.

How Violet wished that were true.

A suited man came over then, looking official with his eyeglasses and a clipboard.

"This is Mr. Jefferson. You are henceforth in his charge." Mrs. Comstock's eyes filled, and she busied herself with checking her bag. She looked haggard from the trip, but she rolled her shoulders back with the consolation that she had done the Lord's work.

Mr. Jefferson looked from list to child, check-marking next to each name.

"You can pull off those numbers, since there are so few of you left," he said.

Violet yanked off the light-blue paper, leaving the pin in her dress, and slipped it into her Bible, not ready to part with it just yet.

Mrs. Comstock shook Mr. Jefferson's hand.

"There's a carriage in front for you, madam," he said.

"Goodbye, children," she said, picking up her bag. "God bless you." Mrs. Comstock pressed her trembling lips together. She did not look at the faces of the stunned children. She walked briskly away.

Violet scraped her heel in the dirt. Next to her, Nettie sobbed, her lank hair hanging over her face. Mr. Jefferson drew back from the girl, repulsed. He checked his watch.

"Order, please. Line up," he said. "Follow me."

The teenagers, William and Patrick, went first, taken as farm hands. A boisterous family of five, who'd come merely to see what the fuss was about, couldn't bear to leave little Hans standing there, looking around on the makeshift platform.

They spoke to him in German—it was the first time Violet had seen him smile—and led him off the stage to the dappled applause of sparse onlookers.

Violet had noticed the woman earlier, sturdy in body, shiny in face, wearing a uniform like a servant's, a simple black dress with a white apron, her graying hair pinned in a high bun. Now she approached the stage, her hands behind her back, and, though she paused briefly at Nettie, she moved to stand in front of Violet, motioning her forward.

"This is rather strange, isn't it," the woman said.

"Ma'am."

"Was the trip all right?"

"It was pleasant," Violet said, Mrs. Comstock echoing in her ears.

"How old are you?"

"Twelve," Violet lied.

The woman blew air out through puffed cheeks. "I'd hoped for a little older," she said, quietly, not wanting Nettie to hear her. "You know how to bake?"

"I can make biscuits, is about it." Violet crinkled her nose. "But I learn quick."

"What's your name?"

"Violet."

"Well, Violet. I can't offer you a mum and a dad, if that's what you're holding out for."

"I'm not holding out for nothing," Violet said.

"It's a small hospital. I'm the matron. We need help in the kitchen."

She was brisk but not cold, and Violet thought she seemed more trustworthy than most.

"I can do that," Violet said. It was not what she had hoped for, but neither was it what she had feared.

"Helen can teach you all her secrets. Her special confections and such. She makes some fancy things I never even heard of." The woman smiled. "Room and board. The residents keep to themselves, but it's a lovely place, really. On a lake."

"Are there fish in it?" Violet asked.

"Oh, sure. Walleye for certain. Bluegill and bass and the like. You can ask the doctor about that. He's a fair and kind sort."

"What shall I call you?"

"The name is Clara Moody. Miss Moody. So it's settled then?"

Violet nodded once. So this was it. There was no rush of excitement, no giddy whoop, no tearful hug, no doll to unwrap, no silver locket to slip around her neck. She had left those childish notions behind on the train. Relief was new to her, and she felt its heaviness sink her shoulders. There was nothing more to fight.

"I'll go fill out the papers," Miss Moody said. "Come along if you'd like."

Violet turned to look at Nettie, who would not meet her eyes, and Frank, whose ears burned red in the sun. They were on their own, but she didn't have enough left to feel sorry for them. She was just glad not to be last. She jumped off the stage.

The carriage bumped along north. Miss Moody pointed out Lake Kegonsa on the right, and then a few miles later,

Lake Waubesa on the left. In the endless space, with the lulling sound of the horse's hooves, Violet thought about the Fourth Ward, which felt so distant from her now, and thought that if she were to go back there, she would feel like a stranger. She thought of Nino, whose family slept like sardines in their low-ceilinged rooms, and wondered how he would look in all this vastness.

"I go to Madison once a week," Miss Moody said. "You can come with me on the next trip if you want."

"What's it like?" Violet asked.

"It's the state capital, you know. And the university is there. Two big lakes. A bustling city."

Miss Moody did not ask Violet about herself, and Violet did not offer. Her old life seemed faded and cracked, inaccessible almost, and to explain it to Miss Moody in this wide-open air, where it was quiet enough to hear the mourning doves when the horses paused, seemed impossible. Violet decided she would heed Mrs. Comstock's instructions after all: from here on she would not talk about the orphan train and what came before. Her story would be her own, and she would start again.

"I'm really just eleven," Violet said.

Miss Moody pressed her lips together with a sigh, but she did not scold her or turn the carriage around.

"Anything else you would like to tell me?"

"No, ma'am."

They rode up to the east of Lake Monona, the sun hot on Violet's head. She wiped her hands on her already soiled dress.

"We'll have to burn that, I suspect," Miss Moody said.

"I won't miss it."

Violet closed her eyes for a moment and listened to the wind and the papery shake of tree leaves, and smelled the green.

She thought about little Elmer, who had sat next to her all the way to Illinois, and she was happy he'd gotten a family, even if he'd had to leave his sister. She gathered Irish Patrick would be indentured, and wondered if he would run away. She hoped well for all the others and guessed that some would get lucky and some would not. She knew she was being taken to a new home by a woman who seemed straightforward, even kind, and that she, Violet, might have a chance for more than she would have had in New York.

"It's a hospital," Miss Moody said, as they turned onto a wooded lane. "Did I mention that already? A rest home for women with female troubles. But it's quiet. And your room will be near the doctor's quarters on a different floor."

A room, she thought. I will have a room.

Soon Lake Mendota came into view, flashes of blue and light through the trunks of the ash and walnut trees. The surface of the lake shimmered, rippling from the breeze. She had missed beauty in the Fourth Ward, missed the subtle sounds of birds and bugs, wind and water.

A mansion appeared as they rounded the thumb of the lake. It was imposing, almost lavish, but for the cracks in the sandstone walls and the missing slate tiles on the roof. This was the hospital, airy and warmly ramshackle, with sweeping views of the lake. She hoped it would someday feel like home.

Violet worked alongside Helen in the kitchen, more like an apprentice than hired help, and eventually took over the des-

serts, the cakes, the puddings, and—the doctor's favorite—
Conserve of Roses on angel-food cake. Miss Moody picked
out books for her from the library in town—*A Wonder
Book for Girls and Boys, Black Beauty, The Prince and the
Pauper*—but Violet left them unopened to explore the woods,
to climb trees, to play games with the residents for whom she
was a mascot of sorts, a communal daughter. Mrs. Benton,
who'd gone hysterical after her fourth baby died at birth,
taught her how to knit. And Violet grew fond of the old doctor. Sometimes they fished together in early summer morn-
ings, and in winter they skated on the lake. He was good to
her, and, if not quite a father, he showed her a kind of love,
and for that she was grateful.

A few years later, while in Madison picking up kitchen
provisions on market day, Violet ran into Frank, now tall
and filled out, having grown into his once too-large ears.
He smiled when he saw her, and then blushed, as if remembering how they'd left it between them. He told her he'd
been picked by an old widow from Monroe who died a
month later, and then a cheese maker across town took him
on. A decent man, he said, kind of like an uncle, and he
didn't make Frank work too hard.

"Have you heard about anyone else?" she asked.

"I saw Hans once when I went on a delivery to Stoughton. There he was, throwing a ball in the schoolyard with
the other kids. Still doesn't talk good English. But it worked
out for him. He's part of the family and everything. He said
he calls them Mama and Papa, even." Frank cleared his
throat and looked down at his shoes, trying to cover the
longing in his voice.

"What about the girl, Nettie? She get picked in the end?"

Frank squinched up his face trying to remember. "I don't think so. Probably sent up to Black River Falls, to the industrial home and broom factory up there. That's what I hear happens to the ones left over."

Violet nodded, not all that surprised. "I guess we did okay," she said.

Neither of them spoke about what they had left behind.

"Good thing we didn't get off in Beloit," he said.

She snorted but smiled, resisting the urge to remind him that one of them did, in fact, jump off the train.

"Good to see you," she said.

"Yeah," he said. "It's good."

It was the last Violet saw of Frank, and the last time she talked about the train.

When she was eighteen, after the doctor had died, she married Samuel Olsen, a farmer whom she met at a dry goods shop in Madison, a man who was quiet and hardworking and loyal, a man who didn't ask too many questions, a man who, for the most part, left her be. She said goodbye to her makeshift family at the rest home, and she and Samuel moved to a farm over the state line in Minnesota. After three miscarriages, she gave birth to a glacial-eyed baby she named Iris, and in that moment when she felt split open and re-formed, when the doctor placed the little warm thing in her arms, she forgave her mother—for letting her go—as mothers often do. Violet had feared she might have little reserves of tenderness for a child, having pined for her own lost mother for so long, but Iris tapped into a small, secret well within her.

Miss Moody stopped first at the supply closets.

"A toothbrush, a flannel, soap. Let's see. A dress. Some underclothes. They'll be a bit big, but it's a start. We'll get you some more dresses in town tomorrow. Follow me now."

Past the doctor's quarters, Miss Moody pushed open a door to a small lemon-painted room with a window that looked out on the lake. There was a narrow bed, a dresser, a lamp, and a night table.

"Your room. And your key." Miss Moody struggled to get it off her ring. "Here."

"A key to my room," was all Violet could get out, from the tumble of emotion and exhaustion that washed through her.

Miss Moody smiled. "The mosquitoes'll start soon, so best not to leave your window open at night."

Violet nodded. To worry about mosquitoes almost made her laugh.

"Clara?" a male voice called from down the hall. Footsteps clacked against the polished wooden floor.

The doctor appeared in the doorway, a white beard obscuring half his face, his eyes shiny and dark, and Violet put her hand up in a small wave. He looked inquisitively at Miss Moody.

"Well, hello—"

"Violet," Miss Moody said.

"Violet. I'm Dr. Marlowe. Welcome."

"Thank you, sir. Doctor," Violet said.

"How old are you, Violet?"

"She's thirteen, Doctor. Same age as the scullery girl here before."

"Huh," he said, glancing again at Violet's young face.

"Well, I suspect Clara will see to everything. See you at supper."

Violet never returned to New York City, to its endless struggle and brutality and life. She wanted to leave it as it was, to stay ignorant of what it had become. She did not know that, a year after she left, Nino had died in a gang fight, bleeding to death on the docks in a warm summer rain. But she knew it was better not to know what had become of him, as it would surely have cracked her heart in two. As an old woman, Violet would daydream about Nino and the other boys—the wild freedom of the street—and in her bones she would feel an ache for that teeming city of her youth, for the rotting, howling, reeking adventure of it. For those gritty quicksilver days, so long ago.

After her husband died—that patient man who through time had become her friend—and with Iris married, with a son and another baby on the way, Violet felt set free. She lived alone on what remained of the farm, where she had experienced joy and sadness and where she now welcomed solitude. She was content to busy her restless hands knitting sweaters for Samantha, her new grandchild, watching her stories on TV, and watching the sun come up each morning.

She would never know that, a few months after she left on the train, Lilibeth had gone back to the Aid Society to try to get her back but was told there was no record of any child with that name and birth date. Or that she had married a man, an eccentric old railroad executive, and moved uptown, or that she had died at the age of forty-three, her body riddled with cancer, asleep on a woven straw mat at Madam Tang's. But with the long view of her life, Violet wondered sometimes about her girlhood migration, what she had gained—clean clothes, good food, her own bed, stability, and the kindness of Dr. Marlowe; a fair chance, really—and what she had lost—her mother. The lack Violet felt had never gone away. All the comforts of her life in Wisconsin had only changed its shape.

"Miss Moody?"

"Yes, Violet."

"Do I go to work now?"

"Oh, no. Not today."

"What should I do then?"

"Why don't you rest. You must be tired from your travels. The kitchen can wait. We'll start fresh tomorrow."

Violet sat on the bed, her feet not quite touching the floor, and placed her dusty Bible on the bedside table.

"Supper at five-thirty." Miss Moody pulled the door closed behind her.

Violet swung her feet and then jumped off the bed to look out the window. She saw a young woman sitting down by the water, rocking back and forth, as if there were a baby in her arms. Violet sat back on the bed and fell to the side, her head landing on the pillow. What an extraordinary thing that I am here, she thought. It was so very quiet. She wished again for the photograph of her mother. She was already forgetting the details of it, her mother's expression, her borrowed dress. She missed her mother as if it had been years already, a memory faint and bittersweet. But she was drifting now, sleep tugging her into a dream of a sun-hazy Kentucky morning, flies buzzing against the door. She awakened and moved her feet up onto the bed, too tired to take off her dirty boots.

AUTHOR'S NOTE

In the mid-nineteenth century, tens of thousands of children—orphaned, homeless, poverty-stricken, neglected, or delinquent—roamed the streets of New York City. Charles Loring Brace, a young minister, founded the Children's Aid Society to help this teeming underclass. He decided to enact a controversial social experiment: remove these children from their circumstances, put them on trains, and send them west to new Christian homes in rural America.

Children of all ages boarded trains without knowing their destinations, and efforts were made to ensure that families would not be able to track them down. Upon arrival, children were cleaned up and paraded before prospective parents on makeshift stages. There were successes. But there were many failures. With no oversight of the adopters and scant follow-up of children placed, orphan train riders were vulnerable to abuse and indenture, often treated as free farmhands in labor-starved agricultural areas.

The Orphan Train Movement operated from 1854 to 1929, relocating 150,000 to 200,000 children. It is considered the forerunner of foster care in the United States.

ACKNOWLEDGMENTS

My love and gratitude go to my dear Meadows and Darrow families for their unwavering support, encouragement, and inspiration. Special thanks to Susannah Meadows for her terrific suggestions, Jessica Darrow for her unbridled enthusiasm, and Jane Meadows for first telling me about the orphan trains.

An enormous thank you to my editor, Helen Atsma, for her wise direction and generous vision. Thank you to Sarah Bowlin for championing *Mercy Train*. Her guidance and support have been invaluable. Thank you also to the wonderful teams at Henry Holt and St. Martin's Griffin.

I'm so incredibly grateful for my friend, advocate, and agent, Elisabeth Weed, for her perseverance and faith in me. Thank you as well to Jenny Meyer for believing in this book and running with it.

I owe so much to my first and most trusted reader, Alex Darrow. Thanks also to Michelle Wildgen for her invaluable insight, and to Jesse Lee Kercheval, Susanna Daniel, and Judy Mitchell for their close reads and guidance.

My sincere appreciation goes to Cathy Stephens, for generously sharing her Madison history research, and to the Wisconsin Historical Society.

Thank you to the friends near and far who have steadfastly supported my writing over the years: Jennifer Sey, Mark Sundeen, Lewis Buzbee, Lynn Kilpatrick, Jean Johnson, Meredith and Jennifer Bell, Carolyn Frazier, Lance McDaniel, Melissa Kantor, Emma Straub, April Saks, Doe Yamashiro, Kristin Farr Costello, Jody Maxmin, Amy Sweigert, Christopher Sey, Andrew Wilcox, Katie Gerdes, Denise Wood Hahn, and, always, my friends from the Creative Writing Program at the University of Utah.

ABOUT THE AUTHOR

RAE MEADOWS is the author of *No One Tells Every-thing*, a Poets & Writers Notable Novel, and *Calling Out*, which received the 2006 Utah Book Award for fiction and was named one of the best books of the year by the *Chicago Tribune*. She lives with her husband and two daughters in Minneapolis, Minnesota.

MERCY TRAIN

by Rae Meadows

About the Author

- An Interview with Rae Meadows
- On Writing *Mercy Train*
- An Interview with Rae Meadows and Her Mom, Jane Meadows

Keep on Reading

- Reading Recommendations
- Reading Group Questions

For more reading group suggestions,
visit www.readinggroupgold.com.

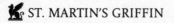 ST. MARTIN'S GRIFFIN

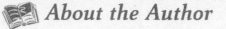# About the Author

Born in Brussels, Rae Meadows grew up in Cleveland and San Diego before attending Stanford University as an art history major. After years in unsatisfying advertising jobs in San Francisco, she wrote her first story, which led to local workshops and eventually the MFA program at The University of Utah.

While in Salt Lake City, she answered phones at an escort service, the experience of which inspired her first novel. *Calling Out* received the 2006 Utah Book Award for fiction and was named an *Entertainment Weekly* Must-Read, a Book Sense Notable Novel, a Barnes & Noble Discover Great New Writers selection, and one of the Best Books of 2006 by the *Chicago Tribune*. Meadows was also named one of five *Poets & Writers* Debut Writers to Watch. Her second novel, *No One Tells Everything*, was named a Notable Novel by *Poets & Writers*, and it was awarded Honorable Mention in the 2008 Anne Powers Fiction Prize. Her stories have appeared in various literary magazines.

She lives with her husband and two daughters in Minneapolis, Minnesota.

"'No More donuts.... Basically, it means get to work.'"

📖 *An Interview with Rae Meadows:*

Q: **What is the best piece of writing advice anyone ever gave you?**

A: No More donuts. My first writing teacher, Lewis Buzbee, gave me a pencil printed with that advice. Basically, it means get to work.

Q: **What is the question most commonly asked by your readers? What is the answer?**

A: Were you an escort? No! (Meadows's first novel, *Calling Out*, featured a character who worked at an escort service.)

Q: **What are some books that have been important to you as a writer?**

A: *Jesus' Son*, by Denis Johnson
As I Lay Dying, by William Faulkner
The Sun Also Rises, by Ernest Hemingway
Gilead, by Marilynne Robinson
Beloved, by Toni Morrison
Winesburg, Ohio, by Sherwood Anderson
To the Lighthouse, by Virginia Woolf
Last Night at the Lobster, by Stewart O'Nan
In the Lake of the Woods, by Tim O'Brien
The Sheltering Sky, by Paul Bowles

Q: **What are your hobbies and outside interests?**

A: My main interest is pottery. I have my wheel in the basement. Since becoming a mother, I have not been able to devote much time to it, but working with clay will be a lifelong pursuit.

Q: **What is your favorite quote?**

A: From a fortune cookie: All things have beauty, but not everyone sees it.

*About the
Author*

Q: What was your inspiration for *Mercy Train*?

A: I wanted to write a novel from three perspectives, and when I learned of the orphan trains, I knew immediately that one of the characters would be eleven-year-old Violet. At the time I thought I would write the whole novel as historical fiction, but then I became a mother and everything changed. Motherhood became the lens, and the multigenerational story fell into place.

Q: How did your own entry into motherhood affect your novel and your characters?

A: It was huge. This idea of displacement that motherhood brings was certainly something I experienced. You engage with the world one way and then all of a sudden you make a dramatic shift to focusing on the well-being of your child. I wasn't sure where the writer part of me fit in anymore. The three characters in the novel deal with their recalibrations of self in their own ways.

Q: Tell us about your stylistic choice to weave the three story lines together moving in and out through time and perspective.

A: Memory is rarely linear. A smell can take you back thirty years in an instant. I wanted the juxtaposition of perspectives and time periods to have a kaleidoscopic effect, particularly since memory is such a big part of the novel. I wanted to show how the stories of Violet, Iris, and Sam are inextricably interconnected. I also liked the challenge that interweaving these stories posed to me as a writer. I had to make sure the jumping around worked thematically and rhythmically, and didn't leave a reader feeling lost.

"The subject of my fiction often seems to emerge from a serendipitous collision of ideas."

On *Writing* Mercy Train

The subject of my fiction often seems to emerge from a serendipitous collision of ideas. For *Mercy Train*, I began wanting to write about my grandfather. He was the youngest of eight children, born into rural poverty in Barren County, Kentucky. When he was three, his family moved north to Illinois so his father could take a job in a lumber mill. I planned a sweeping story about family history and migration, imagining my great-grandparents at the turn of the twentieth century, packing a wagon, seeking more for their children than they could eke out from their small parcel of Kentucky land.

Then my mom happened to ask me if I'd ever heard of the orphan trains. I hadn't, and I was immediately enthralled. Beginning in the mid-nineteenth century, under the direction of The Children's Aid Society, orphaned, delinquent, and poor children from New York City were shipped out on trains in the hopes they would be adopted by Christian farm families in the Midwest—without anything set up in advance or any screening of potential adopters. Whoever showed up at the makeshift viewings could simply take home a child, as if picking up a sack of cornmeal from the mercantile.

I was shocked I'd never heard of this fascinating piece of American history. But the orphan trains were no secret; there has been plenty written about them, mainly devoted to personal accounts of orphan train riders. Most of what I read on the subject was folksy and sentimental. It wasn't until I turned to the history of child welfare that the underside of the Orphan Train Movement became apparent: there was no protest or regulation of the trains because they were effectively draining New York City of a poor, useless class, delivering these children to labor-starved areas where they could be put to work for very little or for free.

I started to envision a novel about two disparate characters brought together by one of the trains. One would be a girl who leaves Kentucky with her mother and ends up in New York City's dismal Fourth Ward. The other would be an ex–Civil War doctor who runs the Wisconsin Insane Asylum, allowing me to delve into the history of Madison, where I'd lived for the past five years. I spent hours poring over photographs and asylum records at the Wisconsin Historical Society, and I read everything I could about the orphan trains and New York City in the last years of the nineteenth century. I was ready to write.

And then I had a baby.

Motherhood turned my life on its head and made me question myself in a way that was scary and new. The first year was a time of euphoric highs and soul-doubting lows, and as the months slid by, I feared I would never want to write again.

When my daughter was a year old, I finally sat down with all my old notes and creaked out some pages. But I was a different woman than I'd been before becoming a mother, in the obvious ways, of course, but also in subtle shifts of perception, longing, and contentedness. And I was a different writer, too. When I wrote about the doctor, it felt clunky and studied, dark and gothic in a way that no longer felt right. What I wanted to write about—what I now felt compelled to write about—was motherhood. Admitting this allowed the novel to take shape. Springing from the original inspiration of my grandfather's life, it became an exploration of mothers and daughters through three generations, anchored by the story and legacy of a scrappy girl named Violet who boards an orphan train in 1900.

"Mercy Train...is a manifestation, I hope, of the writer I have become."

Mercy Train melds my family history, the orphan trains, and the experience of becoming a mother. It is a manifestation, I hope, of the writer I have become.

An Interview with Rae Meadows and Her Mom, Jane Meadows

Q: Jane, after reading Rae's novel, do you feel like you have a different sense of the complexity of the relationship between the two of you? Rae, did you think differently of your relationship with your mother after you had spent so much time with Iris, Sam, and Violet?

J: I have always thought my relationship with Rae was pretty straightforward. However, it occurred to me at one point while reading *Mercy Train* that since Rae's characters had complicated relationships with their mothers, that perhaps complexity had been part of our relationship, at least for her, and that I had been unaware of its presence. The self-reprimand soon followed that if indeed this was a factor, then I should have caught it and tapped into it.

R: My mom and I have had a remarkably unfraught relationship, but I did think about her often while I was writing this book. She has lived so much life— she's beautiful and amazing at eighty-one—and I think in pondering questions for the characters, it made me wonder what it would be like to see my mom as a young single woman or newly married or a first-time mother. This past Christmas she mentioned that she once had dated a professional hockey player named Moose, and I was reminded of how even though I have heard a lot of stories about her life, there is an endless supply of things I don't know.

Q: **Do you think (as Iris mentions) that having children is a way to try and understand one's own mother? Jane, did you learn a lot about your mother when you had children? Rae, did you?**

J: Perhaps many might find this to be helpful, but personally I never sought to better understand my mother. I didn't need to. She was an honest, loving, demonstrative being whom I loved and trusted.

R: Although for me it wasn't a conscious thing, I feel like I have learned so much about my mom since becoming a mother. That intense, unfailing love mixed with worry that she exuded is something I know now on a gut level. My mom had breast cancer when her daughters were eight, five, and three, and I don't think I fully understood what strength and courage this required until I became a mother and tried to imagine myself in the same position.

"I feel like I have learned so much about my mom since becoming a mother."

Q: **The existence of the orphan trains is such a fascinating yet seemingly forgotten part of American history. Rae has said that you introduced her to the subject, Jane, which sparked her to write *Mercy Train*. How did you hear about the orphan trains? What was your initial reaction to this piece of history?**

J: I was waiting for Rae to arrive at the airport in Cleveland, and I struck up a conversation with the woman sitting next to me who was also waiting for her daughter. She mentioned that her daughter had done some research on the Orphan Train Movement of the early part of the twentieth cen-

tury. I had never heard of the orphan trains and was fascinated and full of questions. I, of course, relayed all this to Rae in baggage claim.

R: And good thing she did! I didn't know at the time that the orphan trains would be the basis for my next novel, but I knew instantly they had rich narrative possibilities and I needed to find out more.

Q: As Rae was writing *Mercy Train*, did she come to you for advice? If not, what kind of advice would you have given her in writing about a mother-daughter relationship? Rae, what advice was the most helpful to you in developing these complex characters?

J: Rae is an inspired, gifted writer who needed no advice about writing *Mercy Train*. The only advice I'd have given her, had she asked, is the same advice I would have given her had she been writing about balloons: make the characters interesting and make it a good story. She seems to have done exactly this without anyone's help.

R: Although I didn't seek advice exactly, I did use details from my mom's life in developing these characters. For instance, I remember my mom telling me how when she first got married, she would get all done up and have a cocktail ready for my dad when he came home from work. Iris is from the same generation as my mom, and she enacts a similar scene. And then in a larger sense, my mom has told me about the great agony she felt when her mother was dying in regards to intervention and resuscitation, and this was on my mind in the flashbacks of Iris and Sam.

Q: Which character—Sam, Violet, or Iris—did each of you connect with the most? Why?

J: My younger self of fifty years ago strongly identifies with Sam in her relationship to her baby, in her procrastination and lack of focus in returning to her creative work, and in her guilt and subsequent self-chastisement over the aborted Down syndrome fetus. But it's Iris who is closest to my own age and who has faced some of life's tougher moments. She's accepting and talks to herself in a down-to-earth way, without self-pity. Her self-admonishment to "buck up" is one I plan to adopt. It very much suits those of us who are facing our eighties.

R: Violet is very unlike how I was as a child and, in that sense, she is the most fictional of the three characters. Iris definitely has some of me in her, though she is in such a different stage of life. So, I have to say I connected most with Sam, since her character sprang from some of my experiences as a new mother, particularly the anxiety about where creative pursuits fit in after motherhood. From the outside, her life is similar to mine.

Q: Iris mentions that the relationship between her and her daughter has grown closer now that Sam is an adult. Jane and Rae, how has your relationship changed from when Rae was younger versus now?

J: When a child has become a responsible adult, there is little responsibility for the mother to guide or instruct. Rae and I are friends and, as such, tolerant of each other's differences and all the best that friendship infers. We are each committed to a helpful, thoughtful, appreciative, and always loving relationship toward each other. Rae was an appealing, charming, loving child. She remains so to this day, only the package is taller.

R: Thanks, Mom. I think our relationship has grown into an adult friendship, which I have come to cherish and depend on. My mom is such a neat woman: an accomplished painter, a writer of lovely old-fashioned letters, a believer in alternative medicine and health long before it was fashionable, a person of great faith, a true original. As I get older, I have really come to appreciate that she finds joy in the everyday—she's happy puttering around her house and garden. I also love that my mom had a renaissance later in life when she came into her voice, and she is unapologetic about speaking what she believes in, which makes her a great person to talk to.

Q: **Rae, how difficult was it to write about the struggles of being a daughter—and a mother—knowing that your mom would eventually read it? Did you find that the writing process became harder with this in mind?**

R: My mom has always been my most ardent supporter, so I didn't hesitate in exploring the mother-daughter dynamic between these characters. Luckily my mom is not like Iris or Violet as a mother, so I wasn't too worried that she would see herself and possibly be hurt by the book. Besides, she survived me writing about an escort service in my first novel, so I figured she would be okay with this one!

Q: **As a mother, there is always that fear of having your children repeat your mistakes. What things did you try to avoid passing on to your children? What advice or wisdom have you tried to instill?**

J: I don't remember imparting any earthshaking advice. I suppose I thought to teach by example, as my own mother had. It was, of course, a given that there would be no drinking, smoking, or drugs.

*About the
Author*

R: Can I just say my mom's first response was, "But I didn't make any mistakes." She was joking of course, but in a way, she's right. I had the luxury of having a stay-at-home mom who loved being a mom and exuded contentment, and was unendingly supportive. My sisters and I were incredibly lucky. Though her advice on clean living I'm afraid I didn't quite follow in my younger years. (Sorry, Mom!)

"My sisters and I were incredibly lucky."

Recommended Reading

Some suggestions from Rae Meadows about books to grab after you put down *Mercy Train*

ON MOTHERHOOD:
Unless, by Carol Shields
Anne Sexton: A Biography, by Diane Middlebrook

PULITZER PRIZE WINNERS I APPLAUD:
Olive Kitteridge, by Elizabeth Strout
A Visit from the Goon Squad, by Jennifer Egan

WONDERFUL STORY COLLECTIONS FROM SMALL PRESSES:
In the House, by Lynn K. Kilpatrick
The Pale of Settlement, by Margot Singer
The End of the Straight and Narrow,
         by David McGlynn

NEWLY RELEASED GEMS:
The Man Who Quit Money, by Mark Sundeen
Laura Lamont's Life in Pictures, by Emma Straub

OTHER GREAT READS:
Home, by Marilynne Robinson
Driftless, by David Rhodes
Shadow Tag, by Louise Erdrich

*Keep on
Reading*

Reading Group Questions

1. How much did you know about orphan trains before reading this novel? What touched you most about Violet's story? Did reading *Mercy Train* make you want to learn more?

2. We are introduced to Violet as a rambunctious young girl living with an adventurous zeal for life—that is, until she is sent off on the orphan train. In what ways has Violet changed from a little girl to the older woman Iris remembers as her mother? Why do you think she has changed? How has she remained the same?

3. Which mother/daughter relationship resonated most with you? Why?

4. Has there ever been a time in your life when you've been forced to make a hard decision regarding a loved one's health like Sam is? What do you think of the decision she ultimately made?

5. Do you think each of the mothers in this book represents her particular generation? What about them is specific to the environment in which they grew up?

6. Iris tells Sam that women don't know what they will be like as mothers. Why do you think she tells her this? Do you think this is true? Do women really have no control over the mothers they become?

7. There is a running theme of identity and self throughout the novel. Iris feels that she put up a façade as a mother. Samantha loses her will to create art after having Ella. Is losing one's identity part of becoming a mother? Do the women in this novel think that motherhood is worth the sacrifice?

8. There are a lot of secrets that are kept by the women in the novel (eg., Violet's abandonment by her mother; Iris's trip to the Drake Hotel; Sam's abortion). Why do you think they keep these secrets—even from those closest to them?

9. Are there any questions that this book brought up that you've ever wanted to ask your mother but couldn't? What are they?

10. Iris's reading played a big role in this novel. Are there any books that you and your mother or children have connected over? Why?

11. Did reading this novel make you think about your own family history? What memories did it bring up? Did it make you want to learn more about your family's past?

12. Violet chooses her path and suggests being sent on the orphan train. "She wanted what her mother could never give her." Do you think she made the right decision? How would her life have been different?

13. How are Violet, Iris, and Sam similar? How are they different? What do you think Ella's inheritance will be from the family?